Thomas D'Urfey

Songs Complete, Pleasant and Divertive; Set to Music

Vol. III

Thomas D'Urfey

Songs Complete, Pleasant and Divertive; Set to Music
Vol. III

ISBN/EAN: 9783744762533

Printed in Europe, USA, Canada, Australia, Japan

Cover: Foto ©Andreas Hilbeck / pixelio.de

More available books at **www.hansebooks.com**

SONGS Compleat,

Pleasant and Divertive;

SET TO

MUSICK

By Dr. JOHN BLOW, Mr. HENRY PURCELL, and other Excellent Masters of the Town.

Ending with some ORATIONS, made and spoken by me several times upon the PUBLICK STAGE in the THEATER. Together with some Copies of VERSES, PROLOGUES, and EPILOGUES, as well for my own PLAYS as those of other Poets, being all Humerous and Comical.

VOL III.

Written by Mr. D'URFEY.

LONDON:

Printed by *W. Pearson*, for *J. Tonson*, at SHAKESPEAR'S Head, against *Catherine* Street in the *Strand*, 1719.

A N
Alphabetical TABLE
OF THE
SONGS and POEMS
Contain'd in this
B O O K.

A

An Alphabetical TABLE.

My

An Alphabetical TABLE.

There's

An Alphabetical TABLE.

POEMS.

SONGS

Songs Compleat,

Pleasant and Divertive, &c.

VOL. III.

The CLOAK's KNAVERY.

OME buy my new Ballad,
I hav't in my Wallet,
But 'twill not I fear please every Pallat;
Then mark what ensu'th,
I swear by my Youth,
That every Line in my Ballad is truth:
A ballad of Wit, a brave Ballad of worth,
'Tis newly printed, and newly come forth.
'Twas made of a Cloak that fell out with a Gown,
That crampt all the Kingdom and crippl'd the Crown.

I'll tell you in brief,
A story of Grief,
Which happen'd when *Cloak* was Commander in Chief;
It tore Common Prayers,
Imprison'd Lord Mayors,
In one day it Voted down Prelates and Players:
It made People perjur'd in point of Obedience,
And the *Covenant* did cut off the Oath of Allegiance.
  Then let us endeavour to pull the Cloak *down,*
  That cramp'd all the Kingdom and crippl'd the Crown.

It was a black *Cloak,*
In good time be it spoke,
That kill'd many Thousands, but never struck stroke;
With Hatchet and Rope,
The forlorn Hope,
Did joyn with the Devil to pull down the Pope:
It set all the Sects in the City to work,
And rather than fail 'twould have brought in the *Turk.*
  Then let us endeavour, &c.

It seiz'd on the Tow'r Guns,
Those fierce Demi-Gorgons,
It brought in the Bagpipes and pull'd down the Organs;
The Pulpits did smoak,
The Churches did choak,
And all our Religion was turn'd to a *Cloak:*
It brought in Lay-Elders could not write nor read,
It set *Publick Faith* up, and pull'd down the *Creed.*
  Then let us endeavour, &c.

This pious Imposter,
Such Fury did foster,
It left us no Penny, nor no *Pater Noster;*
It threw to the Ground
Ten Commandments down,
And set up twice Twenty times Ten of its own:
It routed the King, and Villains elected,
To plunder all those whom they thought Disaffected.
  Then let us endeavour, &c.

To

To blind Peoples Eyes,
This *Cloak* was so Wise,
It took off Ship-money, but set up Excise;
Men brought in their Plate,
For Reasons of State,
And gave it to *Tom Trumpeter* and his Mate:
In Pamphlets it writ many specious Epistles,
To cozen poor Wenches of Bodkins and Whistles.
  Then let us endeavour to pull the Cloak *down,*
  That cramp'd all the Kingdom and crippl'd the Crown.

In Pulpits it moved,
And was much approved,
For crying out —— *Fight the Lord's Battles beloved;*
It bobtayl'd the Gown,
Put Prelacy down,
It trod on the Mitre to reach at the Crown:
And into the Field it an Army did bring,
To aim at the Council, but shot at the King.
  Then let us endeavour, &c.

It raised up States,
Whose politick Pates,
Do now keep their Quarters on the City Gates;
To Father and Mother,
To Sister and Brother,
It gave a Commission to kill one another:
It took up Mens Horses at very low rates,
And plunder'd our Goods to secure our Estates.
  Then let us endeavour, &c.

This *Cloak* did proceed,
To a damnable Deed,
It made the best mirror of Majesty bleed;
Tho' *Cloak* did not do't,
He set it on Foot,
By rallying and calling his Journey-men to't:
For never had come such a bloody disaster,
If *Cloak* had not first drawn a Sword at his Master.
  Then let us endeavour, &c.

B 2

Though

    Though some of them went hence,
    By sorrowful Sentence,
This lofty long *Cloak* is not mov'd to Repentance,
    But he and his Men,
    Twenty Thousand times ten,
Are plotting to do their Tricks over again :
But let this proud *Cloak* to Authority stoop,
Or *DUN* will provide him a Button and Loop.
   Then let us endeavour to pull the Cloak *down,*
   That basely did Sever the Head from the Crown,

    Let's pray that the King,
    And his Parliament,
In Sacred and secular Things may consent;
    So Righteously firm,
    And Religiously free,
That Papists and Atheists suppressed may be:
And as there's one Deity doth over-reign us,
One Faith, and one Form, and one Church may contain us,
Then Peace, Truth and Plenty, our Kingdom will crown,
And all Popish Plots, and their Plotters shall down.

Blanket-Fair, *or the History of* Temple-
street. *Being a Relation of the merry
pranks play'd on the River of* Thames
during the great Frost: Tune Packing-
ton's Pound.

COME listen a while (tho' the Weather be cold,)
    In your Pockets and Plackets your hands you
      may hold;
I'll tell you a Story as true as 'tis rare,
Of a *River* turn'd into a *Bartholomew* Fair :
    Since old *Christmass* last,
    There has been such a *Frost,*
That the *Thames* has by half the whole Nation been
    crost :

                      Oh

Oh *Scullers* I pity your fate of extreams,
Each *Land-man* is now become free of the *Thames*.
'Tis some *Lapland* Acquaintance of Conjurer *Oats*,
That has ty'd up your hands and Imprisoned your Boats;
You know he was ever a Friend to the Crew,
Of all those that to Admiral *James* have been true :
  Where Sculls did once Row,
  Men walk to and fro,
But e're four Months are ended, 'twill hardly be so ;
Should your hopes of a Thaw by this weather be crost,
Your Fortune will soon be as hard as the Frost.

In Roast-Beef and Brandy, much Money is spent,
And Booths made of Blankets that pay no ground-rent ;
With old fashion'd Chimneys the Rooms are secur'd,
And the Houses from danger of Fire are insured :
  The chief place you meet,
  Is call'd *Temple-street*,
If you do not believe me, then you may go and see't ;
From the Temple the Students do thither resort,
Who were always great Patrons, of Revels and sport.

The Citizen comes with his Daughter and Wife,
And swears he ne're saw such a sight in his Life ;
The Prentices starv'd at home for want of Bread,
To catch them a heat, do flock thither in shoals :
  While the Country Squire
  Does stand and admire,
At the wondrous Conjunction of Water and Fire ;
Straight comes an arch Wag, a young Son of a Whore,
And lays the Squire's head where his heels were before.

The *Rotterdam Dutchman* with fleet cutting Scates,
To pleasure the Crowd, shews his Tricks and his Feats ;
Who like a Rope-dancer (for his sharp Steels)
His Brains and Activity lie in his Heels,
  Here all things like Fate,
  Are in slippery state,
From the soal of the Foot to the crown of the Pate ;
While the Rabble in Sledges run giddily round,
And nought but a Circle of Folly is found.

Here

Here Damsels are handled like Nymphs in the Bath,
By Gentlemen-Ushers, with Legs like a Lath;
They slide to a Tune, and cry give me your Hand,
When the tottering Fops are scarce able to stand:
      Then with fear and with care,
      They arrive at the Fair,
Where Wenches sell Glasses and crackt Earthen-ware;
To shew that the World and the Pleasures it brings,
Are made up of Brittle and Slippery things.

A Spark of the Bar with his Cane and his Muff,
One day went to treat his new rigg'd Kitchin-stuff;
Let slip from her Gallant, the gay Damsel try'd,
(As oft she had done in the Country) to slide:
      In the way lay a stump,
      That with a damn'd thump,
She broke both her Shoe-strings and crippl'd her Rump;
The heat of her Buttocks made such a great Thaw,
She had like to have drowned the Man of the Law.

All you that are warm both in Body and Purse,
I give you this warning for better for worse;
Be not there in Moonshine, pray take my advice,
For slippery things have been done on the Ice:
      Maids there have been said,
      To lose Maiden-head,
And Sparks from full Pockets gone empty to Bed;
If their Brains and their Bodies had not been too warm,
It is forty to one they had come to less harm.

The Praise of the Dairy-Maid, *with a lick at the* Cream-Pot, *or a Fading* Rose. *To the foregoing Tune.*

LET Wine turn a Spark, and Ale huff like a *Hector*,
   Let *Pluto* drink *Coffee*, and *Jove* his rich *Nectar*;
     Neither Syder nor Sherry,
     Metheglin nor Perry,

Shall

Shall more make me Drunk, which the vulgar call merry:
These Drinks o'er my fancy no more shall prevail,
But I'll take a full soop at the merry Milk-pail.

In praise of a Dairy I purpose to sing,
But all things in order first, *God save the King;*
    And the Queen I may say,
    That ev'ry *May-day,*
Has many fair Dairy-Maids, all fine and gay :
Assist me fair Damsels, to finish this Theam,
And inspire my fancy with Strawberries and Cream.

The first of fair Dairy-Maids if you'll believe,
Was *Adam's* own Wife, your Great-Grandmother *Eve;*
    She milk'd many a Cow,
    As well she knew how,
Tho' Butter was then not so cheap as 'tis now :
She hoarded no Butter nor Cheese on a Shelf,
For the Butter and Cheese in those days made it self.

In that Age or time there was no damn'd Money,
Yet the Children of *Israel* fed upon Milk and Honey ;
    No Queen you could see
    Of the highest Degree,
But would milk the Brown Cow with the meanest she :
Their Lambs gave them Cloathing, their Cows gave
    them Meat,
In a plentiful Peace all their Joys were compleat.

But now of the making of Cheese we shall treat,
That Nurser of Subjects, bold *Britain's* chief Meat ;
    When they first begin it,
    To see how the Rennet
Begets the first Curd, you wou'd wonder what's in it :
Then from the blue Whey, when they put the Curd by,
They look just like Amber, or Clouds in the Sky.

Your *Turkey* Sherbet and *Arabian* Tea,
Is Dish-water stuff to a dish of new Whey ;
    For it cools Head and Brains,
    Ill Vapours it drains,
· And tho' your Guts rumble 'twill ne'er hurt your Brains,

Court

Court Ladies i' th' Morning will drink a whole Pottle,
And send out their Pages with Tankard and Bottle.

Thou Daughter of Milk, and Mother of Butter,
Sweet Cream thy due praises how shall I now utter?
     For when at the best,
     A thing's well express'd,
We are apt to reply, *that's the Cream of the Jest:*
Had I been a Mouse, I believe in my Soul,
I had long since been Drowned in a Cream bowl.

The Elixir of Milk, the *Dutchmen's* delight,
By motion and tumbling thou bringest to light;
     But oh, the soft stream,
     That remains of the Cream,
Old *Morpheus* ne'er tasted so sweet in a Dream:
It removes all Obstructions, depresses the Spleen,
And makes an old Bawd like a Wench of fifteen.

Amongst the rare Virtues that Milk does produce,
A thousand more Dainties are daily in use;
     For a Pudding I'll tell ye,
     E'er it goes in the Belly,
Must have both good Milk, and the Cream and the Jelly:
For dainty fine Pudding without Cream, or Milk,
Is like a Citizen's Wife without Sattin or Silk.

In the Virtue of Milk there's more to be muster'd,
The charming delights of Cheese-Cakes and Custard;
     For at *Tottenham Court,*
     You can have no sport,
Unless you give Custards and good Cheese Cakes for't:
And what's *Jack Pudding* that makes us to Laugh,
Unless he hath got a great Custard to quaff.

Both Pancakes and Fritters of Milk have good store,
But a *Devonshire* Wite-pot requires much more;
     No state you can think,
     Tho' you study and wink,
From the lusty Sack-posset to poor Posset-drink;

But

But Milk's the Ingredient, tho' Sack's ne'er the worse,
For 'tis Sack makes the Man, tho' Milk makes the
    Nurse.

But now I shall treat of a Dish that is cool,
A rich clouted Cream, or a Gooseberry-Fool ;
      A Lady I heard tell,
      Not far off did dwell,
Made her Husband a Fool, and yet pleas'd him full
    well :
Give thanks to the Dairy then every Lad,
That from good natur'd Women such Fools may be
    had.

When the Damsel has got the Cows Teat in her Hand ;
How she merrily sings, while smiling I stand ;
      Then with a pleasure I rub,
      Yet impatient I scrub,
When I think of the Blessing of a Syllibub ;
Oh Dairy-Maids, Milk-maids, such bliss ne'er oppose ;
If e'er you'll be happy, I speak under the Rose.

This *Rose* was a Maiden once of your profession,
Till the Rake and the Spade had taken possession ;
      At length it was said,
      That one Mr. *Ed——mond*,
Did both dig and sow in her Parsly-Bed :
But the Fool for his labour deserves not a Rush,
For grafting a Thistle upon a Rose Bush.

Now Milk-maids take warning by this Maidens fall,
Keep what is your own, and then you keep all :
      Mind well your Milk-pan,
      And ne'er touch a Man,
And you'll still be a Maid, let him do what he can
I am your well-wisher, then listen to my Word,
And give no more Milk than the Cow can afford.

A true Relation of the dreadful Combate between More *of* More-Hall, *and the* Dragon *of* Wantley.

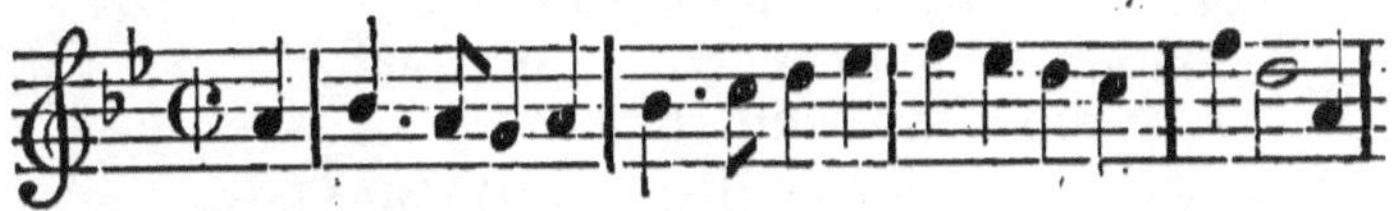

OLD Stories tell how *Hercules*
    A Dragon slew at *Lern;*
With seven Heads and fourteen Eyes,
    To see and well discern:
      But he had a Club,
      This Dragon to drub,
Or he had ne'er don't, I warrant ye;
      But *More* of *More-Hall,*
      With nothing at all,
He slew the Dragon of *Wantley.*

This Dragon had two furious Wings,
Each one upon each Shoulder;

With

With a Sting in his Tayl,
As long as a Flayl,
Which made him bolder and bolder ;
He had long Claws,
And in his Jaws
Four and forty Teeth of Iron ;
With a Hide as tough, as any Buff,
Which did him round Inviron.

Have you not heard that the *Trojan* Horse,
Held Seventy Men in his Belly ?
This Dragon was not quite so big,
But very near, I'll tell ye :
Devour did he,
Poor Children three,
That could not with him grapple ;
And at one Sup,
He eat them up,
As one should eat an Apple.

All sorts of Cattle this Dragon did eat,
Some say he'd eat up Trees ;
And that the Forest sure he would
Devour up by Degrees :
For Houses and Churches,
Were to him Gorse and Burches,
He eat all, and left none behind ;
But some Stones, dear *Jack*,
Which he could not crack,
Which on the Hills you will find.

In *Yorkshire*, near fair *Rotherham*,
The Place I know it well ;
Some two or three Miles, or there-abouts,
I vow I cannot tell ;
But there is a Hedge,
Just on the Hill edge,
And *Matthew's* House hard by it ;
Oh there and then,
Was this Dragon's Den,
You could not chuse but spy it.

Some

Some say this Dragon was a Witch,
　Some say he was the Devil;
For from his Nose a Smoak arose,
　And with it burning Snivel;
　　Which he cast off,
　　When he did Cough,
In a Well that he did stand by;
　　Which made it look,
　　Just like a Brook,
Running with burning Brandy.

Hard by a furious Knight there dwelt,
　Of whom all Towns did ring;
For he could Wrestle, play at Quarter-Staff,
Kick, Cuff, Box, Huff,
Call Son of a Whore,
　Do any kind of thing:
　　By the Tail, and the Main,
　　With his Hands twain,
He swong a Horse till he was dead;
　　And that which was stranger,
　　He for very Anger,
Eat him all up but his Head.

These children as I told being eat,
　Men, Women, Girls, and Boys;
Sighing and Sobbing, came to his Lodging,
　And made a hedious Noise:
　　Oh save us all,
　　More of *More-Hall,*
Thou pearless Knight of these Woods;
　　Do but stay this Dragon,
　　We won't leave us a Rag on,
We'll give thee all our Goods.

Tut, tut, quoth he, no Goods I want,
　But I want, I want in sooth;
A fair Maid of Sixteen that's brisk,
　And smiles about the Mouth:
　　Hair as black as a Sloe,
　　.Both above and below,

With

With a Blush her Cheeks adorning;
   To 'noynt me o'er Night,
   E'er I go to Fight,
And to dress me in the Morning.
This being done, he did engage
   To hew this Dragon down;
But first he went New Armour to
   Bespeak at *Sheffield* Town:
     With Spikes all about,
     Not within, but without,
Of Steel so sharp and strong;
     Both behind and before,
     Arms, Legs, all o'er,
Some five or six inches long.

Had you but seen him in this Dress,
   How fierce he look'd and big;
You would have thought him for to be,
   An *Ægyptian* Porcu-Pig:
     He frighted all,
     Cats, Dogs, and all,
Each Cow, each Horse, and each Hog
     For fear did flee,
     For they took him to be
Some strange outlandish Hedghog.

To see this Fight, all People there
   Got upon Trees and Houses;
On Churches some, and Chimneys too,
   But they put on their Trowzes:
     Not to spoil their Hose,
     As soon as he rose,
To make him strong and mighty,
     He drank by the Tale,
     Six Pots of Ale,
And a Quart of *Aqua-vitæ*.

It is not Strength that always wins,
   For Wit doth Strength excel;
Which made our cunning Champion,
   Creep down into a Well:

Where

Where he did think,
This Dragon would drink,
And so he did in Truth,
And as he stoop'd low,
He rose up and cry'd boe,
And hit him in the Mouth.

Oh, quoth the Dragon, pox take you come out,
Thou that distrub'st me in my Drink;
And then he turn'd and shit at him,
Good lack how he did stink!
Beshrew thy Soul,
Thy Body is foul,
Thy Dung smells not like Balsam;
Thou Son of a Whore,
Thou stink'st so sore,
Sure thy Diet it is unwholesome.

Our Politick Knight on the other side
Crept out upon the brink;
And gave the Dragon such a doust,
He knew not what to think:
By Cock, quoth he,
Say you so, do you see,
And then at him let flie;
With Hand, and with Foot,
And so they went to't,
And the Word it was, Hey boys, hey.

Your Word, quoth the Dragon, I don't understand,
Then to't they fell at all:
Like to Wild Bears, so fierce, I may
Compare great things with small:
Two Days and a Night
With this Dragon did Fight,
Our Champion on the Ground;
Tho' their Strength it was great,
Yet their Skill was neat,
They never had one wound.

At

At length the hard Earth began for to quake,
  The Dragon gave him such a knock,
Which made him to Reel;
And straight way he thought
  To lift him as high as a Rock:
    And thence let him fall,
    But *More* of *More-hall,*
Like a Valiant Son of *Mars;*
    As he came like a Lout,
    So he turned him about,
And hit him a Kick on the Arse.

Oh! quoth the Dragon, with a Sigh,
  And turned six times together;
Sobbing, and tearing, Cursing and Swearing,
  Out of his Throat of Leather:
    Oh thou Raskal,
    More of *More-hall,*
Would I had seen you never;
    With the thing at thy Foot,
    Thou hast prickt my Arse Gut,
Oh, I am quite undone for ever.

Murder, Murder, the Dragon cry'd
  Alack, alack, for Grief;
Had you but mist that Place, you could
  Have done me no Mischief:
    Then his Head he shak'd,
    Trembled, and Quak'd,
And down he laid and cry'd;
    First on one Knee,
    Then on back tumbled he,
So Groan'd, Kick'd, Shit, and Dyed.

The

The Old Man's WISH.

If

I F I live to grow old (for I find I go down)
   Let this be my Fate, in a fair Country Town ;
Let me have a warm House, with a Stone at the Gate,
And a cleanly young Girl to rub my bald Pate :
   May I govern my Passion with an absolute sway,
   And grow wiser and better, as my Strength wears
      away ;
   Without Gout, or Stone, by a gentle decay.

In a Country Town by a murmuring Brook,
With the Ocean at distance whereon I may look ;
With a spacious Plain without Hedge or Stile,
And an easie Pad-Nag, to ride out a Mile :
   May I govern, &c.

With *Horace,* and *Petrarch,* and two or three more,
Of the best Wits that liv'd in the Ages before ;
With a Dish of Roast Mutton, not Venison nor Teal,
And clean (tho' course) Linnen at every Meal :
   May I govern, &c.

With a Pudding on Sundays, and stout humming Liquor,
And remnants of *Latin* to welcome our Vicar ;
With a hidden reserve of *Burgundy* Wine,
To Drink the King's Health in as oft as I Dine :
   May I govern, &c.

When the days are grown short, and it Freezes & Snows,
May I have a Coal-fire as high as my Nose ;
A Fire (which once stirr'd up with a Prong)
Will keep the Room temperate all the Night long :
   May I govern, &c.

With a Courage undaunted may I Face my last day,
And when I am Dead may the better sort say ;
In the Morning when sober, in the Evening when mellow,
He's gone, and left not behind him his Fellow :
   For he govern'd his Passion with an absolute sway,
   And grew wiser and better as his strength wore away ;
   Without Gout, or Stone, by a gentle decay.

The Old Woman's Wish. To the foregoing Tune.

WHEN my Hairs they grow Hoary, and my
　　Cheeks they look pale,　　　[sight doth fail;
When my Forehead hath Wrinkles, and my Eye-
Let my words both and Actions be free from all harm,
And have my Old Husband to keep my Back warm:
　The Pleasures of Youth, are Flowers but of May,
　Our Life's but a Vapour, our Body's but Clay;
　Oh! Let me live well, though I live but one day.

With a Sermon on Sunday, and a Bible of good Print,
With a Pot o'er the fire, and good Victuals in't;
With Ale, Beer, and Brandy, both Winter and Summer,
To drink to my Gossip, and be pledg'd by my Gummer:
　The Pleasures of Youth, &c.

With Pigs, and with Poultry, with some Money in store,
To lend to my Neighbour, and give to the Poor;
With a Bottle of *Canary,* to drink without Sin,
And to Comfort my Daughter when that she lies Inn:
　The Pleasures of Youth, &c.

With a Bed soft and easie, to rest on at Night,
With a Maid in the Morning to rise when 'tis light;
To do her work Neatly, to obey my desire,
To make the House clean, and to blow up the Fire:
　The Pleasures of Youth, &c.

With Coals, and with Bavins, and a good warm Chair,
With a thick Hood & Mantle, when I ride on my Mare:
Let me dwell near my Cupboard, and far from my Foes,
With a pair of Glass Eyes to clap on my Nose:
　The Pleasures of Youth, &c.

And when I am Dead, with a sigh let them say,
Our honest old Gammer is laid in the Clay;
When young she was cheerful, no Scold, nor no Whore,
She helped her Neighbours and gave to the Poor,
　Tho' the Flower of her Youth in her Age did decay,
　Though her Life was a Vapour that vanish'd away;
　She liv'd well and Happy until the last day.

The

The Old Woman's Wish.   To the same Tune.

IF I live to be Old, which I never will own,
  Let this be my Fortune in Country or Town;
Let me have a warm Bit, with two more in store,
And a Lusty young Fellow to rub me before:
  May I give to my Passion an absolute sway,
  Till with Mumping and Grunting, my Breath's worn
     away;
  Without Ach or Cough, by a tedious decay.

In a dry Chimny Nook with a Rug and warm Cloaths,
A swinging Coal-fire still under my Nose;
With a large Elbow Chair to sit at the Fire,
And a Crutch, or a Staff to the Bed to retire:
  May I give to my Passion, &c.

With a Pudding on Sunday, with Custard and Plums,
When my Teeth are all out, for to ease my old Gums;
With a Dram of the Bottle, each day a fresh Quart,
Reserv'd in a Corner to Cheer up my Heart:
  May I give to my Passion, &c.

With a Neighbour or two to tell me a Tale,
And to Sing *Chevy-Chase,* o'er a Pot of good Ale;
A Snuff-box, and short Pipe snug under the Range,
And a clean Flannel Shift, as oft as I change:
  May I give to my Passion, &c.

Without *Palsey* or *Gout,* may I dye in my Chair,
And when Dead, may my *Great, Great Grandchild,*
    declare
She's gone, who so long had cheated the Devil,
And the World is well rid of a troublesome evil:
  That gave to her Passion an absolute sway,
  Till with Mumping and Grunting, her Breath wore
     away;
  Without Ach, or Cough, by a tedious decay.

 The

The BLACK-SMITH.

OF all the Trades that ever I see,
   There's none to a *Blacksmith* compared may be ;
With so many several Tools works he,
   Which no Body can deny.

The first that ever Thunder-bolt made,
Was a *Cyclops* of the *Blacksmith's* Trade ;
As in a learned Author is said,
   Which no Body, &c.

When Thund'ring like we strike about,
The Fire like Lightning flashes out ;
Which suddenly with Water we d'out,
   Which no Body, &c.

The fairest Goddess in the Skies,
To Marry with *Vulcan* did advise ;
And he was a *Blacksmith* Grave and Wise
   Which no Body &c.

Vulcan

Vulcan he to do her right,
Did Build her a Town by Day and by Night,
And gave it a Name which was *Hammersmith* hight,
    Which no Body, &c.

Vulcan, further did acquaint her,
That a pretty Estate he would appoint her ;
And leave her *Seacole-lane* for a Joynter,
    Which no Body, &c.

And that no Enemy might wrong her,
He Built her a Fort you'd wish no stronger ;
Which was in the Lane *Ironmonger,*
    Which no Body, &c.

Smithfield he did cleanse from Dirt,
And sure there was reason for't ;
For there he meant she should keep her Court,
    Which no Body, &c.

But after in a good time and Tide,
It was by the *Blacksmith* rectifi'd ;
To the Honour of *Edmond Ironside,*
    Which no Body, &c.

Vulcan after made a Train,
Wherein the God of War was ta'en ;
Which ever since hath been call'd *Paul's chain,*
    Which no Body, &c.

The Common Proverb as it is read,
That a Man must hit the Nail on the head ;
Without the *Blacksmith* cannot be said,
    Which no Body, &c.

Another must not be forgot,
And falls unto the *Blacksmith's* Lot ;
That he must strike while the Iron is hot,
    Which no Body, &c.

Another

Another comes in most proper and fit,
The *Blacksmith's* Justice is seen in it ;
When you give a Man Roast-meat and beat him with
    the Spit,
    Which no Body can deny.

Another comes in our *Blacksmith's* way,
When things are safe as old Wives say ;
We have them under Lock and Key,
    Which no Body, &c.

Another that's in the *Blacksmith's* Books,
And only to him for remedy looks ;
Is when a Man is quite off the hooks,
    Which no Body, &c.

Another Proverb to him doth belong,
And therefore let's do the *Blacksmith* no wrong ;
When a Man's held hard to it buckle and thong,
    Which no Body, &c.

Another Proverb doth make me laugh,
Wherein the *Blacksmith* may challenge half ;
When a Reason's as plain as a Pike-staff,
    Which no Body, &c.

Though your Lawyers Travel both near and far,
And by long Pleading a good Cause may mar ;
Yet your *Blacksmith* takes more pains at the Bar,
    Which no Body, &c.

Tho' your Scrivener seeks to crush and to kill,
By his Counterfeit Deeds, and thereby doth ill ;
Yet your *Blacksmith* may Forge what he will,
    Which no Body, &c.

Tho' your Bankrupt Citizens lurk in their holes,
And Laugh at their Creditors and their catch-poles ;
Yet your *Blacksmith* can fetch them over the coals,
    Which no Body, &c.

                             Though

Though *Jockey* in the Stable be never so neat,
To look to his Nag and prescribe him his meat;
Yet your *Blacksmith* knows better how to give him a
    heat,
    Which no Body, &c.

If any Taylor have the Itch,
The *Blacksmith's* water as black as Pitch;
Will make his Hands go thorough stitch,
    Which no Body, &c.

There's never a Slut if filth o'er smutch her,
But owes to the *Blacksmith* for her Leacher;
For without a pair of Tongs there's no Man would
    touch her,
    Which no Body, &c.

Your Roaring Boys who every one quails,
Fights, Domineers, Swaggers, and rails;
Could never yet make the *Smith* Eat his Nails,
    Which no Body, &c.

If any Scholar be in doubt,
And cannot well bring this matter about;
The *Blacksmith* can Hammer it out,
    Which no Body, &c.

Now if to know him you would desire,
You must not scorn but rank him higher;
For what he gets is out of the Fire,
    Which no Body, &c.

Now here's a good Health to *Blacksmiths* all,
And let it go round, as round as a Ball;
VVe'll drink it all off though it cost us a fall,
    Which no Body, &c.

The

The BREWER.   *To the foregoing Tune.*

THere's many Clinching Verse is made,
   In Honour of the *Blacksmith's* Trade;
But more of the *Brewer* may be said,
   Which no Body can deny.

I need not much of this repeat,
The *Blacksmith* cannot be Compleat;
Unless the *Brewer* do give him a heat,
   Which no Body, &c.

VVhen Smug unto the Forge doth come,
Unless the *Brewer* doth Liquor him home;
He'll never strike, my Pot, and thy Pot, *Tom,*
   Which no Body, &c.

Of all professions in the Town,
The *Brewer's* Trade hath gain'd renown;
His Liquor reaches up to the Crown,
   Which no Body, &c.

Many new Lords from him there did spring,
Of all the Trades he still was their King;
For the *Brewer* had the VVorld in a sling,
   Which no Body, &c.

He scorneth all Laws and Marshal stops,
But whips an Army as round as tops,
And cuts off his Foes as thick as Hops,
   Which no Body, &c.

He dives for Riches down to the Bottom,
And crys my Masters when he has got 'em;
Let every Tub stand upon his own bottom,
   Which no Body, &c.

In

In Warlike Acts he scorns to stoop,
For when his Army begins to droop ;
He draws them up as round as a Hoop,
   Which no Body can deny.

The Jewish *Scot* that scorns to Eat
The flesh of Swine, and Brewers beat ;
Twas the sight of his Hogs-head made 'em retreat,
   Which no Body, &c.

Poor *Jockey* and his Basket Hilt
Was beaten, and much Blood was spilt ;
And their Bodies like Barrels did run a tilt,
   Which no Body, &c.

Though *Jemmy* gave the first Assault,
The Brewer at last made him to halt ;
And gave them what the Cat left in the Malt,
   Which no Body, &c.

They cry'd that Anti-christ came to settle,
Religion in a Cooler and a Kettle ;
For his Nose and Copper were both of one Metal,
   Which no Body, &c.

Some Christian Kings began to quake,
And said with the Brewer no quarrel we'll make ;
We'll let him alone, as he Brews let him Bake,
   Which no Body, &c.

He hath a strong and very stout Heart,
And thought to be made an Emperor for't ;
But the Devil put a Spoke in his Cart,
   Which no Body, &c.

If any intended to do him disgrace,
His Fury would take off his Head in the place ;
He always did carry his Furnace in his Face,
   Which no Body can deny.

                                   But

But yet by the way you must understand,
He kept his Foes so under Command ;
That Pride could never get the upper hand,
   Which no Body can deny.

He was a stout Brewer of whom we may brag,
But now he is hurried away with a Hag ;
He Brews in a Bottle, and Bakes in a Bag,
   Which no Body, &c.

And now may all stout Soldiers say,
Farewel the glory of the Day ;
For the Brewer himself is turn'd to Clay,
   Which no Body, &c.

Thus fell the brave Brewer, the bold Son of slaughter,
We need not to fear, what shall follow after ;
For he dealt all his time in Fire and Water,
   Which no Body, &c.

And if his Successor had had but his might,
Then we had not been in a pitiful plight ;
But he was found many grains too light,
   Which no Body, &c.

Let's leave off Singing, and Drink off our Bub,
We'll call up a Reckoning, and every Man Club ;
For I think I have told you a Tale of a Tub,
   Which no Body can deny.

A

A Song *made on the Power of Women.* *To the foregoing Tune.*

WILL you give me leave, and I'll tell you a story,
Of what has been done by your Fathers before ye,
It shall do more good than Ten of *John Dory*,
  Which no Body can deny.

'Tis no Story of *Robin Hood*, nor of his Bow-men,
I mean to Demonstrate the power of Women;
It is a Subject that's very common,
  Which no Body, &c.

What tho' it be, yet I'll keep my Station,
And in spite of Criticks give you my Narration:
For Women now are all in Fashion,
  Which no Body, &c.

Then pray give me advice as much as you may,
For of all things that ever bore sway;
A Woman beareth the Bell away,
  Which no Body, &c.

The greatest Courage that ever rul'd,
Was baffled by Fortune, tho' ne'er so well school'd;
But this of the Women can never be cool'd,
  Which no Body, &c.

I wonder from whence this power did spring,
Or who the Devil first set up this thing;
That spares neither Peasant, Prince, nor King,
  Which no Body, &c.

Their Scepter doth rule from *Cæsar* to Rustick,
From finical *Kit*, to Soldier so lustick;
In fine, it Rules all, tho' ne'er so Robustick,
  Which no Body can deny.

For where is he that writes himself Man,
'That ever saw Beauty in *Betty* or *Nan;*
But his Eyes turn'd Pimp, and his Heart trapan,
    Which no Body, &c.

I fain would know one of *Adam's* Race,
Tho' ne'er so Holy a Brother of Grace ;
If he met a loose Sister, but he wou'd embrace,
    Which no Body, &c.

What should we talk of Philosophers old,
Whose Desires were hot, tho' their Natures cold :
But in this kind of Pleasure they commonly rowl'd,
    Which no Body, &c.

First *Aristotle*, that jolly old fellow,
Wrote much of *Venus*, but little of *Bellow;*
Which shew'd he lov'd a Wench that was mellow,
    Which no Body, &c.

From whence do you think he derived Study,
Produc'd all his Problems, a Subject so muddy ;
'Twas playing with her at Cuddle my Cuddy,
    Which no Body, &c.

The next in order is *Socrates* grave,
Who Triumph'd in Learning and Knowledge yet gave
His Heart to *Aspatia*, and became her Slave,
    Which no Body, &c.

Demosthenes to *Corinth* he took a Voyage,
We shall scarce know the like on't in thy Age or my Age
And all was for a Modicum Pyeage,
    Which no Body, &c.

The *Proverb* in him a whit did not fail,
For he had those things which make Men prevail ;
A sweet Tooth and a Liquorish tayl,
    Which no Body can deny.

                                                Ly-

Lycurgus and *Solon* were both Law-makers,
And no Men I'm sure are such Wise-acres;
To think that themselves would not be partakers,
   Which no Body can deny.

An Edict they made with Approbation,
If the Husband found fault with his Wives consolation;
He might take another for Procreation,
   Which no Body, &c.

If the Wife found coming in short,
The same Law did right her upon report;
Whereby you may know, they were Lovers o'th' Sport,
   Which no Body, &c.

And now let us view the State of a King,
Who is thought to have the World in a string;
By a Woman is Captivated, poor thing,
   Which no Body, &c.

Alexander the Great, who conquered all,
And Wept because the World was so small;
In the Queen of *Amazon's* pit did fall,
   Which no Body, &c.

Antonius, and *Nero,* and *Caligula,*
Were *Rome's* Tormentors by Night and by Day;
Yet Women beat them at their own Play,
   Which no Body can deny.

The

The Infallible Doctor.

From

FROM *France*, from *Spain*, from *Rome* I come,
   And from all Parts of *Christendom ;*
For to Cure all strange Diseases,
Come take Physick he that pleases :
Come ye broken Maids that scatter,
And can never hold your Water,
     I can teach you it to keep ;
     And other things are very meet,
     As groaning backward in your Sleep.

Come an ugly dirty Whore,
That is at least Threescore or more ;
Whose Face and Nose stands all awry,
As if you'd fear to pass her by ;
I can make her Plump and Young,
Lusty, lively and also strong ;
     Honest, Active, fit to Wed,
     And can recall her Maiden-head,
     All this is done as soon as said.

If any Man has got a Wife,
That makes him weary of his Life
With Scolding, yoleing in the House,
As tho' the Devil was turn'd loose :
Let him but repair to me,
I can Cure her presently
     With one Pill, I'll make her civil,
     And rid her Husband of that evil,
     Or send her Headlong to the Devil.

The Pox, the Palsey, and the Gout,
Pains within, and Aches without ;
There is no Disease but I
Can find a present Remedy :
Broken Legs and Arms, I'm sure,
Are the easiest Wounds I Cure ;
     Nay, more than that I will maintain,
     Break your Neck, I'll set it again,
     Or ask you nothing for my pain.

                       Or

Or if any Man has not
The Heart to fight against the *Scot;*
I'll put him in one, if he be willing,
Shall make him fight and ne'er fear killing :
Or any that has been Dead,
Seven long Years and Buried ;
     I can him to Life restore,
     And make him as sound as he was before,
     Else let him never trust me more.

If any Man desire to Live
A Thousand Ages, let him give
Me a Thousand Pounds, and I
Will warrant him Life, unless he Dye ;
Nay more I'll teach him a better Trick,
Shall keep him well, if he ne'er be sick;
     But if I no Money see,
     And he with Diseases troubled be,
     Than he may thank himself, not me.

A Song *made on the Downfall, or pulling
down of* Chairing-Cross : *An. Dom.* 1642.

Undone ! undone ! the Lawyers are,
   They wander about the Town ;
And cannot find the way to *Westminster*,
   Now *Chairing-Cross* is down :
At the end of the *Strand*, they make a stand,
   Swearing they are at a loss ;
And Chaffing say, that's not the way,
   They must go by *Chairing-Cross*.

The Parliament to Vote it down,
   Conceived very fitting ;
For fear't should fall and Kill 'em all,
   I'th' House as they were sitting :
They were inform'd't had such a Plot,
   Which made 'em so hard Hearted ;
To give express command, it should be
   Taken down and Carted.

Men talk of Plots, this might been worse,
   For any thing I know ;
Than that *Tomkins* and *Chalenour*,
   Was Hang'd for long ago ;
But as our Parliament from that,
   Themselves strangely defended ;
So still they do discover Plots,
   Before they be intended.

For neither Man, Woman, nor Child,
  Will say I am confident;
They ever heard it speak one Word,
  Against the Parliament:
T' had Letters about it some say,
  Or else it had been freed;
Fore-God I'll take my Oath that it,
  Could neither Write, nor Read.

The Committee said, Verily
  To Popery 'twas bent;
For ought I know it might be so,
  For to the Church it never went:
What with Excise, and other loss,
  The Kingdom doth begin;
To think you'll leave 'em ne'er a Cross
  Without Door, nor within.

Methinks the Common-Council should,
  Of it have taken pity;
Cause good old Cross, it always stood,
  So strongly to the City:
Since Crosses you so much disdain,
  Faith if I was as you;
For fear the King should Rule again,
  I'd pull down Tyburn too.

Cas-

CASSANDRA *in Mourning.*

A Wake my Lute, arise my string,
   And to my sad *Cassandra* sing ;
Like the old Poets,
When the Moon had put her Sable Mourning on :
Aloud they sounded with a merry strain,
Until her brightness was restor'd again.

Too

Too well I know from whence proceeds,
Thy wearing of these Mournful weeds ;
In cruel Flames for thee I Burn,
And thou for me dost therefore Mourn ;
So sits a glorious Goddess in the Skies,
Clouded i'th' Smoak of her own Sacrifice.

Wear other Virgins what they will,
Cassandra loves her Mourning still ;
Thus the Milky-way so white,
Is never seen but in the Night ;
The Sun himself, altho' so bright he seem,
Is black, as are the *Moors* that Worship him.

But tell me thou Deformed Cloud,
How dar'st thou such a Body shroud ?
So *Satyrs*, with black hedious Face,
Of old did lovely Nymphs Embrace :
That Mourning e'er should hide such glorious Maids,
Thus Deities of Old did live in Shades.

Her words are Oracles, and come,
(Like those) from out some darkned Room ;
And her Breath proves that Spices do,
Only in scorched Countries grow :
If she but speak, an *Indian* she appears,
Tho' all o'er black, at Lips she Jewels wears.

Methinks I now do *Venus* spy,
As she in *Vulcan's* Arms did lie ;
Such is *Cassandra* and her shroud,
She looks like Snow within a Cloud :
Melt then and yield, throw off thy Mourning Pall,
Thou never canst look White, until thou Fall.

A

A SONG.

YOnder comes a courteous Knight,
   Lustily raking over the hay,
He was well ware of a bonny lass,
   As she came wandering over the way :
Then she sang down a down,
   Hey down derry ; than she, &c.

Jove

Jove you speed, fair Lady, he said,
    Amongst the leaves that be so green ;
If I. were a King, and wore a Crown,
    Full soon fair Lady, should thou be a Queen.
        Then she sang, *&c.*

Also *Jove* save you, fair Lady,
    Among the Roses that be so red ;
If I have not my will of you,
    Full soon fair Lady, shall I be dead.
        Then she sang, *&c.*

Then he lookt East, then he lookt West,
    He lookt North, so did he South :
He could not find a privy place,
    For all lay in the Devil's mouth.
        Then she sang, *&c.*

If you will carry me gentle Sir,
    A maid unto my father's hall ;
Then you shall have your will of me
    Under purple and under Pall.
        Then she sang, *&c.*

He set her upon a steed,
    And himself upon another ;
And all the day he rode her by,
    As tho' they had been sister and brother.
        Then she sang, *&c.*

When she came to her fathers hall,
    It was well walled round about ;
She rode in at the wicket gate,
    And shut the four ear'd fool without.
        Then she sang, *&c.*

You had me (quoth she) abroad in the field,
    Among the corn, amidst the hay,
Where you might had your will of me,
    For, in good faith Sir, I ne'er said nay.
        Then she sang, *&c.*

You

You had me also amid the field,
 Among the rushes that were so brown ;
Where you might had your will of me,
 But you had not the face to lay me down.
  Then she sang, *&c.*

He pull'd out his nut-brown sword,
 And wip'd the rust off with his sleeve :
And said ; *Joves* Curse come to his heart,
 That any Woman would believe.
  Then she sang, *&c.*

When you have your own true love,
 A mile or twain out of the Town,
Spare not for her gay cloathing,
 But lay her body flat on the ground.
  Then she sang, *&c.*

Reciprocal Love.

I Love a Lass but cannot show it,
  I keep a fire that burns within,
Rak'd up in embers : Ah ! could she know it,
  I might perhaps be lov'd again :
    For a true love may justly call,
    For friendship love reciprocal.

Some gentle courteous winds betray me,
  A sigh by whispering in her ear,
Or let some pitious shower convey me,
  By dropping on her breast a tear,
    Or two, or more ; the hardest flint,
    By often drops receive a dint.

Shall I then vex my heart and rend it,
  That is already too, too weak ;
No, no, they say Lovers may send it,
  By writing what they cannot speak :
    Go then my muse, and let this Verse,
    Bring back my Life, or else my Hearse.

The

The Country-Man's Ramble thro' Bartholomew-Fair.

A Dzooks ches went the other day to *London* Town,
In *Smithfield* such gazing,
Zuch thrusting and squeezing,
Was never known :
A Zitty of Wood, some Volk do call it *Bartledom*-Fair,
But ches zure nought but Kings and Queens live there.

In Gold and Zilver, Zilk and Velvet each was drest,
A Lord in his Zatting,
Was buisy prating,
Among the rest :
But one in blew Jacket came, which some do *Andrew* call,
Adsheart, talk'd woundly wittily to them all.

At

At last Cutzooks, he made such sport I laugh'd aloud,
    The Rogue, being fluster'd,
    He flung me a Custard,
    Amidst the Croud:
The Volk vell a laughing at me; then the Vezen zaid,
Bezure *Ralph*, give it to *Doll* the Dairy-maid.

I *zwallowed* the affront, but staid no longer there;
    I thrust and I scrambled,
    Till further I rambled,
    into the Fair.
Where *Trumpets* and *Bagpipes*, *Kettle-drums*, *Fidlers*,
    were *all* at work,
And the *Cook* zung, *Here's your delicate Pig and Pork*.

I look'd around, to see the Wonders of the Vair,
    Where Lads and Lasses,
    With Pudding-bag arses,
    Zo nimble were;
Heels over head, as round as a wheel they turn'd
    about,
Old Nick zure, was in their breeches without doubt.

Most woundy *pleas'd*, I up and down the Vair did range,
    To zee the vine Varies,
    Play all their Vagaries,
    I vow 'twas strange.
I ask'd them aloud, *What Country little Volk they were?*
A cross brat answer'd me, *Che were Cuckold-shire.*

I thrust and shov'd *along as well* as e'er I *could*,
    At *last did I grovel*,
    Into a dark Hovel,
    Where Drink was *sold;*
They brought me Cans, which cost a penny apiece,
    adsheart,
I'm zure twelve *ne'er could fill a* Country-quart.

Che went to draw her Purse, to pay them for their beer,
    The *Devil* a Penny.
    Was left of my Money,
    Che'll vow and zwear:
                They

They doft my Hat for a Groat, then turn'd me out of
    doors :
Adswounds, *Ralph*, did ever zee zuch Rogues and
    Whores.

TOM a BEDLAM.

Forth from the dark and dismal Cell,
    And from the deep Abyss of Hell,
Mad *Tom* is come to view the World again,
To see if he can cure his distemper'd Brain.

Fears and Cares oppress my Soul,
Hark how the angry Furies howl,
Pluto laughs, and *Proserpine* is glad,
To see poor naked *Tom* of *Bedlam* mad.

Thro' the World I wander Night and Day,
    To find my stragling Senses,
In an angry Mood Old *Time*,
    With his Pentateuch of Tenses.

When me he spyes, away he flies,
    For Time will stay for no Man ;
In vain with Cries I rend the Skies,
    For Pity is not common.

Cold and Comfortless I lye,
Help ! oh help ! or else I die ;
Hark I hear *Apollo's* Team,
    The Carman gins to whistle,
Chast *Diana* bends her Bow,
    And the Boar begins to bristle.

                                  Come

Come *Vulcan* with Tools and Tackles,
And knock off my troublesome Shackles :
Bid *Charles* make ready his Wain,
To find my lost Senses again.

Last Night I heard the Dog-star bark,
Mars met *Venus* in the Dark :
Limping *Vulcan* heat an Iron Bar,
And furiously ran at the God of War.

Mars with his Weapon laid about,
Limping *Vulcan* had the Gout,
For his broad Horns hung so in his Light,
That he could not see to aim aright.

Mercury, the nimble Post of Heaven,
   Stay'd to see the Quarrel,
Gorrel Belly *Bacchus* giantly bestrid
   A Strong Beer Barrel.

To me he drank, I did him thank,
   But I could drink no Sider ;
He drank whole Butts 'till he burst his Guts,
   But mine were ne'er the wider.

Poor *Tom* is very dry,
A little Drink for Charity :
Hark ; I hear *Acteon's* Hounds,
   The Hunts-man whoops and Hallows,
Ringwood, Rockwood, Jowler, Bowman,
   All the Chace doth follow.

The Man in the Moon drinks Clarret,
   Eats powder'd Beef, Turnep and Carret,
But a Cup of old *Malago* Sack,
   Will fire the Bush at his Back.

The

The Prodigal's Resolution :

Or, my Father was born before me.

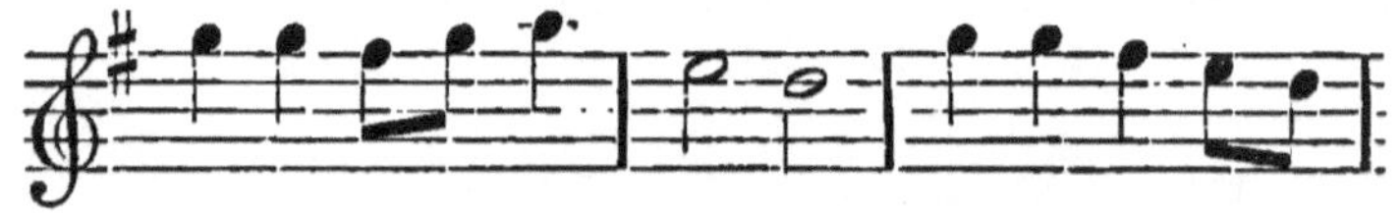

I Am a lusty lively Lad,
  Now come to One and Twenty,
My Father left me all he had,
  Both Gold and Silver plenty :
Now he's in Grave, I will be brave,
  The Ladies shall adore me ;
I'll court and kiss, what hurt's in this,
  My Dad did so before me.

My

My Father was a thrifty Sir,
  Till Soul and Body sundred,
Some say he was an Usurer,
  For thirty in the Hundred :
He scrapt and scratcht, she pincht and patcht,
  That in her Body bore me ;
But I'll let fly, good cause why,
  My Father was born before me.

My Daddy has his Duty done,
  In getting so much Treasure,
I'll be as dutiful a Son,
  For spending it in Pleasure ;
Five Pound a Quart shall cheer my Heart,
  Such Nectar will restore me,
But I'll let fly, good cause why,
  My Father was born before me.

My Grannum liv'd at *Washington,*
  My Grandsir delv'd in Ditches,
The Son of old *John Thrashington,*
  Whose Lantern Leather Breeches,
Cry'd, whither go ye ? whither go ye ?
  Tho' Men do now adore me,
They ne'er did see my Pedigree,
  Nor who was born before me.

My Gransir striv'd, and wiv'd, and thriv'd,
  'Till he did Riches gather,
And when he had much Wealth atchiev'd,
  Oh, then he got my Father :
Of happy Memory, cry I,
  That e'er his Mother bore him,
I ne'er had been worth one Penny,
  Had I been born before him.

To Free-school, *Cambridge,* and *Grays-Inn,*
  My gray-coat Gransir put him,
Till to forget he did begin,
  The Leathern Breech, that got him ;

One

One dealt in Straw, the other in Law,
  The one did ditch and delve it,
My Father store of Sattin wore,
  My Gransir Beggar's Velvet.

So I get Wealth, what care I if
  My Grandsir were a Sawyer,
My Father prov'd to be a chief,
  And subtile, Learned Lawyer:
By Cook's Reports, and Tricks in Courts,
  He did with Treasure store me,
That I may say, Heavens bless the Day,
  My Father was born before me.

Some say of late, a Merchant that
  Had gotten store of Riches,
In's Dining-Room hung up his Hat,
  His Staff, and Leathern Breeches:
His Stockings gartred up with Straw,
  E'er providence did store him,
His Son was Sheriff of *London*, cause
  His Father was born before him.

So many Blades now rant in Silk,
  And put on Scarlet Cloathing,
At first did spring from Butter-milk,
  Their Ancestors worth nothing;
Old *Adam*, and our Grandam *Eve*,
  By digging and by Spinning,
Did to all Kings and Princes give
  Their radical Beginning.

My Father to get my Estate,
  Tho' selfish, yet was slavish,
I'll spend it at another rate,
  And be as lewdly lavish;
From Mad-men, Fools, and Knaves he did
  Litigiously receive it;
If so he did, Justice forbid,
  But I to such should leave it.

At

At Play-houses, and Tennis Court,
    I'll prove a noble Fellow,
I'll court my Doxies to the Sport
    Of o'brave Bunchinello :
I'll drink and drab, I'll Dice and stab,
    No Hector shall out-roar me ;
If Teachers tell me Tales of Hell,
    My Father is gone before me.

Our aged Counsellors would have
    Us live by Rule and Reason,
'Cause they are marching to their Grave,
    And Pleasure's out of Season :
I'll learn to dance the Mode of *France,*
    That Ladies may adore me ;
My thrifty Dad no Pleasure had,
    Tho' he was born before me.

I'll to the Court, where *Venus* Sport
    Doth revel it in Plenty,
I'll deal with all, both great and small,
    From twelve to five and twenty ;
In Play-houses I'll spend my Days,
    For they're hung round with Plackets,
Ladies make room, behold I come,
    Have at your knocking Jackets.

Power of Love.

Since

Since love hath in thine, and mine Eye,
    Kindled a holy flame,
What pity 'twere to let it die,
    What sin to quench the same?
The stars that seem extinct by day,
    Disclose their flames at night,
And in a sable sense convey,
    Their loves in beams of light.

So when the jealous Eye, and Ear,
    Are shut or turn'd aside,
Our Tongues, our Eyes, may talk sans fear
    Of being heard or spy'd.
What tho' our bodies cannot meet,
    Love's fuel's more divine ;
The fixt stars by their twinkling greet,
    And yet they never joyn.

False Meteors that do change their place,
    Tho' they shine fair and bright ;
Yet when they covet to embrace,
    Fall down and lose their light.
Thus while we shall preserve from waste,
    The flame of our desire,
No Vestal shall maintain more chaste,
    Or more immortal fire.

If thou perceive thy flame decay,
    Come light thine eyes at mine ;
And when I feel mine waste away,
    I'll take new fire from thine.

A SONG.

IN the merry month of *May*,
  On a morn by break of day,
Forth I walk'd the wood so wide,
When as *May* was in her pride :
There I spy'd all alone, all alone,
Phillida and *Choridon.*

Much ado there was God wot,
He did love, but she could not ;
He said his love was to woo,
She said none was false to you ;
He said he had lov'd her long,
She said love should take no wrong.

Choridon would have kist her then,
She said Maids must kiss no Men,
Till they kiss for good and all ;
Then she bad the shepherd call,

All

All the Gods to witness truth,
Ne'er was loved so fair a youth.

Then with many a pretty Oath,
As Yea and Nay, and Faith and Troth;
Such as silly Shepherds use,
When they would not love abuse;
Love which had been long deluded,
Was with Kisses sweet concluded.

And *Phillida* with Garlands gay,
Was Crowned the Lady *May*.

The TINKER.

HE that a *Tinker*, a *Tinker* would be,
  Let him leave other Loves,
And come listen to me;
Tho' he travels all the day
  He comes home late at night,
And Dallies, and Dallies, with his Doxey,
  And Dreams of delight.

His Pot and his Toast, in the morning he takes,
  And all the day long good Musick he makes;
He wanders the world, to Wakes, and to Fairs,
  And casts his Cap, and casts his Cap,
At the Court and her Cares,
  When to the Town the Tinker doth come,
O! how the wanton Wenches run.

Some bring him Basons, some bring him Bowls,
  All Wenches pray him to stop up their holes;
Tink goes the Hammer, the Skillet and the Scummer
  Come bring me the Copper Kettle,
For the *Tinker*, the *Tinker*,
  The merry, merry *Tinker*,
O! he is the Man of Mettle.

A Forsaken Lover's Complaint.

As

AS I walk'd forth one summers day,
　　To view the meadows green and gay,
A pleasant Bower I espied,
Standing fast by a River side ;
And in't a Maiden, I heard cry,
Alas ! Alas ! there's none e'er lov'd as I.

Then round the meadow, did she walk,
Catching each flower by the stalk :
Such flowers as in the meadow grew,
The *Dead-man's Thumb*, an Herb all blew,
　　And as she pull'd them, still cry'd she,
　　Alas ! Alas ! none ever lov'd like me.

The Flowers of the sweetest scents,
She bound about with knotty Bents,
And as she bound them up in Bands,
She wept, sigh'd, and wrung her hands,
　　Alas ! Alas ! Alas ! cry'd she,
　　Alas ! none ever lov'd like me.

When she had fill'd her Apron full,
Of such green things as she could cull,
The green leaves serv'd her for a Bed,
The Flowers were the Pillows for her head :
　　Then down she laid, ne'er more did speak ;
　　Alas ! Alas ! with Love her heart did break.

Love's

Love's Bacchanal.

Lay

L Ay that sullen Garland by thee,
    Keep it for th' Elisium shades ;
Take my wreath of lusty Ivy,
    Not of that faint Mirtle made.

When I see thy soul descending,
    To that cold unfertile Plain ;
Of sad Fools, the Lake attending,
    Thou shalt wear this Crown again.
       Cho.
Now drink Wine, and know the odds,
    'Twixt that *Lethe,* 'twixt that *Lethe,*
'Twixt that *Lethe,* and the Gods.

Rouse thy dull and drowsie Spirits,
    Here's the soul reviving streams,
The stupid Lovers brain inherits,
    Nought but vain and empty Dreams.

Think not thou these dismal trances,
    Which our raptures can content,
The Lad that laughs, and sings and dances,
    Shall come soonest to his end.
       Cho.
Sadness may some pity move,
Mirth and Courage, mirth and courage,
Mirth and Courage, conquers Love.

Fy then on that cloudy forehead,
    Ope those vainly crossed arms ;
Thou may'st as well call back the buried,
    As raise Love, by such like charms.

Sacrifice a glass of Claret,
    To each letter of her Name ;
Gods have oft descended for it,
    Mortals must do more the same.
       Cho.
If she comes not at the flood,
Sleep will come, sleep will come,
Sleep will come, and that's as good.

                          Amyn-

Amyntor *Distracted Complains.*

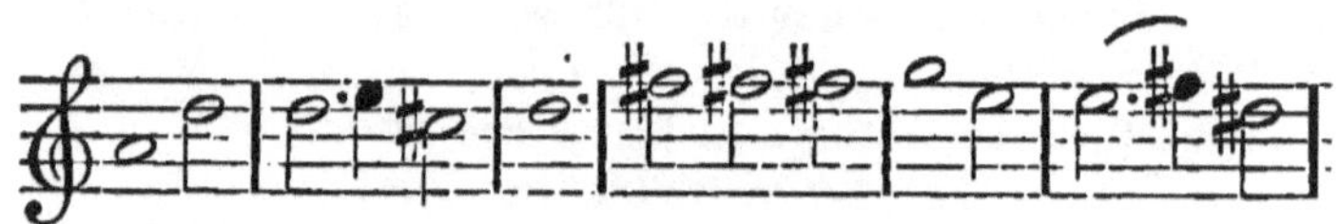

I Had a *Chloris* my Delight,
    Hey down, hey down,
With Hair as brown as Berries ;
Her Cheeks like Roses, red and white,
    Her Lips more sweet than Cherries.

Tho' lovely Black dwelt in her Eyes,
    Hey down, hey down,
Like brightest Day that shin'd ;
And Hills of Snow upon her Breast,
    Made me, and all Men blind.

She was so sweet, so kind, so free,
    Hey down, hey down,
To kiss, to sport, and play ;
But all this was with none but me,
    So Envy 't self will say.

She fed her Flock on yonder Plain,
    Hey down, hey down,
'Tis wither'd now, and dry ;
How can *Amyntor* longer live,
When such Things for her die ?

Her

Her wandring Kids look in my Face,
    Hey down, hey down,
And with dumb Tears express,
The want of *Chloris*, my true Love,
    And their kind Shepherdess.

She lov'd me without Fraud or guile,
    Hey down, hey down,
But not for Flocks or Treasure ;
And I was happy all the while,
    But no Woe worth all Pleasure.'

When she liv'd, I went fine and gay,
    Hey down, hey down,
With Flowers and Ribbons deck'd ;
But now I am (as Shepherds say)
    The Emblem of Neglect.

Where are those pretty Garlands now,
    Hey down, hey down,
Of Ivy and of Bays,
Which *Chloris* platted on my Brow,
    For singing in her Praise ?

With naked Legs and Arms I go,
    Hey down, hey down,
For why ? the Clothes I wore,
With Bonnets, Scarfs, and many more,
    Upon her Grave lie tore.

For woe is me, I should be warm,
    Hey down, hey down,
Or any Comfort have,
As long as my dear *Chloris* lies
    So cold within her Grave.

I'll gather Sticks, and make a Fire,
    Hey down, hey down,
So warm her where she lies,
Of Myrtles, Cypress, and Sweet Bryer,
    And then perhaps she'll rise.

To

To Young Virgins.
A SONG.

Virgins, if e'er at length it prove,
    My Destiny to be, to be in Love,
  Pray wish me such a Fate :
May Wit and Prudence be my Guide,
And may a little decent Pride,
    My Actions regulate.
♀ Virgins, if e'er I am in Love,
Pray wish me such a Fate.

Such Stateliness I mean, as may
Keep nauseous Fools and Fops, and Fops away,
    But still oblige the Wise :
That may secure my Modesty,
And Guardian to my Honour be,
    When Passion does arise,
♀ Virgins, if e'er I am in Love, &c.

When first a Lover I commence,
May it be with a Man, a Man of Sence,
    And learned Education :
May all his Courtship easy be,
Neither too formal nor too free,
    But wisely show his Passion.
♀ Virgins, &c.

May his Estate agree with mine,
That nothing look like a Design,
    To bring us into Sorrow :
Grant me all this that I have said,
And willingly I'll live a Maid
    No longer than to Morrow.
♀ Virgins, if e'er I am in Love,
Pray wish me such a Fate.

A

A SONG.

FOur and twenty Fidlers all in a Row,
   And there was fiddle fiddle, and twice fiddle
     fiddle,
'Cause 'twas my Lady's Birth-day,
Therefore we kept Holiday,
And all went to be merry.

Four and twenty Drummers all in a Row,
And there was tantarra rara, tan, tantarra rara, rara,
    rara rar, there was rub, *&c.*

Four and twenty Tabors and Pipers all in a Row,
And there was whif and dub,
   And tan tarra rara, *&c.*

Four

Four and twenty Women all in a row,
And there was tittle tatile, and twice prittle prattle ;
  And Whif and Dub, *&c.*

Four and twenty Singing Men all in a row,
And there was Fa la, la, la, la, ; Fa, la, la, la, la, la,
  And there was Tittle, *&c.*

Four and twenty Fencing-Masters all in a row,
And this and that, and down to the Legs clap, Sir,
  And cut 'em off, and Fa, *&c.*

Four and twenty Lawyers all in a row,
And there was *Omne quod exit in um damno sed
Plus Damno Decorum,* and there was this and that, *&c.*

Four and twenty Vintners all in a row,
And there was rare Claret and White, I ne'er drunk
Worse in my life, and excellent good Canary drawn off
The Lees of Sherry, if you do not like it,
  Omne Quod, &c.

Four and twenty Parliament Men all in a Row,
And there was Loyalty and Reason, without a word
Of Treason, and there was rare Claret, *&c.*

Four and twenty *Dutch* Men all in a row,
And there was *Alter Malter Van tor Dyken Skapen
Kopen de Hogue, Van Rottyck, Van tonsick de Brille,
Van Boerstyck Van Foerstick and Soatrag Van Hogan
  Herien-Van-Donck,*
Rare Claret and white, *&c.*

A SONG.

A Beggar got a Beadle,
　A Beadle got a Yeoman ;
A Yeoman got a Prentice,
　And a Prentice got a Freeman ;
The Freeman got a Master,
　The Master got a Lease,
The Lease made him a Gentleman,
　And Justice of the Peace.

The Justice being Rich,
　And Gallant in desire ;
He marry'd with a Lady,
　And so he got a Squire :
The Squire got a Knight
　Of Courage bold and stout ;
The Knight he got a Lord,
　And so it came about.

The Lord he got an Earl,
　His Country he forsook ;
He travell'd into *Spain*,
　And there he got a Duke :

The

The Duke he got a Prince,
　The Prince a King of Hope :
The King he got an Emperor,
　The Emperor got a Pope.

Thus as it was feigned,
　The Pedigree did run ;
The Pope he got a *Fryer*,
　The Fryer he got a Nun :
The Nun by chance did stumble,
　And on her Back she sunk,
The Fryer fell a top of her,
　And so they got a Monk.

The Monk he had a Son,
　With whom he did inhabit,
Who when the Father died,
　The Son became Lord Abbot :
Lord Abbot had a Maid,
　And he catcht her in the Dark,
And something he did to her,
　And so begot a Clark.

The Clark he got a Sexton,
　The Sexton got a Digger ;
The Digger got a Preband,
　The Preband got a Vicar ;
The Vicar got an Attorney,
　The which he took in snuff ;
The Attorney got a Barrister,
　The Barrister got a Ruff.

The Ruff did get good Counsel,
　Good Counsel got a Fee,
The Fee did get a Motion,
　That it might Pleaded be ;
The Motion got a Judgment,
　And so it came to pass ;
A Beggar's Bratt, a scolding Knave,
　A Crafty Lawyer was.

A

A New BALLAD *upon a Wedding.*

THE Sleeping *Thames* one Morn I cross'd,
By two contending *Charons* tost ;
I Landed and I found,
By one of *Neptune's* jugling Tricks,
Enchanted *Thames* was turn'd to *Styx*,
Lambeth th' Elysian Ground.

The Dirty Linkboy of the Day,
To make himself more fresh and gay,
Had spent five Hours, and more ;
Scarce had he Comb'd and Curl'd his Hair,
When out there comes a brighter Fair,
Eclips'd him o'er, and o'er.

The dazl'd Boy wou'd have retir'd,
But durst not, because he was hir'd,

To light the Purblind Skies;
But all on Earth, will Swear and say,
They saw no other Sun that Day,
        Nor Heav'n, but in her Eyes.

Her starry Eyes, both warm and shine,
And her dark Brows, do them enshrine,
        Like Love's Triumphal Arch;
Their Firmament is Red and White,
Whilst the other Heav'n is but bedight,
        With *Indigo* and *Starch.*

Her Face a Civil War had bred,
Betwixt the White Rose and the Red,
        Then Troops of Blushes came;
And charg'd the White with might and main,
But stoutly were repuls'd again,
        Retreating back with shame.

Long was the War, and sharp the Fight,
It lasted dubious until Night,
        Which wou'd to the other yield;
At last the Armies both stood still,
And left the Bridegroom at his Will,
        The Pillage of the Field.

But, oh, such Spoils! which to compare,
A Throne is but a rotten Chair,
        And Scepters are but sticks;
The Crown it self, 'twere but a Bonnet,
If her Possession lay upon it,
        What Prince wou'd not here fix.

Heaven's Master-piece, Divinest frame,
That e'er was spoke of yet by Fame,
        Rich Nature's utmost Stage;
The Harvest of all former years,
The past's Disgrace, the future's fears,
        And glory of this Age.

Thus

Thus to the Parson's Shop they trade,
And a slight Bargain there is made,
    To make Him her Supreme;
The Angels pearch'd about her Light,
And Saints themselves had Appetite,
    But I will not Blaspheme.

The Parson did his Conscience ask,
If he were fit for such a Task,
    And cou'd perform his Duty;
Then straight the Man put on the Ring,
The Emblem of another thing,
    When strength is joyn'd to Beauty.

A modest Cloud her Face invades,
And wraps it up in Sarsnet Shades,
    While thus they mingle Hands;
And then she was oblig'd to say,
Those Bug-bear Words, *Love and Obey*,
    But meant her own Commands.

The envious Maids lookt round about,
To see what One wou'd take them out,
    To terminate their Pains;
For tho' they Covet, and are Cross,
Yet still they value more one Loss,
    Than many Thousand Gains.

Knights of the Garter, two were Call'd,
Knights of the Shoe-string, two install'd,
    And all were bound by Oath;
No further than the Knee to pass,
But oh! the Squire of the Body was
    A better place than both.

A tedious Feast protracts the time,
For eating now, was but a Crime,

        And

      And all that interpos'd ;
For like two Duellists they stood,
Panting for one another's Blood,
      And longing till they clos'd.

Then came the Jovial Musick in,
And many a merry *Violin*,
      That Life and Soul of Legs ;
Th' impatient Bridgroom would not stay,
Good Sir, cry they, what Man can play,
      Till he's wound up his pegs.

But then he Dances till he reels,
For Love and Joy had Wing'd his Heels,
      And puts the Hours to flight ;
He leapt and skipt, and seem'd to say,
Come Boys, I'll drive away the Day,
      And shake away the Night.

The lovely Bride, with Murd'ring Arts,
Walks round, and Brandishes her Darts,
      To give the deeper Wound ;
Her Beauteous Fabrick, with such grace,
Ensnares a Heart, at every pace,
      And Kills at each rebound.

She glides as if there were no Ground,
And slily draws her Nets around,
      Her Lime-twigs are her Kisses ;
Then makes a Curtsie with a Glance,
And strikes each Lover in a Trance,
      That Arrow never misses.

Thus have I oft a Hobby seen,
Daring of Larks over a Green,
      His fierce occasion tarry ;
Dances about them as they fly,
And gives them sport before they Die,
      Then stoops and Kills the Quarry.

Her Sweat, like Honey-drops did fall,
And Stings of Beauty pierc'd us all,
    Her shape was so exact ;
Of Wax she seemed fram'd alive,
But had her Gown too been a Hive,
    How Bees had thither flock'd.

Thus envious Time prolong'd the Day,
And stretch'd the Prologue to the Play,
    Long stopp'd the sluggish Watch ;
At last a Voice came from above,
Which call'd the Bridegroom and his Love,
    To Consummate the Match.

But (as if Heav'n wou'd it retard)
A Banquet comes, like the Night-Guard,
    Which stay'd them half the Night ;
The Bridegroom then with's Men retir'd,
The Train was laying to be fir'd,
    He went his Match to light.

When he return'd, his Hopes was crown'd,
An Angel in the Bed he found,
    So glorious was her Face ;
Amaz'd he stopt —— but then, quoth He,
Tho' 'tis an Angel, 'tis a She,
    And leap'd into his Place.

Thus lay the Man with Heav'n in's Arms,
Bless'd with a Thousand pleasing Charms,
    In Raptures of Delight ;
Reaping at once, and Sowing Joys,
For Beauty's Manna never cloys,
    Nor fills the Appetite.

But what was done, sure was no more,
Than that which had been done before,
    When she her self was Made ;
Something was lost, which none found out,
And He that had it cou'd not shew't,
    Sure 'tis a Jugling Trade.

A

A SONG.

PHillis at first seem'd much afraid,
    Much afraid, much afraid,
Yet when I Kiss'd, she soon repay'd ;
Could you but see, could you but see,
What I did more, you'd Envy me,
What I did more, you'd Envy me,
You'd Envy me.

We

We then so sweetly were employ'd,
The height of Pleasure we enjoy'd ;
Could you but see, could you but see,
You'd say so too, if you saw me,
You'd say so too, if you saw me,
If you saw me.

She was so Charming, Kind, and Free,
None ever could more Happy be ;
Could you but see, could you but see,
Where I was then, you'd wish to be,
Where I was then, you'd wish to be,
You'd wish to be.

All the Delights we did express,
Yet craving more still to possess ;
Could you but see, could you but see,
You'd Curse, and say, why was't not me,
You'd Curse, and say, why was't not me,
Why was't not me.

Ladies, if how to Love you'd know,
She can inform what we did do ;
But cou'd you see, but cou'd you see,
You'd cry aloud, the next is me,
You'd cry aloud, the next is me,
The next is me.

A SONG.

FROM Twelve years old, I oft have been told,
   A Pudding it was a delicate bit ;
I can Remember my Mother has said,
What a Delight she had to be Fed
                                With a Pudding.

Thirteen being past, I long'd for to taste,
What Nature or Art, could make it so sweet ;
For many gay Lasses, about my Age,
Perpetually speak on't, that puts me in a rage
                                 For a Pudding.

Now at Fifteen, I often have seen,
Most Maids to admire it so ;
That their Humour and Pride is to say,
O what a Delight they have for to play
                                 With a Pudding.
                                       When

When I am among, some Wives that are young,
Who think they shall never give it due praise ;
It is sweet, It is good, It is pleasant still,
They cry, they think they shall ne'er have their fill
Of a Pudding.

The greater sort of the Town and the Court,
When met, their Tongues being tipp'd with Wine ;
How merry and Jocund their Tattles do run,
To tell how they ended, and how they begun
With a Pudding.

Some Ancient Wives, who most of their Lives,
Have daily tasted of the like Food ;
Now for want of Supplies, do Swear and Grumble,
That still they're able enough to Mumble
A Pudding.

Now, now I find, Cat will to kind,
Since all my Heart, and Blood is on fire ;
I am resolv'd whatever comes on't,
My Fancy no longer shall suffer the want
Of a Pudding.

For I'll to *John*, who says he has one,
That's cramm'd as close as a Cracker or Squib ;
Who ever is telling me when we do meet,
Of the wishing desires and sweetness they get
In a Pudding.

I thought at first, it never would burst,
It was as hard as Grissel or Bone ;
But by the Rowling and Trowling about,
How kindly and sweetly the Marrow flew out
Of his Pudding.

Well, since I ne'er was fed with such geer,
Until my *John* did prove so kind ;
I made a request to prepare again,
That I might continue in Love with the strain
Of his Pudding.
Then

Then straight he brought, what I little thought,
Could ever have been in its former plight ;
He Rumbl'd and Jumbl'd me o'er, and o'er,
Till I found he had almost wasted the store
Of his Pudding.

Then the other Mess, I begg'd him to dress,
Which by my Assistance was brought to pass ;
But by his dulness and moving so slow,
I quickly perceiv'd the stuffing grew low
In his Pudding.

Tho' he grew cold, my Stomach did hold,
With Vigour to relish the other bit ;
But all he could do, could not furnish again,
For he swore he had left little more than the Skin
Of his Pudding.

A SONG.

IF Musick be the Food of Love,
  Sing on, sing on, sing on, sing on,
Till I am fill'd, am fill'd with Joy;
  For then my listning Soul you move,
  For then my listning Soul you move,
With Pleasures that can never cloy:
Your Eyes, your Mein, your Tongue declare,
That you are Musick ev'ry where.

Pleasures invade both Eye, and Ear,
  So fierce the transports are, they Wound;
And all my Senses feasted are,
  Tho' yet the Treat is only sound.
Sure I must Perish by your Charms,
Unless you save me in your Arms.

A

A New Song, *upon the* Robin-red-breast's *attending Queen* Mary's *Hearse in* Westminster Abby.

ALL you that lov'd our Queen alive,
　　Now Dead lament Her fate;
And take a walk to *Westminster*,
　　To see Her lie in State.

Amongst all other glorious sights,
　　A Wonder you may see;
A Bird, or something like a Bird,
　　Attend Her Majesty.

Sometimes it Hops, sometimes it Flys,
　　Then Perches o'er the Hearse;
Then strains its Throat, and Sings a Note,
　　That's neither Prose nor Verse.

The Tune is Solemn as if Set
　　To fit some doleful Ditty;
In Lamentation for the Queen,
　　To move all Hearts to pity.

A perfect Bird, it seems to be,
　　In Feathers, Bill, and Wings;
Nor is their Feather'd Creatures else,
　　That Hops, and Flies, and Sings.

But

But what Bird 'twas not known, until,
  One Wiser than the rest ;
Affirm'd that he a *Robin* was,
  And prov'd it by his Breast.

I call it He, not She, because,
  It Sings, and Cocks its Tail ;
Which that no Female *Robin* doth,
  I'll hold a Pot of Ale.

This Bird abides about the Hearse,
  Most part of every Day ;
Nor can you fail to hear him Sing,
  Unless the Organs play.

For Organ Pipes, b'ing wider much,
  Than *Robin-red-Breast's* Throat ;
Their noise must needs be loud enough,
  To drown one *Robin's* Note.

Some say this Bird an Angel is,
  If so, we hope 'tis good ;
But why an Angel? why forsooth,
  They say, he takes no food.

But that the *Robin* lives by meat,
  Is true, without dispute ;
For tho' none ever saw him eat,
  Enough have seen him Mute.

And that sometimes undecently,
  Upon the Statue-Royal ;
Which made some call him *Jacobite*,
  Or otherwise Illoyal.

The *Papists* say, this Bird's a Fiend,
  Which haunts Queen *MARY'S* Ghost ;
And by its wrestless motion shews,
  How her poor Soul is tost.

But

But why then is this pretty Bird,
  So lively brisk and merry ;
This rather proves the Queen at ease,
  And safe from *Purgatory.*

An old Star-gazing * Taylor says,   * Gadbury *a*
  This frolick Bird proclaims ;   *Jacobite Alma-*
How glad all such as he would be,   *nack maker.*
  To welcome home King *JAMES.*

And *Patridge*, who can make both Shoes,   † Patridge
  And Almanacks to boot ;   *a Shoe-maker*
Says by this Bird assuredly,   *now makes Al-*
  Some Plot is still on Foot.   *manacks.*

For having like an Augur, watch'd,
  Which way he took his flight ;
The *Robin* flew on his left-hand,
  And not upon the right.

A Bird once in *Rome's* Capitol,   ‖ ἤ ςαι πᾱντα
  Said all ‖ things shall be well ;   καλῶς. Sueto-
And why this harmless *Robin* should,   nius *in the Life*
  Bode ill I cannot tell.   *of* Domitian.

All we can guess, is from this Bird's
  Appearing still alone ;
Which represents our King's Sole case,
  Now his fair Queen is gone.

The *Robin* may have lost his Mate,
  So hath King *William* his ;
And that he may well match again,
  Our hearty Prayer is.

A

A SONG. *New Set by Mr.* Church.

L Eave off fond *Hermite*, leave thy Vow,
  And fall again to Drinking;
That Beauties that want Sack allow,
  Is hardly worth thy thinking:
Dry Love or small can never hold,
And without *Bacchus*, *Venus* soon grows cold.

Dost think by turning Anchorite,
  Or a dull *Small-Beer* sinner;
Thy cold embraces can invite,
  Or sprightly Courtship win her:
No, 'tis *Canary* that inspires,
'Tis *Sack* like Oyl, gives Flames to Am'rous fires.

This

This makes thee chant thy Mistress name,
    And to the Heavens raise her ;
And range this Universal frame,
    For Epithets to praise her :
Low Liquors render Brains unwitty,
And ne'er provoke to Love, but move to pity,

Then by thy self, and take thy Glass,
    Leave off this dry Devotion ;
Thou must like *Neptune*, court thy Lass,
    Wallowing in *Nectar's* Ocean :
Let's offer to each Ladies shrine,
A full crown'd Bowl, here's Health to thine.

A SONG.   *New Set by Mr.* Church.

Ho

H O Boy, hey Boy,
 Come, come away Boy,
And bring me my longing desire ;
A Lass that is Neat, and can well do the Feat,
 When lusty young Blood is on fire.

Let her Body be Tall,
And her Wast be Small,
 And her age not above Eighteen ;
Let her care for no Bed, but here let spread,
 Her Mantle upon the Green.

Let her Face be fair,
And her Breasts be bare,
 And a Voice let her have that can Warble
Let her Belly be Soft, but to mount me aloft,
Let her Bounding Buttocks be Marble.

Let her have a Cherry Lip,
Where I *Nectar* may sip,
 Let her Eyes be as Black as a Sloe ;
Dangling Locks I do love, so that those hang above,
Are the same with what grows Below.

Oh such a bonny Lass,
May bring wonders to pass,
 And make me grow younger, and younger ;
And whene'er we do part, she'll be Mad at the Heart,
That I'm able to tarry no longer.

The Devil's Progress on Earth, or Huggle Duggle, &c.

F*Rier Bacon* walks again,
  And Doctor *Forster* too,
Proserpine and *Pluto*,
  And many a Goblin more :
With that a merry Devil
  To make the Airidge vow'd ;
Huggle Duggle Ha ! ha ! ha !
  The Devil laugh'd aloud.

Why

Why think you that he laugh'd,
  Forsooth he came from Court ;
And there amongst the Gallants
  Had spy'd such pretty Sport :
There was such cunning Jugling,
  And Ladies gone so proud ;
  Huggle Duggle, &c.

With that into the City
  Away the Devil went,
To view the Merchant's Dealings
  It was his full Intent,
And there along the brave Exchange
  He crept into the croud,
  Huggle Duggle, &c.

He went into the City,
  To see all there was well ;
Their Scales were false, their Weights were light,
  Their Conscience fit for Hell :
And *Panders* chosen Magistrates,
  And *Puritans* allow'd,
  Huggle Duggle, &c.

With that into the Country
  Away the Devil goeth,
For there is all plain Dealing,
  For that the Devil knoweth :
But the Rich Man Reaps the Gains,
  For which the poor Man Plough'd ;
  Huggle Duggle, &c.

With that the Devil in hast,
  Took post away to Hell ;
And call'd his Fellow Furies,
  And told them all on Earth was well :
That Falshood there did flourish,
  Plain Dealing was in a Cloud ;
Huggle Duggle Ha ! ha ! ha !
  The Devils laugh'd aloud.

G 2

A

A SONG, *New set by Mr.* Church.

LIKE a Ring without a Finger,
   Or a Bell without a Ringer,
Like a Horse was never ridden,
Or a Feast, and no Guest bidden ;
Like a Well without a Bucket,
Or a Rose if no Man pluck it ;
   Just such as these may she be said,
   That lives, ne'er loves, but dies a Maid.

The Ring, if worn, the Finger decks,
The Bell pull'd by the Ringer speaks,
The Horse doth ease, if he be ridden,
The Feast doth please, if Guest be bidden ;

The

The Bucket draws the Water forth,
The Rose when pluckt is still more worth;
  Such is the Virgin in my Eyes,
  That lives, loves, marries, e'er she dies.

Like to the Stock not grafted on,
Or like a Lute not play'd upon;
Like a Jack without a Weight,
Or a Barque without a Freight;
Like a Lock without a Key,
Or a Candle in the Day,
  Just such as these may she be said,
  That lives, ne'er loves, but dies a Maid.

The grafted Stock doth bear best Fruit,
There's musick in the finger'd Lute,
The Weight doth make the Jack go ready;
The Freight doth make the Bark go steady:
The Key the Lock doth open right,
The Candle's useful in the Night:
  Such is the Virgin in my Eyes,
  That lives, loves, marries, e'er she dies.

Like a Call with *Anon* Sir,
Or a Question, and no Answer:
Like a Ship was never rigg'd,
Or a Mine was never digg'd:
Like a Wound without a Tent,
Or Silver Box without a Scent:
  Just such as these may she be said,
  That lives, ne'er loves, but dies a Maid.

Th' *Anon* Sir, doth obey the Call,
The civil Answer pleaseth all:
Who rigs a Ship, sails with the Wind,
Who digs a Mine doth Treasure find:
The Wound by wholsome Tent hath ease,
The Box perfum'd the Senses please:
  Such is the Virgin in my Eyes,
  That lives, loves, marries, e'er she dies.

Like

Like Marrow-bone was never broken,
Or Commendation, and no Token :
Like a Fort, and none to win it,
Or like the Moon, and no Man in it;
Like a School without a Teacher,
Or like a Pulpit, and no Preacher ;
   Just such as these may she be said,
   That lives, ne'er loves, but dies a Maid.

The broken Marrow-bone is sweet,
The Token doth adorn the Greet ;
There's Triumph in the Fort being won,
The Man rides glorious in the Moon :
The School is by the Teacher still'd,
The Pulpit by the Preacher fill'd :
   Such is the Virgin in my Eyes,
   That lives, loves, marries, e'er she dies.

Like a Cage without a Bird,
Or a thing too long deferr'd :
Like the Gold was never tried,
Or the Ground unoccupied ;
Like a House that's not possessed,
Or a Book was never pressed :
   Just such as these may she be said,
   That lives, ne'er loves, but dies a Maid.

The Bird in Cage doth sweetly sing,
Due Season sweetens every thing ;
The Gold that's try'd from Dross is pur'd,
There's profit in the Ground mannur'd ;
The House is by Possession graced,
The Book well press'd is most embraced :
   Such is the Virgin in my Eyes,
   That lives, loves, marries, e'er she dies.

A

A SONG.

I Went to the Alehouse as an honest Woman shou'd,
  And a Knave follow'd after, as you know Knaves
     wou'd,
Knaves will be Knaves in every Degree,
I'll tell you by and by how this Knave serv'd me.

I call'd for my Pot as an honest Woman shou'd,
And the Knave drank't up, as you know Knaves wou'd,
  Knaves will be Knaves, &c.

I went into my Bed, as an honest Woman shou'd,
And the Knave crept into't, as you know Knaves
     wou'd,
  Knaves will be Knaves, &c.

I proved with Child as an honest Woman shou'd,
And the Knave ran away, as you know Knaves wou'd,
Knaves will be Knaves in every Degree,
And thus I have told you how this Knave serv'd me.

A

A Scotch SONG.

AS I sat at my Spinning-Wheel,
  A bonny Lad there passed by,
I kenn'd him round, and I lik'd him weel,
  Geud Feth he had a bonny Eye :
My Heart new panting, 'gan to feel,
But still I turn'd my Spinning-Wheel.

Most gracefully he did appear,
As he my Presence did draw near,
And round about my slender Waste
He clasp'd his Arms, and me embrac'd :
  To kiss my Hand he down did kneel,
  As I sat at my Spinning-Wheel.

My

My Milk white Hand he did extol,
And prais'd my Fingers long and small,
And said, there was no Lady fair,
That ever could with me compare :
   Those pleasing Words my Heart did feel,
   But still I turn'd my Spinning-Wheel.

Altho' I seemingly did chide,
Yet he would never be deny'd,
But did declare his Love the more,
Until my Heart was Wounded sore ;
   That I my Love cou'd scarce conceal,
   But yet I turn'd my Spinning-Wheel.

As for my Yarn, my Rock and Reel,
And after that my Spinning-Wheel,
He bid me leave them all with Speed
And gang with him to yonder Mead :
   My panting Heart strange Flames did feel,
   Yet still I turn'd my Spinning-Wheel.

He stopp'd and gaz'd, and blithly said,
Now speed the Wheel, my bonny Maid,
But if thou'st to the Hay-Cock go,
I'll learn thee better Work I trow,
   Geud Feth, I lik'd him passing weel,
   But still I turn'd my Spinning-Wheel.

He lowly veil'd his Bonnet oft,
And sweetly kist my Lips so soft ;
Yet still between each Honey Kiss,
He urg'd me on to farther Bliss :
   'Till I resistless Fire did feel,
   Then let alone my Spinning-Wheel.

Among the pleasant Cocks of Hay,
Then with my bonny Lad I lay,
What Damsel ever could deny,
A Youth with such a Charming Eye ?
   The Pleasure I cannot reveal,
   It far surpast the Spinning-Wheel.

A

A SONG.

D*Amon* why will you die for Love,
  Yet ne'er your flames discover;
Be wise and soon that pain remove,
Or tell the Nymph (or tell the Nymph) you Love her:
  As in each of her fierce disdain,
So in Love's cruel Anguish:
  He who wants Sense to beg for ease,
Deserves, (deserves in pain, in pain,
  Deserves) in pain to Languish.

Women like Fortune Love the bold,
  Like her their minds they vary;
Perhaps this day tho' *Celia's* Cold,
  With you the next She'll Marry:
Be sure be true if She is kind,
  If cruel then forget her;
With little pains you soon will find,
  A Nymph who'll use you better.

A SONG.

YOU understand no tender Vows,
   Of fervent and eternal Love;
That Lover will his labour lose,
   Who does with sighs and tears propose,
     Your Heart to move:
But if he talk of settling Land,
   A House in Town, and Coach maintain'd,
   You understand, you understand.

You understand no Charm in Wit,
   In Shape, in Breeding, or in Air;
To any Fop you will submit,
   The Nauseous Clown, or fulsome Citt,
     If rich they are,
Who Guineas can may you command,
   Put Gold, and then put in your ——
   You understand, you understand.

A

A SONG.

S Ince roving of late,
    Is as fatal as War ;
And no Female sinner,
    Will deal on the square ;
Since to keep's out of Fashion,
    And drains the poor Cully ;
While his Miss at his cost,
    Keeps some rascally Bully.

Since Mistresses fell,
    And Wives buy the Pleasure ;
And to wed or be constant's
    The same in some Measure ;
As soon as I can,
    I will leave Fornication,
And get a good Wife,
    If there's one in the Nation.

One modestly free,
    Not too proud of her Means ;
And tho' she writes Woman,
    Not out of her Teens,
Not indebted to Art,
    For her Wit nor her Beauty,
Yet whose Charms daily prompt me,
    To Family Duty.

Who visits the Church,
    Tho' custom can't move her,
To play there at Bo-peep,
    Cross Pew with a Lover :
Yet let her with care,
    Sun a contrary evil,
Lest Angel at Church,
    Prove at home a meer Devil.

Not one who to noose,
    Some young *Bubble* bestows,
Her whole slender Fortune,
    In Trifles and Cloaths ;

Nor

Nor an over-fond Dotard,
  Who Palls ev'ey pleasure,
While for Bottle or Friend,
  She would leave me no leisure.

Nor one kind and gay,
  Like some before Wedlock,
Then a Slut and a Shrew,
  When she holds me in Fetlock :
Nor will I in haste,
  My dear liberty barter,
Lest, thinking to catch,
  I am caught by a *Tartar.*

My Mistress much Sense,
  And all Vertues admit,
And joyn to good humour,
  Wealth, Beauty and Wit ;
With a fervent affection,
  She always must love me,
And no Beauty but hers,
  E'er be able to move me.

Oh ! such may she be,
  Who shall tempt me to Marry ;
If there is no such she,
  'Till there is, I must tarry :
And when she is found,
  I'll no more be a Rover,
But wed her with speed,
  And, what's strange, I'll Love her.

The

The surpriz'd Nymph.   *A SONG.*

THe four and twentieth day of May,
   Of all days in the year ;
A Virgin Lady fresh and gay,
   Did privately appear :
Hard by a River side got she,
   And did sing loud the rather ;
Cause she was sure, she was secure,
   And had intent to bathe her.

With

With glittering, glancing, jealous Eyes,
  She slily looks about;
To see if any lurking Spies
  Were hid to find her out:
And being well resolv'd that none,
  Could see her Nakedness,
She pull'd her Robes off one by one,
  And did her self undress.

Her purple Mantle fring'd with Gold,
  Her Ivory Hands unpinn'd;
It wou'd have made a Coward bold,
  Or tempted a Saint to 'a sinn'd:
She turn'd about and look'd around,
  Quoth she, I hope I'm safe;
Then her rosie Petticoat,
  She presently put off.

The snow white Smock which she had on,
  Transparently to deck her,
Look'd like Cambrick or Lawn,
  Upon an Alablaster Picture:
Thro' which Array I did faintly spy
  Her Belly and her Back;
Her Limbs were straight, and all was white,
  But that which should be Black.

Into a fluent Stream she leapt,
  She lookt like *Venus* Glass;
The Fishes from all Quarters crept,
  To see what Angel 'twas:
She did so like a Vision look,
  Or Fancy in a Dream;
'Twas thought the Sun the Skies forsook,
  And dropt into the Stream.

Each Fish did wish himself a Man,
  About her all was drawn,
And at the Sight of her began
  To spread abroad their Spawn;

She turn'd to swim upon her Back,
   And so display'd her Banner;
If *Jove* had then in Heaven been,
   He would have dropt upon her.

A Lad that long her Love had been,
   And cou'd obtain no Grace,
For all her prying lay unseen,
   Hid in a secret place:
Who had often been repuls'd,
   When he did come to Wooe her;
Pull'd off his Cloaths, and furiously
   Did run and leap into her.

She squeak'd, she cry'd, and down she div'd,
   He brought her up again;
He brought o'er upon the Shore,
   And then——and then——and then——
As *Adam* did Old *Eve* enjoy,
   You may guess what I mean;
Because she all uncover'd lay,
   He cover'd her again.

With water'd Eyes she pants and crys,
  ' I'm utterly undone;
If you will not be wed to me,
   E'er the next Morning Sun:
He answer'd her he ne'er would stir,
   Out of her Sight till then;
We'll both clap Hands in Wedlock Bands,
   Marry, and to't again.

A SONG,

New sett by Mr. Church.

A

A *Beggar*, a *Beggar*, a *Beggar* I'll be,
　There's none leads a Life more jocund than he,
A *Beggar* I was, and a *Beggar* I am,
A *Beggar* I'll be, from a *Beggar* I came,
If as it begins our Tradings do fall,
We in the Conclusion shall *Beggars* be all,
　　Tradesmen are unfortunate in their Affairs,
　　And few Men are thriving, but Courtiers and Players.

A Craver my Father, a Maunder my Mother,
A Filer my Sister, a Filcher my Brother,
A Canter my Uncle that car'd not for Pelf,
A Lifter my Aunt, and a *Beggar* my self;
In white wheaten Straw, when their Bellies were full,
Then I was got between a Tinker and a Trull.
　　And therefore a Beggar, a Beggar I'll be,
　　For there's none leads a Life more jocund than he.

When Boys do come to us, and that their Intent is
To follow our Calling, we ne'er bind 'em prentice;
Soon as they come to't, we teach them to do't,
And give them a Staff and a Wallet to boot,
We teach them their *Lingua*, to Crave and to Cant,
The Devil is in them if then they can want.
　　And he, or she, that a Beggar will be,
　　Without Indentures they shall be made free.

We beg for our Bread, yet sometimes it happens,
We feast it with a Pig, Pullet, Coney, and Capons,
For Churches Affairs, we are no Men-slayers,
We have no Religion, yet live by our Prayers,
　Butif when we beg; Men will not draw their Purses,
We charge, and give Fire with a Volley of Curses.
　　The Devil confound your good Worship, we cry,
　　And such a bold brazen-fac'd Beggar am I.

We do things in Season, and have so much Reason,
We raise no Rebellion, nor never talk Treason,
We bill all our Mates at very low Rates,
Whilst some keep their Quarters as high as the Gates,

With

With *Shinkin* ap *Morgan*, with blue-cap or *Teague*,
We into no Covenant enter, nor League.
   And therefore a bonny bold Beggar I'll be,
   For none lives a Life more merry than he.

For such petty Pledges, as Shirts from the Hedges,
We are not in fear to be drawn upon Sledges,
But sometimes the Whip doth make us to skip,
And then we from Tything to Tything do trip,
For when in a poor Bouzing-kan we do bib it,
We stand more in dread of the Stocks, than the Gibbet.
   And therefore a merry mad Beggar I'll be,
   For when it is Night in the Barn tumbles he.

We throw down no Alter, nor never do falter,
So much as to change a Gold Chain for a Halter;
Tho' some Men do flout us, and others do doubt us,
We commonly bear forty Pieces about us,
But many good Fellows are fine, and look fiercer,
That owe for their Clothes to the Taylor and Mercer.
   And if from the Stocks I can keep out my Feet,
   I fear not the Compter, King's-Bench, nor the Fleet.

Sometimes I do frame my self to be lame,
And when a Coach comes, I hop to my Game,
We seldom miscarry, or ever do marry,
By the Gown, Common-Prayer, or Cloak Directory;
But *Simon* and *Susan*, like Birds of a Feather,
They Kiss, and they laugh, and so lie down together.
   Like Piggs in the Pea-Straw, intangled they lie,
   'Till there they beget such a bold Rogue as I.

A SONG *on a Wedding.   New set by*
Mr. Clark.

NOW that Love's Holiday is come,
  And *Madg* the Maid hath swept the Room,
    And trimm'd her Spit and Pot;
Awake my merry Muse and sing,
The Revels and that other thing,
    That must not be forgot.

As the gray Morning dawn'd, 'tis said,
Clorinda broke out of her Bed,
    Like *Cynthia* in her Pride,
Where all the Maiden Lights that were
Compris'd within our *Hemisphere*,
    Attended at her side.

But

But wot you then, with much ado,
They dress'd the Bride from Top to Toe !
      And brought her from her Chamber ;
Deck'd in her Robes, and Garments gay,
More sumptuous than the live-long Day,
      Or Stars inshrin'd in Amber.

The sparkling Bullies of her Eyes,
Like two Eclipsed Suns did rise,
      Beneath her Chrystal Brow ;
To shew, like those strange Accidents,
Some sudden changeable Events,
      Were like to hap below.

Her Cheeks bestreak'd with white and red,
Like pretty Tell-tales of the Bed,
      Presag'd the blustring Night,
With his encircling Arms and Shade,
Resolv'd to swallow and invade,
      And skreen her Virgin Light.

Her Lips, those Threads of Scarlet die,
Wherein Love's Charms and Quiver lie,
      Legions of Sweets did crown,
Which smilingly did seem to say,
O crop me ! crop me ! whilst you may,
      Anon they're not mine own.

Her Breasts, those melting *Alps* of Snow ;
On whose fair Hills in open show,
      The *God of Love* lay knapping ;
Like swelling Butts of lively Wine,
Upon their Ivory Tilts did shine,
      To wait the lucky tapping.

Her Waste, that tender Type of Man,
Was but a small and single Span,
      Yet I dare safely swear,
He that whole thousands has in Fee,
Would forfeit all, so he might be
      Lord of the Mannor there.

                                             But

But now before I pass the Line,
Pray *Reader*, give me leave to dine,
    And pause here in the middle ;
The *Bridegroom* and the *Parson* knock,
With all the *Hymeneal* Flock,
    The *Plum-cake* and the *Fiddle.*

When as the Priest *Clarinda* sees,
He star'd, as't had been half his Fees,
    To gaze upon her Face :
And if the Spirit did not move,
His Countenance was far above
    Each Sinner in the place.

With mickle stir he joyn'd their Hands,
And hamper'd them in Marriage Bands,
    As fast as fast may be :
Where still methinks, methinks I hear,
That secret Sigh in every Ear,
    Once Love, remember me.

Which done, the Cook he knockt amain,
And up the Dishes in a train
    Came smoaking, two and two :
With that they wip'd their Mouths and sate,
Some fell to quaffing, some to prate,
    Ay, marry, and welcome too.

In pairs they thus impail'd the Meat,
Roger and *Margaret*, and *Thomas* and *Kate*,
    Ralph and *Bess*, *Andrew* and *Maudlin*,
And *Valentine*, eke with *Sybill* so sweet,
Whose Cheeks on each side of her Snuffers did meet,
    As round and as plump as a Codling.

When at the last they had fetched their Frees,
And mired their Stomachs quite up to their Knees
    In Claret and good Cheer ;
Then, then began the merry Din,
For as it was they were all on the pin,
    O ! what kissing and clipping was there.

But

But as Luck would have it, the *Parson* said Grace,
And to frisking and dancing they shuffled apace,
    Each Lad took his Lass by the Fist,
And when he had squeez'd her, and gam'd her, until
The Fat of her Face ran down like a Mill,
    He toll'd for the rest of the Grist.

In Sweat and in Dust having wasted the Day,
They enter'd upon the last Act of the Play,
    The Bride to her Bed was convey'd,
Where Knee-deep each Hand fell down to the Ground,
And in seeking the Garter much Pleasure was found ;
    'Twould have made a Man's Arm have stray'd.

This Clutter o'er *Clarinda* lay,
Half bedded, like the peeping Day,
    Behind *Olympus* Cap ;
VVhilst at her Head each twittering Girl,
The fatal Stocking quick did whirl,
    To know the lucky Hap.

The Bridegroom in at last did rustle,
All disappointed in the Bustle,
    The Maidens had shav'd his Breeches :
But let us not complain, 'tis well,
In such a Storm, I can you tell,
    He sav'd his other Stitches.

And now he bounc'd into the Bed,
Even just as if a Man had said,
    Fair Lady have at all ;
VVhere twisted at the Hug they lay,
Like *Venus* and the sprightly Boy,
    O ! who wou'd fear the Fall ?

Thus both with Love's sweet Tapor fired,
And thousand balmy Kisses tired,
    They could not wait the rest ;
But out the Folk and Candles fled,
And to't they went, and what they did,
    There lies the Cream o'th' Jest.

The

The Wife-Hater.   To the foregoing Tune.

HE that intends to take a Wife,
   I'll tell him what a kind of Life,
      He must be sure to lead ;
If she's a young and tender Heart,
Not documented in Love's Art,
      Much Teaching she will need.

For where there is no Path, one may
Be tir'd before he find the way ;
      Nay, when he's at his Treasure :
The Gap perhaps will prove so strait,
That he for Entrance long may wait,
      And make a toil of's Pleasure.

Or if one old and past her doing,
He will the Chambermaid be wooing,
      To buy her Ware the cheaper ;
But if he chuse one most formose,
Ripe for't, she'll prove libidinous,
      Argus himself shan't keep her.

For when these Things are neatly drest,
They'll entertain each wanton Guest,
      Nor for your Honour care ;
If any give their Pride a Fall,
They've learn'd a Trick to bear withal,
      So you their Charges bear.

Or if you chance to play your Game,
With a dull, fat, gross, and heavy Dame,
      Your Riches to increase,
Alas, she will but jeer you for't,
Bid you to find out better Sport,
      Lie with a Pot of Grease.

If

If meager—— be thy delight,
She'll conquer in veneral Fight,
    And waste thee to the Bones ;
Such kind of Girls, like to your Mill,
The more you give, the more crave they will,
    Or else they'll grind the Stones.

If black, 'tis Odds, she's dev'lish proud ;
If short, *Zantippe* like to loud,
    If long, she'll lazy be :
Foolish (the Proverb says) if fair ;
If wise and comely, Danger's there,
    Lest she do Cuckold thee.

If she bring store of Money, such
Are like to domineer too much,
    Prove Mrs. no good Wife :
And when they cannot keep you under,
They'll fill the House with scolding Thunder,
    What's worse than such a Life.

But if their Dowry only be
Beauty, farewel Felicity,
    Thy Fortune's cast away ;
Thou must be sure to satisfy her,
In Belly, and in Back desire,
    To labour Night and Day.

And rather than her Pride give o'er,
She'll turn perhaps an honour'd Whore,
    And thou'lt *Acteon'd* be ;
Whilst like *Acteon*, thou may'st weep,
To think thou forced art to keep,
    All such as devour thee.

If being Noble thou dost wed,
A servile Creature basely bred,
    Thy Family it defaces ;
If being mean, one nobly born,
She'll swear to exalt a Court-like Horn,
    Thy low Descent it graces.

If

If one Tongue be too much for any,
Then he who takes a Wife with many,
    Knows not what may betide him ;
She whom he did for Learning Honour,
To scold by Book will take upon her,
    Rhetorically chide him.

If both her Parents living are,
To please them you must take great care,
    Or spoil your future Fortune ;
But if departed they're this Life,
You must be Parent to your Wife,
    And Father all be certain.

If bravely Drest, fair Fac'd and Witty,
She'll oft be gadding to the City,
    Nor can you say nay ;
She'll tell you (if you her deny)
Since Women have Terms, she knows not why,
    But still to keep them may.

If thou make choice of Country Ware,
Of being Cuckold there's less fear,
    But stupid Honesty ;
May teach her how to Sleep all Night,
And take a great deal more Delight,
    To Milk the Cows than thee.

Concoction makes their Blood agree,
Too near, where's Consanguinity,
    Then let no Kin be chosen ;
He loseth one part of his Treasure,
Who thus confineth all his Pleasure,
    To th' Arms of a first Couzen.

He'll never have her at Command,
Who takes a Wife at Second hand,
    Than chuse no Widow'd Mother ;
The First Cut of that Bit you love,
If others had, why mayn't you prove,
    But Taster to another.

Besides

Besides if She bring Children many,
'Tis like by thee she'll not have any,
    But prove a Barren Doe ;
Or if by them She nc'er had one,
By thee 'tis likely she'll have none,
    Whilst thou for weak Back go.

For there where other Gardners have been Sowing
Their Seed, but never could find it growing,
    You must expect so too ;
And where the *Terra Incognita*
So's Plow'd, you must it Fallow lay,
    And still for weak Back go.

Then trust not a Maiden Face,
Nor confidence in Widows place,
    Those weaker Vessels may
Spring Leak, or Split against a Rock,
And when your Fame's wrapt in a Smock,
    'Tis easily cast away.

Yet be she Fair, Foul, Short, or Tall,
You for a time may Love them all,
    Call them your Soul, your Life ;
And one by one, them undermine,
As Courtezan, or Concubine,
    But never as a Married Wife.

He who considers this, may end the strife.
Confess no trouble like unto a Wife.

A SONG. *New Set by Mr.* Church.

IN Faith 'tis true, I am in Love,
   'Tis your black Eyes have made me so ;
My resolutions they remove,
   And former niceness overthrow.

Those glowing Char-coals set on fire,
   A Heart that former flames did shun ;
Who as *Heretick* unto desire,
   Now's judg'd to suffer *Martyrdom.*

But Beauty, Since it is thy Fate,
   At distance thus to Wound so sure ;
Thy Vertues I will imitate,
   And see if Distance prove a Cure.

Then farewel Mistress, farewel Love,
   Those lately entertain'd desires ;
Wise Men can from that Plague remove,
   Farewel black Eyes, and farewel Fires.

If ever I my Heart acquit,
   Of those dull Flames, I'll bid a Pox
On all black Eyes, and swear they're fit
   For nothing but a Tinder-box.

A

A SONG.

TOM and *Will* were Shepherds Swains,
  They lov'd and liv'd together;
When fair *Pastora* grac'd their Plains,
  Alas! why came she thither;
For tho' they fed two several Flocks,
  They had but one desire;
Pastora's Eyes, and Amber Locks,
  Set both their Hearts on Fire.

Tom

Tom came of Honest gentle Race,
  By Father, and by Mother;
And *Will* was noble, but alass!
  He was a younger Brother:
Tom was toysome, *Will* was sad,
  He Huntsman, nor no Fowler;
Tom was held a proper Lad,
  But *Will* the better Bowler.

Tom would drink her Health, and Swear,
  The Nation could not want her;
Will could take her by the Ear,
  And with his Voice Inchant her:
Tom kept always in her sight,
  And ne'er forgot his Duty;
Will was Witty, and could write,
  Smooth Sonnets on her Beauty.

Thus did she exercise her Skill,
  When both did Dote upon her;
She graciously did use them still,
  And still preserv'd her Honour:
So Cunning and so Fair a She,
  And of so sweet Behaviour;
That *Tom* thought he, and *Will* thought he
  Was chiefly in her Favour.

Which of these two she loved most,
  Or whether she loved either;
'Tis thought they'll find it to their cost,
  That she indeed lov'd neither:
For to the Court, *Pastora's* gone,
  T' had been no Court without her;
The Queen amongst all her Train had none
  Was half so fair, about Her.

Tom Hung his Dog, and threw away
  His Sheep-crook and his Wallet;
Will burst his Pipes, and Curst the day,
  That e'er he made a Sonnet.

A SONG.

Quoth

QUoth *John* to *Joan*, wilt thou have me?
   I Prithee now wilt, and Ise Marry with thee ;
   My Cow, my Cow, my House and Rents,
Aw my Lands and Tenements :
  Say my Joan, *say my* Joaney, *will that not do ?*
  I cannot, cannot come every day Wooe.

I have Corn and Hay in the Barn hard by,
And three fat Hogs penn'd up in the Sty ;
I have a Mare and she's coal Black,
I Rid on her Tail, to save her Back :
  Say my Joan, *&c.*

I have a Cheese upon the shelf,
I cannot Eat it all my self ;
I have three good Marks that like in a Rag,
In the nook of the Chimney instead of a Bag :
  Say my Joan, *&c.*

To Marry I would have thy consent,
But faith I never could Compliment ;
I can say nought but Hoy gee ho,
Terms that belong to Cart and Plough :
  Say my Joan, *say my* Joaney, *will that not do !*
  I cannot, cannot come every day to Wooe.

St. GEORGE *for* England.

Why

WHY should we boast of *Arthur* and his Knights,
    We know how many Men have perform'd
    fights ;
Or why should we speak of Sir *Lancelot du Lake,*
Or Sir *Tristam du Leon,* that fought for the Ladies sake :
Read old Stories, and there you'll see
How St. *George,* St. *George,* did make the Dragon flee.
    St. *George,* he was for *England,* St. *Dennis* was for
        France,
    Sing *Honi Soit qui mal y pense.*

To speak of the Monarchs, it were too long to tell,
And likewise of the *Romans,* how far they did excell ;
Hannibal and *Scipio,* they many a Field did Fight,
Orlando Furioso he was a valiant Knight :
Romulus and *Remus,* were those that *Rome* did Build,
But St. *George,* St. *George,* the Dragon he hath Kill'd.
    St. George *he was,* &c.

Jeptha and *Gideon,* they led their Men to Fight,
The *Gibeonites* and *Ammonites* they put them all to flight;
Hercules's Labour was in the Vale of Brass,
And *Sampson* slew a thousand, with the Jaw-bone of
    an Ass :
And when he was Blind, pull'd the Temple to the
    ground,
But St. *George,* St. *George,* the Dragon did confound.
    St. George *he was,* &c.

Valentine and *Orson,* they came of *Pipin's* Blood,
Alfred and *Aldrecus,* they were brave Knights and
    good ;
The four Sons of *Ammon* that fought with *Charlemaine,*
Sir *Hugh de Burdeaux,* and *Godfrey de Bolaigne :*
These were all *French* Knights, the *Pagans* did Convert,
But St. *George,* St. *George,* pull'd forth the Dragon's
    heart.
    St. George *he was,* &c.

Henry the Fifth he Conquered all *France,*
He quarter'd their Arms, His Honour to advance ;
He

He Raised their Walls, and pull'd their Cities down,
And garnish'd his Head with a double Tripple Crown ;
He thumped the *French*, and after home He came,
But St. *George*, St. *George*, the Dragon he hath slain.
  St. George *he was*, &c.

St. *David*, you know loves Leeks, and toasted Cheese,
And *Jason* was the Man, brought home the *Golden-*
    Fleece;
St. *Patrick* you know he was St. *George's* Boy,-
Seven years he kept his Horse, and then stole him
    away :
For which Knavish act, a Slave he doth remain,
But St. *George*, St. *George*, he hath the Dragon slain.
  St. George *he was*, &c.

Tamberlain the Emperor, in Iron Cage did Crown,
With his bloody Flag display'd before the Town ;
Scanderberg Magnanimous, *Mahomet's Bashaws* dread,
Whose Victorious Bones, were worn when he was dead.:
His *Beglerbeys*, he scorns like dregs, *George Castriot*
    was he call'd,
But St. *George*, St. *George*, the Dragon he hath maul'd.
  St. George *he was*, &c.

Ottoman the *Tartar*, he came of *Persia's* Race,
The great *Mogul*, with his Chests so full of Cloves and
    Mace :
The *Grecian* Youth, *Bucephalus* he Manly did bestride,
But those with all their Worthies Nine, St. *George* did
    them deride :
Gustavus Adolphus, was *Sweedland's* Warlike King,
But St. *George*, St. *George*, pull'd forth the Dragons
    sting,
  St. George *he was*, &c.

Pendragon and *Cadwalladar* of *British* Blood do boast,
Tho' *John* of *Gaunt* his Foes did daunt, St. *George*
    shall rule the roast ;
Agamemnon, and *Cleomedon*, and *Macedon*, did Feats,
But compared to our Champion, they were but meerly
    cheats :

Brave

Brave *Malta* Knights in *Turkish* fights, their brandisht
    Swords outdrew,
But St. *George*, met the Dragon, and ran him thro' and
    thro'.
  St. George *he was for* England, *St.* Dennis *for* France,
  Sing *Honi Soit qui mal y pense.*

Bidea the Amazon, *Proteus* overthrew,
As fierce, as either *Vandal, Goth, Saracen* or *Jew;*
The Potent *Holophernes*, as he lay on his Bed,
In came Wise *Judith*, and subtilly stole away his
    Head:
Brave *Cyclops* stout, with *Jove* he fought, although he
    show'rd down Thunder,
But St. *George* kill'd the Dragon, and was not that a
    wonder.
  St. George *he was,* &c.

Mark Anthony I'll warrant you, play'd feats with *Egypt's*
    Queen,
Sir *Eglamore* that Valiant Knight, the like was never
    seen;
Grim *Gorgons* might was known in Fight, old *Bevis*
    most Men Frighted,
The *Myrmidons*, and *Prestor Johns*, why were not
    these Men Knighted:
Brave *Spinola* took in *Breda, Nassau* did it recover,
But St. *George,* St. *George*, he turn'd the Dragon over
    and over.
  St. George *he was for* England, *St.* Dennis *was for*
    France.
  Sing *Honi Soit qui mal y pense.*

Old

Old England *turn'd New.*
To the Tune of the Blacksmith.   Pag. 28.

YOU talk of *New England*, I truly believe,
  Old England is grown New, and doth us deceive,
I'll ask you a Question or two by your leave,
  And is not Old England *grown New.*

Where are your old Soldiers with Slashes and Scars,
They never us'd Drinking in no time of Wars,
Nor shedding of Blood in Mad drunken Jars,
  And is not Old England, &c.

New Captains are made that never did Fight,
But with Pots in the Day, and Punks in the Night,
And all their chief Care, is to keep their Swords bright,
  And is not Old, &c.

Where are your old Swords, your Bills and your Bows ?
Your Bucklers, and Targets that never fear'd Blows ?
They are turn'd to Stillettoes, with other fair Shows,
  And is not Old, &c.

Where are your old Courtiers that used to Ride
With forty Blue-Coats, and Footmen beside ?
They are turn'd to six Horses, a Coach with a Guide,
  And is not Old, &c.

And what is become of your old *English* Cloaths ?
Your long sleev'd Doublet, and your trunk Hose ?
They are turn'd to *French* fashions and other gewgaws,
  And is not Old, &c.

Your Gallant and his Taylor, some half year together,
To fit a New Suit, to a New Hat and Feather,
Of Gold, or of Silver, Silk, Cloath, Stuff or Leather.
  And is not Old, &c.

We have new fashion'd Beards, and new fashion'd
    Locks,
And new fashion'd Hats, for your new Pated Blocks,
And more New Diseases, besides the *French* POX,
  And is not Old England *grown New.*

New

New Houses are built, and Old ones pull'd down,
Until the new Houses, fell all the Old Ground,
And the Houses stand like a Horse in the Pound.
   And is not Old England *grown New.*

New fashions in House, New fashions at Table,
Old Servants discharg'd, and New not so able,
And all good Old custom, is now but a Fable,
   And is not Old England, &c.

New Trickings, new Goings, new Measures, new Paces,
New Heads for Men, for your Women new Faces,
And twenty New Tricks to mend their bad Cases.
   And is not Old, &c.

New tricks in the Law, New tricks in the Rolls,
New Bodies they have, they look for New Souls,
When the Money is paid for Building old *Pauls,*
   And is not Old, &c.

Then talk no more of *New England,*
New England is where *Old England* did stand,
New Furnish'd, New Fashion'd, New Woman'd, New
   Man'd
   And is not Old England *grown New.*

A Song.   *To the same Tune.*

I'LL tell you a Story if it be true,
   But look you to that, I am sure it is New,
And only in *Salisbury* known to a few,
   Which no Body can deny.

Some Sages have written as we do find,
The Spirits departed are monstrous kind,
To Friend and Relations left behind,
   Which no Body can deny.

                  That

That this is no Tale, I shall you tell,
A Lady there Died, Men thought her in Hell,
I mean in the Grave, as some expound well,
  Which no Body can deny.

Now as the Devil a Hunting did go,
For the Devil goes oft a Hunting you know,
In a Thicket he heard a sound of much Woe,
  Which no Body, &c.

It was a Lady that Wept, and her Weeping
Made *Satan* go from listning to peeping,
Quoth he, what Slave hath this Lady in keeping?
  Which no Body, &c.

Good Sir, quoth she, if of Woman you came,
Pity my case, and I'll tell you the same,
Quoth the Devil, be quick in your story fair Dame,
  Which no Body, &c.

Quoth she, I left two Children behind,
To whom their Father is very unkind,
If I could but Appear, I shou'd change his mind,
  Which no Body, &c.

Fair Dame, quoth the Devil, are these all your wants?
So she told him her Name, her Uncles and Aunts,
All whom he knew well, for they were no Saints,
  Which no Body, &c.

Then she told him how many Sweet-hearts she had,
How many was good, and how many was bad,
The Devil began to think her Stark-mad,
  Which no Body, &c.

And so she went on with the cause of the Squabble,
Belzebub Scratch'd, and was in great trouble,
For he thought it would prove a two Hours Bubble,
  Which no Body, &c.

He would have been gone, but well I wist,
She caught him fast by the Lilly black Fist,
Nay, then quoth the Devil, even do what you list,
  Which no Body can deny.

Now

Now when she was free, to Earth she flew,
And came with a Vengeance, to give her her due,
Then snap went the Lock, and the Candles burnt blue,
   Which no Body can deny.

Quoth she, will you give my Children their Land !
Her Husband did Sweat, you must understand,
For he did not think her so near at hand,
   Which no Body, &c.

But having recover'd Heart of grace,
Quoth he, you Jade come again in this place,
And *Faustus* his Chamber-pot flies in your Face,
   Which no Body, &c.

When she could not prevail by means so foul,
She sought other ways his Mind to controul,
So she went to a Maid, a very good Soul,
   Which no Body, &c.

In the Name of the Father, and so she went on,
Most Gracious Madam, what would you have done?
I'll do it altho' you'd have me a Nun,
   Which no Body, &c.

Then go to my Husband and bid him do right,
Unto my two Children, or else by this light,
I'll rattle his Curtain-Rings every Night,
   Which no Body, &c.

Tell him I'll hear no more of his Reasons,
I'll sit on his Bed, and Read him such Lessons,
As never were heard at Mr. *Mompessons,*
   Which no Body, &c.

So away went the Virgin, and flew like a Bird,
And told the Spirits Husband every Word,
At which I replyed, I care not a T——
   Which no Body, &c.

For when she was Incarnate, quoth he,
She was as much Devil as e'er she could be,
And then I fear'd her no more than a Flea,
   Which no Body can deny.

Good

Good Sir, quoth she, consider my plight,
I am not able to keep outright,
Three waking Ministers every Night,
    Which no Body can deny.

When the Gentleman heard her Ditty so sad,
Compassion straight his Fury allay'd,
And unto the Boys the Land was convey'd,
    Which no Body, &c.

When the Land as I said, was convey'd to the Boys,
The Virgin went home again to rejoyce,
And away went the Spirit with a Tuneable Voice,
    Which no Body can deny.

A SONG.

HOW Happy's the Mortal,
  That lives by his Mill;
That depends on his own,
  Not on Fortune's Wheel:
By the slight of his hand,
  And the strength of his Back;
How merrily, how merrily,
  His Mill goes *Clack, clack, clack,*
How merrily, how merrily,
  His Mill goes Clack.

If his Wife proves a Scold,
  As too often 'tis seen;
For she may be a Scold,
  Sing God bless the Queen:
With his hand to the Mill,
  And his Shoulder to the Sack;
He drowns all the discord,
  In his Musical *Clack, clack, clack,*
He drowns, &c.

O'er your Wives, and your Daughters,
  He often prevails;
By sticking a Cog, of a Foot,
  In their Tails;
Whilst the Hoyden so willingly,
  He lays upon her Back;
And all the while he sticks it in,
  The Stones cry *Clack, clack, clack,*
And all the while he sticks it in,
  The stones cry Clack.

The

The *Angler's* SONG.

To the Tune my Father was born before me.
Page 45.

OF all the Recreations which
   Attend on Humane Nature;
There's none that is of so high a Pitch,
   Or is of such a Stature:
As is the subtle Angler's Life,
   In all Mens approbation;
For Angler's tricks, do daily mix,
   In every Corporation.

Whilst *Eve* and *Adam* liv'd in Love,
   And had no cause of Jangling;
The Devil did the Waters move,
   The Serpent went to Angling:
He baits his Hook, with Godlike look,
   Thought he this will entangle her;
By this all ye may plainly see,
   That the Devil was first an Angler.

Physicians, Lawyers, and Divines,
   Are almost neat entanglers;
And he that looks fine, will in fine,
   That most of them are Anglers:
Whilst grave Divines do Fish for Souls,
   Physicians like Curmudgeons;
They bait with Health, we Fish for Wealth,
   And Lawyers Fish for Gudgeons.

Upon the Exchange 'twixt Twelve and One,
   Meets many a neat entangler;
'Mongst Merchant-Men, there's not one in ten,
   But what is a cunning Angler:
For like the Fishes in the Brook,
   Brother doth swallow Brother;
There's a Golden bait hangs at the Hook,
   And they Fish for one another.

A

A Shop-keeper I next prefer,
  He's a formal Man in Black, Sir ;
He throws his Angle ev'ry where,
  And cry's, what is't you lack, Sir ;
Fine Silks, or Stuffs, Cravats, or Cuffs,
  But if a Courtier prove th' entangler
My Citizen he must look to't then,
  Or the Fish will catch the Angler.

But there's no such Angling as a Wench,
  Stark naked in the Water ;
She'll make you leave both Trout, and Tench,
  And throw your self in after :
Your Hook and Line she will confine,
  Thus tangled is the Entangler ;
And this I fear hath spoil'd the Gear,
  Of many a Jovial Angler.

But if you'll Trowl for a Scriv'ner's Soul,
  Cast in a Rich young Gallant ;
To take a Courtier by the Pole,
  Throw in a Golden Tallant :
But yet I fear the Draught will ne'er,
  Compound for half the charge on't ;
But if you'll catch the Devil at stretch,
  You must bait him with a Searjeant.

Thus I have made my Anglers Trade,
  To stand above defiance ;
For like the Mathematick Art,
  It runs through every Science :
If with my Angling Song I can,
  To Mirth and Pleasure seize you ;
I'll bait my Hook with Wit again,
  And Angle still to please you.

The

The Cavaliers SONG.

HE that is a cleer
          Cavalier
Will not repine,
          Although
His Substance grow
          So very low,
That he cannot drink Wine.

Fortune is a Lass
          Will embrace,
And soon destroy ;
          Free born,
In Libertine,
          We'll ever be,
Singing *Vive le Roy*.

Vertue is its own reward, Sir,
    And *Fortune* is a Whore ;
There's none but Fools and Knaves regard her,
    Or her Power implore.

He that is trusty *Roger*,
    And hath serv'd his King ;
Altho' he be a tatter'd Souldier,
    Yet he will skip and Sing :
Whilst he that fights for Love,
May in the way of Honour prove,
And they that make sport of us,
May come short of us,

Fate will Flatter them,
And will scatter them,
Whilst the Royalty,
Looks upon Loyalty,
We that live peaceably,
May be successfully,
Crown'd with a Crown at last.

But a real Honest Man,
May be utterly undone,
To show his Allegiance,
His love and Obedience,
But that will raise him up,
Virtue weighs him up,
Honour stays him up,
And we'll praise him ;
Whilst the fine Courtier Dine,
With his full bowls of Wine,
Honour will make him fast.

Freely let's be then,
                Honest Men,
And kick at Fate.
                We
May live to see
                Our Loyalty,
Valued at a higher rate.

He that bears a Word, or a Sword,
   'Gainst the Throne ;
Or doth prophanely prate,
To wrong the State,
   Hath but little for his own,

CHORUS.

What tho' Plummers, Painters, and Players,
   Be the prosperous Men ;
Yet we'll attend our own Affairs,
   When we come to't agen :
                ::   Treachery

Treachery may be fac'd with light,
  And Leachery lin'd with Furr ;
A Cuckold may be made a Knight,
  'Tis Fortune *de la gar :*
But what is that to us Boys,
That now are Honest Men ;
  We'll conquer and come agen,
  Beat up the Drum agen,
    Hey for Cavaliers,
    Joy for Cavaliers,
    Pray for Cavaliers ;
  Dub, a dub, dub,
  Have at old *Belzebub,*
  Oliver stinks for fear.

Fifth-Monarchy must down, Bullies,
  And every Sect in Town :
We'll rally, and to't agen,
Give 'em the rout agen,
When they come agen,
Charge 'em home agen,
Face to the right about, *tantar ar ar a,*
This is the Life of an honest poor Cavalier.

A

A Parley, *between* two West Countrymen *on sight of a* Wedding.

I Tell thee *Dick* where I have been,
Where I the rarest things have seen,
  O things beyond compare ;
Such sights again cannot be found,
In any place on *English* ground,
  Be it at Wake or Fair.

At *Chairing Cross,* hard by the way,
Where we (thou know'st) do sell our Hay,
  There is a House with Stairs ;
And their did I see coming down,
Such Voulks as are not in our Town,
  Vorty at least in pairs.

A-

Amongst the rest one Pestilent fine,
(His Beard no bigger tho' than thine)
　　Walkt on before the rest ;
Our Landlord lookt like nothing to him,
The King (God bless him) 'twould undo him,
　　Should he go still so drest.

At course-a-Park without all doubt,
He should have first been taken out,
　　By all the Maids i'th' Town ;
Tho' lusty *Roger* there had been,
Or little *George* upon the green,
　　Or *Vincent* of the Crown.

But wot you what, the Youth was going,
To make an end of his own Wooing,
　　The Parson for him stay'd ;
Yet by his leave (for all his hast)
He did not so much Wish all past,
　　Perchance as did the Maid.

The Maid (and thereby hangs a Tale)
For such a Maid no *Whitson* Ale,
　　Could ever yet produce ;
No Grape that's kindly ripe could be,
So round, so plump, so soft as she,
　　Nor half so full of Juice.

Her Fingers was so small, the Ring,
Would not stay on, which he did bring,
　　It was too wide a Peck ;
And to say Truth, (for out it must)
It lookt like the great Coller (just)
　　About our young Colt's Neck.

Her Feet beneath her Petticoat,
Like little Mice stole in and out,
　　As if they fear'd the Light ;
But *Dick*, she Dances such away,
No Sun upon a *Easter day*,
　　Is half to fine a sight.

He

He would have kist her once or twice,
But she would not she was so nice,
    She would not do it in Sight;
And then she lookt, as who would say,
I will do what I list to Day,
    And you shall do't at Night.

Her Cheeks so rare a white was on,
No Dazy makes Comparison,
    (Who sees them is undone,)
For streaks of red were mingled there,
Such as are on a Katherine Pear,
    The side that's next the Sun.

Her Lips were red, and one was thin,
Compar'd to that was next her Chin;
    (Some Bee had stung it newly :)
But (*Dick*) her Eyes so guard her Face,
I durst no more upon them gaze,
    Than on the Sun in *July*.

Her Mouth so small when she does speak,
Thou'dst swear her Teeth her Words did break,
    That they might passage get;
But she so handled still the matter,
They came as good as ours, or better,
    And are not spent a whit.

If wishing should be any Sin,
The Parson himself had guilty been,
    She lookt that Day so purely,
And did the Youth so oft the Feat,
At Night, as some did in Conceit,
    It would have spoil'd him surely.

Passion, oh me ! how I run on !
There's *that* that would be thought upon,
    (I trow) besides the Bride :
The Business of the Kitchin's great,
For it is fit that Man should eat;
    Nor was it there deny'd.

Just

Just in the Nick the Cook knockt thrice,
And all the Waiters in a trice
    His Summons did obey,
Each Serving-man with Dish in Hand
March'd boldly up, like our train'd Band,
    Presented, and away.

When all the Meat was on the Table,
What Man of Knife, or Teeth was able
    To stay to be intreated ;
And this very reason was,
Before the Parson could say Grace,
    The Company was seated.

Now Hats fly off, and Youths carouse,
Healths first go round, and then the House,
    The Brides came thick and thick ;
And when 'twas nam'd another's Health,
Perhaps he made it hers by Stealth ;
    And who could help it *Dick ?*

O'th' sudden up they rise and dance,
Then sit again, and sigh and glance ;
    Then dance again and kiss ;
Thus sev'ral ways the Time did pass,
Whilst every Woman wish'd her Place,
    And every Man wish'd his.

By this Time all was stol'n aside,
To counsel and undress the Bride
    But that he must not know :
But 'twas thought he guest her Mind,
And did not mean to stay behind,
    Above an Hour or so.

When in he came (*Dick*) there she lay,
Like new fall'n Snow melting away,
    ('Twas time I trow to part)
Kisses were now the only stay,
Which soon he gave, as who would say
    Good B'w'y ! with all my Heart.

                             But

But just as Heavens would have to cross it,
In came the Bride-maids with the Posset,
       The Bridegroom eat in spight ;
For had he left the Women to't,
It would have cost two Hours to do't,
       Which were too much that Night.

At length the Candle's out, and now,
All that they had not done they do ;
       What that is, you can tell ;
But I believe it was no more,
Than thou and I have done before,
       With *Bridget*, and with *Nell*.

Of the Downfal of one part of the Mitre-
Tavern in Cambridge, *or the sinking
thereof into the Cellar. By Mr.* Tho.
Randolph. *To the Tune of* My Father
was born before me, *Pag.* 45.

L Ament, lament you Scholars all,
       Each wear his blackest Gown,
The *Mitre* that held up your Wits,
    Is now itself fallen down :
The dismal Fire on *London-bridge*,
    Could move no Heart of Mine,
For that but o'er the Water stood,
    But this stood o'er the Wine.

It needs must melt each Christian Heart,
    That this sad News but hears ;
To see how the poor Hogsheads wept,
    Good Sack and Claret Tears :
The zealous Students of that place,
    Change of Religion fear,
Lest this Mischance bring in
    The Heresie of Beer.

Un-

Unhappy *Mitre*, I would know
  The Cause of thy sad Hap;
Came it by making Legs too low,
  To *Pembrook's* Cardinal Cap?
Hence know thy self! and cringe no more,
  Since *Popery* went down,
The Cap should veil to thee, for now
  The *Mitre's* next the Crown.

Or was't because our Company
  Did not frequent thy Cell,
As we were wont to drown those Cares,
  Thou fox'd thy self and fell?
No sure, the Devil was a dry,
  And caus'd that fatal Blow,
'Twas he that made the Cellar sink,
  That he might drink below.

And some do say the Devil did it,
  'Cause he would drink up all;
But I rather think the Pope was drunk,
  And let the *Mitre* fall:
But *Rose* now whither, *Faulcon* mew,
  Whilst *Sam* enjoys his Wishes;
The *Dolphin* too must cast her Crown,
  Wine was not made for Fishes.

That Sign a Tavern best becomes,
  That shews who loves Wine best;
The *Mitre's* then the only Sign,
  For 'tis the Scholar's Crest,
Then drink Sack *Sam*, and cheer thy Heart,
  Be not dismay'd at all;
For we will drink it up again,
  Tho' our selves do catch a Fall.

We'll be thy Workmen Day and Night,
  In spite of Bug-bear Proctors;
We drank like fresh Men all before,
  But now we'll drink like Doctors.

A

A SONG.

To the Tune of the Blacksmith, Pag. 20.

I 'LL sing you a Sonnet that ne'er was in Print,
  'Tis truly and newly come out of the Mint,
I'll tell you beforehand you'll find nothing in't.
    On *nothing* I think, and on *nothing* I write,
    'Tis *nothing* I court, yet *nothing* I slight,
    Nor care I a Pin if I get *nothing* by't.

Fire, Air, Earth and Water, Beasts, Birds, Fish and Men
Did start out of *nothing*, a Chaos, a Den ;
And all things shall turn into nothing agen.
    'Tis *nothing* sometimes that makes many things hit,
    As when Fools amongst wise Men do silently sit,
    A Fool that says *nothing* may pass for a Wit.

What one Man loves is another Man's loathing,
This blade loves a quick thing, that loves a new thing,
And both do in the Conclusion love *nothing*.
    Your Lad that makes Love to a delicate smooth thing,
    And thinking with Sighs to gain her and soothing,
    Frequently makes such ado about *nothing*.

At last when his Patience and Purse is decay'd,
He may to the Bed of a Whore be betray'd,
But she that hath *nothing* must needs be a Maid.
    Your slashing, and clashing, and flashing of Wit,
    Doth start out of *nothing* but Fancy and Fit,
    'Tis little or *nothing* to what hath been writ.

When first by the Ears we together did fall,
Then something got *nothing*, and *nothing* got all ;
From *nothing* it came, and to *nothing* it shall.
    That Party that seal'd to a Cov'nant in haste,
    Tho' made our three Kingdoms & Churches lie waste,
    Their Project and all came to *nothing* at last.

                        They

They raised an Army of Horse and of Foot,
To tumble down Monarchy Branches Root,
They thunder'd, and plunder'd, but *nothing* would do't,
　The Organ, the Altar, and Ministers Cloathing,
　In Presbyter *Jack* begot such a loathing,
　That he must needs raise a petty new *nothing*.

And when he had wrap'd us in sanctify'd Cloathing,
Perjur'd the People by faithing and trothing,
At last he was catcht, and all came to *nothing*.
　In several Factions we quarrel and brawl,
　Dispute and contend, and to fighting we fall,
　I'll lay all to *nothing* that *nothing* wins all.

When War and Rebellion, and plundering grows,
The mendicant Man is the freest from Foes,
For he is most happy hath *nothing* to lose.
　Brave Cæsar and *Pompey*, and great *Alexander*,
　Whom Armies did follow as Goose follow Gander,
　Nothing can say to an Action of Slander.

The wisest great Prince, were he never so stout,
Tho' he conquer'd the World,& gave Mankind the rout,
Did bring *nothing* in, nor shall bear *nothing* out.
　Old *Noll* that arose to High-thing from Low-thing,
　By brewing Rebellion, nicking and frothing,
　In seven Years Space was both all things and *nothing*.

Dick (*Oliver's* Heir) that pitiful slow thing,
Who once was invested with Purple Cloathing,
Stands for a Cypher, and that stands for *nothing*;
　If King-killers bold are excluded from Bliss,
　Old *Bradshaw* (that feels the Reward on't by this)
　Had better been *nothing* than now what he is.

Blind Colonel *Hewson* that lately did crawl,
To lofty Degree from a low Coblers Stall,
Did bring all to *nothing*, when All came to All.
　Your Gallant that rants it in delicate cloathing,
　Tho' lately he was but a pitiful low thing,
　Pays Landlord, Draper, and Taylor with *Nothing*.
The

The nimble tongu'd Lawyer that pleads for his Pay,
When Death doth arrest him and bear him away,
At the General Barr will have nothing to say.
    Whores that in Silk were by Gallants embrac'd, ·
    By a Rabble of Prentices lately were chas'd,
    Thus courting and sporting comes to *nothing* at last.

If any Man tax me with Weakness of Wit,
And say that on *nothing*, I *nothing* have writ ;
I shall answer, *Ex nihilo nihil fit.*
    Yet let his Discretion be never so tall,
    This very Word *nothing* shall give it a fall,
    For writing of *nothing* I comprehend all.

Let every Man give the Poet his due,
Cause then 'twas with him, as now it's with you,
He study'd it when he had *nothing* to do.
    This very Word *nothing*, if took the right way,
    May prove advantageous for what would you say,
    If the Vintner should cry there's *nothing* to pay.

The Scolding Wife : New Sett by Mr.
Akeroyd.

SOme Men they do delight in Hounds,
　And some in Hawks take Pleasure ;
Others joy in War and Wounds,
　And thereby gain great Treasure ;
Some they do love on Sea to sail,
　Others rejoyce in Riding :
But all their Judgments do them fail,
　There's no such Joy as *Chiding.*

When

When soon as Day I open mine Eyes,
  To entertain the Morning ;
Before my Husband he can rise,
  I *Chide* and proudly scorn him :
When at the Board I take my place,
  Whatever be the Feasting ;
I first do *Chide*, and then say Grace,
  If so dispos'd to tasting.

Too fat, too lean, too hot, too Cold,
  I ever am complaining ;
Too raw, too roast, too young, too Old,
  I always am disdaining :
Let it be Fowl, or Flesh, or Fish,
  Tho' I am my own Taster ;
Yet I'll find fault with Meat or Dish,
  With Maid or with the Master.

But when to Bed I go at Night,
  I surely fall a weeping ;
For then I leave my great Delight,
  How can I chide when sleeping :
Yet this my Grief doth mitigate,
  And must asswage my Sorrow :
Altho' to Night be too late,
  I'll early *Chide* to Morrow.

Old Simon *the King.*

IN a humour I was late,
  As many good fellows be ;
To think of no matters of State,
  But seek for good Company :
That best contented me.
  I travell'd up and down ;
No Company I could find ;
  Till I came to the sight of the Crown :
My Hostess was sick of the Mumps,
  The Maid was ill at ease,
The Tapster was drunk in his Dumps ;
  They were all of one disease,
    Says Old *Simon* the King.

Considering in my mind,
  And thus I began to think ;
If a Man be full to the Throat,
  And cannot take off his drink,
And if his drink will not down,
  He may hang himself for shame ;
So may the Tapster at the Crown,
  Whereupon this reason I frame ;
Drink will make a Man Drunk,
  And Drunk will make a Man dry ;
Dry will make a Man sick
  And sick will make a Man Die.
    Says Old *Simon* the King.

If a Man should be drunk to night,
    And laid in his grave to morrow :
Will you or any man say,
    That he died of Care or Sorrow ?
Then hang up sorrow and care,
    'Tis able to kill a Cat,
And he that will drink all night,
    Is never afraid of that !
For drinking will make a man Quaff,
    Quaffing will make a man Sing ;
Singing will make a man Laugh,
    And laughing long life doth bring,
        Says Old *Simon* the King.

If a puritan Skinker cry,
    Dear Brother it is a Sin,
To drink unless you be dry,
    Then straight this Tale I begin,
A Puritan left his Cann,
    And took him to his Jugg,
And there he play'd the man,
    As long as he could tugg :
But when that he was spy'd,
    What did he swear or rail ;
No, no truly, dear Brother he cry'd,
    Indeed all flesh is frail,
        Says Old *Simon* the King.

So Fellows if you'll be drunk,
    Of frailty it is a sin,
Or for to keep a punk,
    Or play at In and In ;
For Drink and Dice and Drabs,
    Are all of one condition,
And will breed want and Scabs,
    In spite of the Physician :
Who so fears every Grass,
    Must never piss in a Meadow,
And he that loves a pot and a Lass,
    Must never cry oh ! my head oh !
        Says Old *Simon* the King.

The

The Cautious Drinker : New set by Mr. Akeroyd.

MY Masters and Friends, who ever intends,
    To trouble this Room with Discourse ;
You that sit by are as guilty as I,
    Be your talk the better or worse :
Now lest you should prate of Matters of State,
    Or any thing else that might hurt us ;
We rather will drink off our Cups to the brink,
    And then we shall speak to the purpose.

Suppose you speak clean from the matter you mean,
    That's not a Pin here or there ;
Yet take this Advice, be both merry and wise,
    Ye know not what Creatures be near ;

Or suppose that some sot, should lurk in this pot,
  To scatter out words that might hurt us ;
To free that same doubt, we'll see all the pot out,
  And then we shall speak to the purpose.

If any man here be in bodily fear,
  Of a Wolf, a Wife or a Tweak ;
Here's Armour of proof, shall keep her a loofe,
  Here's Liquor will make a man speak :
Or if any enter to challenge his Friend,
  Or rail at a Lord that might hurt us,
Let him drink once or twice of this *Helicon* juice,
  And then he shall speak to the purpose.

He that rails at the times, in Prose or in Rhimes,
  Doth bark like a Dog at the Moon ;
Sings, Prophesies strange, and threatens some change,
  And hangs them upon the Queens Tomb :
He is but a Rayler, or Prophecying Taylor,
  To scatter out words that might hurt us,
Let's talk of no matches, but drink and sing Catches,
  And then we shall speak to the purpose.

It is a mad zeal for a Man to reveal,
  His secret thoughts when he bouses ;
He is but a Widgeon, that talks of Religion,
  In Taverns or in tipling houses :
It is not for us, such things to discourse,
  Let's talk of nothing that might hurt us ;
But let's begin a new health to our King,
  And then we shall speak to the purpose.

Amidst of our bliss 'twill not be a miss,
  To talk of our going home late ;
If Constable Kite or a Pis-pot at night,
  Should chance to be split on our pate :
It were all in vain to rage or complain,
  Or scatter out words that might hurt us,
'Twere better to trudge home, to honest kind *Joan,*
  And then we shall speak to the purpose.

The

The Gelding of the Devil by Dick the Baker of Mansfield Town.

NOW listen a while, and I will tell,
  Of the Gelding of the Devil of Hell;
And *Dick* the Baker of *Mansfield* Town,
To *Manchester* Market he was bound,
And under a Grove of Willows clear,
This *Baker* rid on with a merry Cheer:
Beneath the Willows there was a Hill,
And there he met the Devil of Hell.

L 2

Baker,

Baker, quoth the Devil, tell me that,
How came thy Horse so fair and fat ?
In troth, quoth the *Baker*, and by my fay,
Because his Stones were cut away :
For he that will have a Gelding free,
Both fair and lusty he must be :
Oh ! quoth the Devil, and saist thou so,
Thou shalt geld me before thou dost go.

Go tie thy Horse unto a Tree,
And with thy Knife come and geld me ;
The *Baker* had a Knife of Iron and Steel,
With which he gelded the Devil of Hell,
It was sharp pointed for the nonce,
Fit for to cut any manner of Stones :
The *Baker* being lighted from his Horse,
Cut the Devil's Stones from his Arse.

Oh ! quoth the Devil, beshrow thy Heart,
Thou dost not feel how I do smart ;
For gelding of me thou art not quit,
For I mean to geld thee this same Day seven-night.
The *Baker* hearing the Words he said,
Within his Heart was sore afraid,
He hied him to the next Market Town,
To sell his Bread both white and brown.

And when the Market was done that Day,
The *Baker* went home another way,
Unto his Wife he then did tell,
How he had gelded the Devil of Hell :
Nay, a wondrous Word I heard him say,
He would geld me the next Market Day ;
Therefore Wife I stand in doubt,
I'd rather, quoth she, thy *Knaves Eyes* were out.

I'd rather thou should break thy Neck-bone,
Than for to lose any manner of Stone,
For why, 'twill be a loathsome thing,
When every Woman shall call thee Gelding.

Thus

Thus they continu'd both in Fear,
Until the next Market Day drew near ;
Well, quoth the good Wife, well I wot,
Go fetch me thy Doublet and thy Coat.

Thy Hose, thy Shoon and Cap also,
And I like a Man to the Market will go ;
Then up she got her all in hast,
With all her Bread upon her Beast :
And when she came to the Hill side,
There she saw two Devils abide,
A little Devil and another,
Lay playing under the Hill side together.

Oh ! quoth the Devil, without any fain,
Yonder comes the Baker again ;
Beest thou well *Baker*, or beest thou woe,
I mean to geld thee before thou dost go :
These were the Words the Woman did say,
Good Sir, I was gelded but Yesterday ;
Oh ! quoth the Devil, that I will see,
And he pluckt her Cloaths above her Knee.

And looking upwards from the Ground,
There he spied a grievous Wound :
Oh ! (quoth the Devil) what might he be ?
For he was not cunning that gelded thee,
For when he had cut away the Stones clean,
He should have sowed up the Hole again ;
He called the little Devil to him anon,
And bid him look to that same Man.

Whilst he went into some private place,
To fetch some Salve in a little space ;
The great Devil was gone but a little way,
But upon her Belly there crept a Flea :
The little Devil he soon espy'd that,
He up with his Paw and gave her a pat :
With that the Woman began to start,
And out she thrust a most horrible Fart.

Whoop !

Whoop ! whoop ! quoth the little Devil, come again I
    pray,
For here's another hole broke, by my fay ;
The great Devil he came running in hast,
VVherein his Heart was sore aghast :
Fough, quoth the Devil, thou art not sound,
Thou stinkest so sore above the Ground,
Thy Life Days sure cannot be long,
Thy Breath it fumes so wond'rous strong.

The Hole is cut so near the Bone,
There is no Salve can stick thereon,
And therefore, *Baker*, I stand in doubt,
That all thy Bowels will fall out ;
Therefore *Baker*, hie thee away,
And in this place no longer stay.

*To a Friend, who desir'd no more than to
admire the Mind, and the Beauty of
Sylvia.*

THO' *Sylvia's* Eyes a Flame could raise,
  More fit for Wonder than for Praise;
And tho' her Wit were clear and high,
That 'twere resistless as her Eye:
  Yet without Love, she still shall find,
  I'm deaf to one, to th' other blind.

Those Fools that think Beauty can prove,
A Cause sufficient for their Love,
I wish they never may have more,
To try how Looks can cure their Sore:
  'Tis such the Sex so high have set,
  They take it not for Gift, but Debt.

If Love were unto Sight confin'd,
The God of it would not be blind;
Nor would the Pleasure of it be,
So often in Obscurity:
  No, to know Joys each Sense hath right,
  Equal at least to that of Sight.

The Gods, who knew the noblest part
In Love, sought not the Mind, but Heart;
And when hurt by the winged Boy,
What they admir'd they did enjoy;
  Knowing a Kindness Love could prove,
  The Hope, Reward, and Cure of Love.

I'll rather my Affections keep
For Nymphs only enjoy'd in Sleep,
Than cast away an Hour of Care
On any, 'cause she's only fair:
  Nay, Sleep more pleasing Dreams do move,
  Than are your waking ones of Love.

The

The Frenzy's less Love to endure,
Then after to decline the Cure ;
Yet do both, aiming no higher
Than for to see, and to admire :
   An Idol you'll not only frame,
   But you will too adore the same.

Had there in *Sylvia* nothing shin'd,
But the unseen Charms of her Mind ;
You would have had the like Esteem
For her, that I have still for them :
   If Flesh and Blood your Flame inspire,
   Then make those only your Desire.

And Friend, that you may clearly prove,
'Tis not her Mind alone you love ;
Let her 'twixt us her self impart,
Give you her Mind, and me her Heart :
   As little Cause then you will find
   As I do now, to love her Mind.

Cælia's *Complaint.*

POor *Cælia* once was very fair,
  A quick bewitching Eye she had,
Most neatly look'd her braided Hair,
  Her dainty Cheek would make you mad ;
Upon her Lips, did all the Graces play,
And on her Breast ten Thousand (Thousand) *Cupids* lay.

Then many a doting Lover came,
  From Seventeen to Twenty one ;
Each told her of his mighty Flame,
  But she forsooth affected none :
One was not handsom, the other was not fine ;
This of Tobacco smelt, and that of Wine.

But th' other Day it was my Fate,
  To walk along that way alone,
I saw no Coach before her Gate,
  But at her Door I heard her Mone ;
She dropt a Tear, and sighing seem'd to say,
Young Ladies marry, marry while you may.

Amyn-

AMYNTOR's *Welladay.*

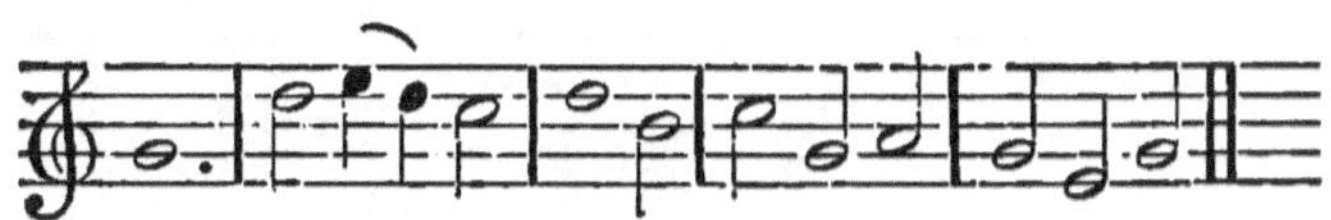

CHloris now thou art fled away,
    Amyntor's sheep are gone astray ;
And all the joy he took to see,
His pretty Lambs run after thee,
   Is gone, is gone, and he alone,
   Sings nothing now but welladay (welladay).

His Oaten Pipe that in thy praise,
Was wont to play such round delays :
Is thrown away, and not a Swain,
Dares pipe, or sing, within his plain ;
   'Tis death for any one to say,
   One word to him, but cowelladay.

The

The May-pole where thy little feet,
So roundly did in measures meet,
Is broken down, and no Content,
Comes near *Amyntor* since you went,
 All that I ever heard him say,
 Was *Chloris, Chloris,* welladay.

Upon those Banks you us'd to tread,
He ever since hath laid his head ;
And whisper'd there such pining woe ;
As not a blade of Grass will grow :
 O Chloris ! Chloris ! come away,
 And hear *Amyntor's* Welladay.

A Lady to a Young Courtier.

L Ove thee ! good Sooth, Not I,
 I've something else to do ;
Alas ! you must go Learn to talk,
Before you Learn to woo ;
Nay fie, stand, off, go too, go too.

Because

Because you're in the fashion,
And newly come to Court ;
D'ye think your Cloaths are Orators,
T' invite unto the sport ?
Ha ! ha ! who will not jeer thee for't !

Ne'er look so sweetly Youth,
Nor fiddle with your Band ;
We know you trim your borrow'd Curls,
To shew your pretty hand :
But 'tis too young for to command.

Go practice how to jeer,
And think each word a Jest,
That's the Court Wit : Alas ! you're out,
To think when finely drest,
You please me or the Ladies :

And why so confident,
Because that lately we,
Have brought another lofty word,
Unto our Pedigree ?
Your inside seems the worse to me.

Mark how Sir *Whacham* fools ;
Ay marry, there's a Wit,
Who cares not what he says or swears,
So Ladies laugh at it ;
Who can deny such blades a bit ?

A

A Description of CHLORIS.

HAve you e'er seen the Morning Sun,
From fair *Aurora's* bosom run?
Or have you seen on *Flora's* Bed,
The Essences of white and red?
Then you may boast, for you have seen,
My Fairer *Chloris*, Beauties Queen.

Have you e'er pleas'd your skilful Ears,
With the sweet Musick of the Spheres?
Have you e'er hear'd the Syrens sing,
Or *Orpheus* play to Hells black King?
If so, be happy and rejoyce,
For thou hast heard my *Chloris* voice.

Have

Have you e'er smelt what Chymick Skill,
From Rose or Amber doth distill?
Have you been near that sacrifice
The Phœnix makes before she dies?
Then you can tell (I do presume)
My *Chloris* is the World's Perfume.

Have you e'er tasted what the Bee,
Steals from each fragrant Flower or Tree?
Or did you ever taste that meat,
Which Poets say that Gods did eat?
O then I will no longer doubt
But you have found my *Chloris* out.

AMYNTOR'S *Dream.*

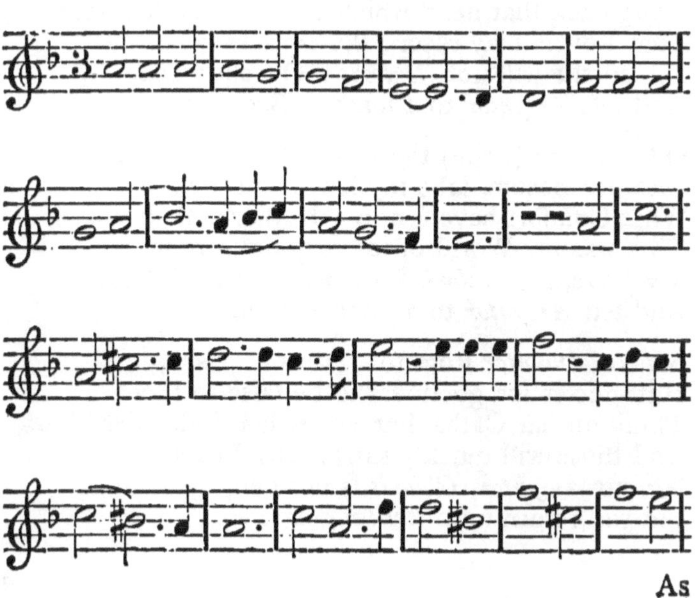

As

AS sad *Amyntor* in a Meadow lay,
Slumbring upon a bed of new made Hay,
A Dream, a fatal Dream unlock'd his Eyes,
Whereat he wakes, and thus *Amyntor* crys ;
Chloris, where art thou *Chloris ?*   Oh, she's fled,
And left *Amyntor* to a loathed Bed.

Hark how the Winds conspire with storm and rain,
To stop her course, and beat her back again :
Hark how the Heavens chide her in her way,
For robbing poor *Amyntor* of his joy :
And yet she comes not *Chloris*, O ! she's fled,
And left *Amyntor* to a loathed Bed.

Come, *Chloris*, come, see where *Amyntor* lies,
Just as you left him, but with sadder eyes ;
Bring back that heart which thou hast stolen from me,
That Lovers may record thy constancy :
O ! no she will not, *Chloris ?* O ! she's fled,
And left *Amyntor* to a loathed Bed.

O ! lend me (Love) thy wings that I may fly,
Into her Bosom, take my leave and die ;
What Comfort have I now i'th' World since she,
That was my World of joy is gone from me :
My Love, my *Chloris ? Chloris*, O ! she's fled,
And left *Amyntor* to a loathed Bed.

Awake *Amyntor* from this Dream for she,
Hath too much goodness to be false to thee;
Think on her Oaths, her Vows, her Sighs, her Tears,
And those will quickly satisfie thy Fears:
No, no *Amyntor*, *Chloris* is not fled,
But will return unto thy longing Bed.

A

A SONG.

Calm

CAlm was the Ev'ning, and clear was the Sky,
    And the sweet budding Flowers did spring;
When all alone went *Amyntor*, and I,
    To hear the sweet Nightingale sing;
    I sate, and he laid him down by me
    And scarcely his breath he could draw:
But when with a fear, he began to come near,
    He was dash'd with a *Ha, ha, ha, ha, ha, ha, ha,*
    ha, ha, ha, ha, ha, ha, ha, ha, ha, ha.

He blush'd to himself, and laid still for a while,
    His modesty curb'd his desire:
But straight I convinc'd all his fears with a smile,
    And added new flames to his fire,
    Ah, *Sylvia!* said he, you are cruel,
    To keep your poor Lover in awe;
Then once more he prest, with his hand to my breast,
    But was dash'd with a *Ha, ha, ha, ha, ha, ha, ha,*
    ha, ha, ha, ha, ha, ha, ha, ha, ha, ha, ha.

I knew it was his Passion that caused his fear,
    And therefore I pity'd his case;
I whisper'd him softly, there's no body near,
    And laid my Cheek close to his face:
    But as we grow bolder and bolder,
    A Shepherd came by us and saw:
    And straight as our bliss, began with a kiss,
    He laught out with a *Ha, ha, ha, ha, ha, ha, ha,*
    ha, ha, ha, ha, ha, ha, ha, ha, ha, ha, ha.

A SONG.

THUS all our lives long we're Frolick and gay,
    And instead of Court Revels we merrily Play
At Trap, and Kettles, and Barley-break run,
At Goff, and at Stool-ball, and when we have done
These innocent Sports, we Laugh and lie down,
And to each pretty Lass we give a green Gown.

We

We teach our little Dogs to fetch and to carry,
The Patridge, Hare, the Pheasant our Quarry,
The nimble Squirrels, with Cudgel we chase,
And the little pretty Lark, betray with a glass :
And when we have done, we Laugh and lie down,
And to each pretty Lass we give a green Gown.

About the May-pole we Dance all around,
And with Garlands of Pinks and Roses are crown'd ;
Our little kind Tribute we merrily pay,
To the gay Lad, and bright Lady o'th' *May :*
　And when we have done, &c.

With our delicate Nymphs we Kiss and we Toy,
What others but Dream of, we daily enjoy ;
With our Sweet-hearts we dally, so long till we find,
Their pretty Eyes say their Hearts are grown kind :
　And when we have done, we Laugh and lie down,
　And to each pretty Lass, we give a green Gown.

A SONG.

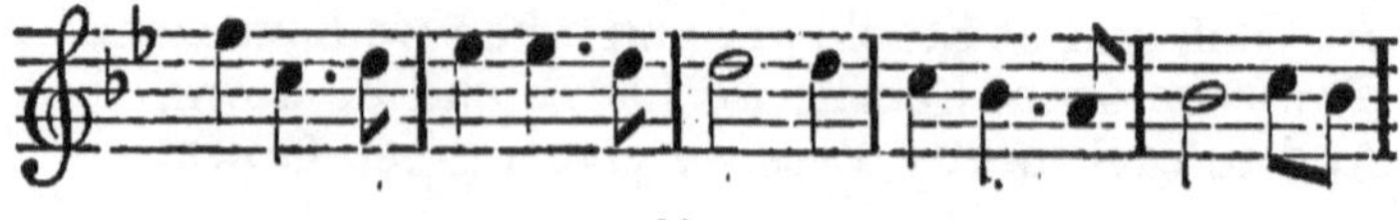

WHere ever I am, or whatever I do,
    My *Phillis* is still in my Mind;
When Angry I mean not to *Phillis* to go,
    My Feet of themselves the way find :
Unknown to my self, I am just at her Door,
And when I would rail, I can bring out no more
    Then *Phillis*, too fair and Unkind :
    Then *Phillis*, too fair and Unkind.

When

When *Phillis* I see, my Heart burns in my Breast,
  And the Love I would stifle is shown ;
But asleep or awake, I am never at rest,
  When from mine Eyes *Phillis* is gone :
Sometimes a sweet Dream doth delude my sad Mind,
But alas ! when I wake, and no *Phillis* I find,
  Then I sigh to my self all alone !
  Then I sigh to my self all alone !

Should a King be my Rival, in her I adore,
  He should offer his Treasure in vain ;
O let me alone to be Happy and Poor,
  And give me my *Phillis* again :
Let *Phillis* be mine, and ever be kind,
I could to a Desart, with her be confin'd,
  And envy no Monarch his Reign :
  And envy no Monarch his Reign.

Alas ! I discover too much of my Love,
  And she too well knows her own Pow'r ;
She makes me each Day a new Martyrdom prove,
  And makes me grow Jealous each Hour :
But let her each Minute Torment my poor Mind,
I had rather love *Phillis*, both false and unkind,
  Than ever be freed from her pow'r :
  Than ever be freed from her pow'r.

A

A SONG.

HOW

HOW unhappy a Lover am I,
   Whilst I sigh for my *Phillis* in vain ;
All my hopes of Delight, are another Man's right,
   Who is Happy, whilst I am in Pain :
Since her Honour affords no relief,
   But to pity the Pains which you bear ;
'Tis the best of your Fate, in a hopeless estate,
   To give o'er, and betimes to despair.

I have try'd the false Medicine in vain,
   Yet I Wish what I hope not to win ;
For without my desire has no Food to its fire,
   But it burns and consumes me within :
Yet at least, 'tis a Comfort to know,
   That you are not unhappy alone ;
For the Nymph you adore, is as wretched or more,
   And accounts all your suff'rings her own.

O you Pow'rs ! let me suffer for both,
   At the Feet of my *Phillis* I'll lie ;
I'll resign up my Breath, and take pleasure in death,
   To be pity'd by her when I Dye :
What her Honour deny'd you in Life,
   In her Death she will give to her Love ;
Such a flame as is true, after Fate will renew,
   When the Souls do meet closer above.

A SONG.

As

AS I walk'd in the Woods one Ev'ning of late,
   A Lass was deploring her hapless Estate ;
In a Languishing posture, poor Maid she appears,
All swell'd with her sighs, and blubber'd with her Tears :
   She Cry'd and she Sobb'd, and I found it was all,
   For a little of that which Harry *gave* Doll.

At last she broke out, Wretched, she said,
Will not Youth come succour a languishing Maid ?
With what he with ease and pleasure may give,
Without which alass, poor I cannot live !
   Shall I never leave Sighing, and Crying, and Call,
   For a little of that which Harry *gave* Doll.

At first when I saw a young Man in the place,
My Colour would fade, and then flush in my Face ;
My Breath it grew short, and I shiver'd all o'er,
My Breast never Popp'd up and down so before :
   I scarce knew for what, but now I find it was all,
   For a little of that which Harry *gave* Doll.

A

A SONG.

Be-

BEneath a Mirtle shade,
  Which Love for none but Lovers made,
I slept, and straight my Love before me brought,
Phillis the Object of my waking thought:
Undrest she came, my Flames to meet,
Whilst Love strew'd Flow'rs beneath her Feet,
So prest by her, became, became more sweet.

From the bright Vision's head,
A careless Veil of Lawn was loosely spread;
From her white Temples, fell her shaded Hair,
Like cloudy Sun-shine, not too Brown or fair:
Her Hands, her Lips, did Love inspire,
Her ev'ry Grace, my Heart did fire,
But most her Eyes, which languish'd with desire.

Ah, charming Fair, said I,
How long can you, my Bliss and yours deny;
By Nature and by Love, this lovely shade,
Was for Revenge of suff'ring Lovers made:
Silence and shades with Love agree,
Both shelter you, and favour me,
You cannot Blush, because I cannot see.

No, let me Dye, she said,
Rather than lose the Spotless name of Maid;
Faintly she spoke me-thought for all the while,
She bid me not believe her, with a Smile:
Then dye said I, she still deny'd,
And is it thus, thus, thus she cry'd,
You use a harmless Maid? and so she Dy'd.

I Wak'd, and straight I knew,
I Lov'd so well, it made my Dream prove true;
Fancy the kinder Mistress of the two,
Fancy had done what *Phillis* would not do:
Ah, cruel Nymph, cease your disdain,
While I can Dream you scorn in vain,
Asleep, or waking you must ease my pain.

A

A SONG.

Me-

Ethinks the poor Town has been troubled too
        long,
With *Phillis* and *Chloris* in every Song ;
By Fools who at once, can both Love and Dispair,
And will never leave calling them Cruel and Fair :
VVhich justly provokes me in Rhime to express,
The truth that I know of my Bonny black *Bess.*

This *Bess* of my Heart, this *Bess* of my Soul,
Has a Skin white as Milk, but Hair black as a Coal ;
She's plump, yet with ease you may span round her
        VVaste,
But her round swelling Thighs can scarce be embrac'd :
Her Belly is soft, not a word of the rest,
But I know what I mean, when I drink to the Best.

The Plow-man, and Squire, the Erranter Clown.
At home she subdu'd in her Paragon Gown,
But now she adorns the Boxes and Pit,
And the proudest Town Gallants are forc'd to submit :
All Hearts fall a leaping wherever she comes,
And beat Day and Night, like my Lord —s Drums ;

But to those who have had my dear *Bess* in their Arms,
She's gentle and knows how to soften her Charms
And to every Beauty can add a new Grace,
Having learn'd how to Lisp, and trip in her pace :
And with Head on one side, and a languishing Eye,
To Kill us with looking, as if she would Dye.

A SONG.

O The time that is past,
    When she held me so fast,
And declar'd that her Honour no longer could last;
When no light but her languishing Eyes did appear,
To prevent all excuses of Blushes and Fear.

When she sigh'd and unlac'd,
    With such Trembling and hast,
As if she had long'd to be closer Imbrac'd;
My Lips the sweet pleasure of Kisses enjoy'd,
While my Mind was in search of hid Treasure imploy'd.

My

My Heart set on fire,
With the flames of desire,
I boldly pursu'd what she seem'd to require ;
But she cry'd for pity-sake, change your ill Mind,
Pray *Amyntas* be Civil, or I'll be unkind.

Dear *Amyntas* she crys,
Then casts down her Eyes,
And in Kisses she gives, what in words she denys ;
Too sure of my Conquest, I purpose to stay,
Till her free Consent had more sweetned the Prey.

But too late I begun,
For her Passion was done,
Now *Amyntas* she crys, I will never be won ;
Your Tears and your Courtship no pity can move,
For you've slighted the Critical minute of Love.

The TOWN *Gallant.*

L ET us drink and be merry, Dance, Joke, &
      Rejoice,
With Claret and Sherry, Theorbo and Voice ;
The changeable World to our Joy is unjust,
All Treasure's uncertain, then down with your dust :
In Frolicks dispose your Pounds Shillings and Pence,
For we shall be nothing a Hundred years hence.

We'll Kiss and be free with *Moll*, *Betty*, and *Nelly*,
Have Oysters and Lobsters, and Maids by the Belly,
Fish Dinners will make a Lass spring like a Flea,
Dame *Venus* (Love's Goddess) was born of the Sea :
With *Bacchus* and with her we'll tickle the sence,
For we shall be past it a Hundred years hence.

Your most Beautiful Bit, that hath all Eyes upon her,
That her Honesty sells for a Hogo of Honour ;
Whose lightness and brightness doth shine in such
      splendor,
That none but the stars, are thought fit to attend her :
Tho' now she be pleasant and sweet to the sence,
Will be damnable Mouldy a Hundred years hence.

The Usurer that in the Hundred takes Twenty,
Who wants in his Wealth, and pines in his Plenty,
Lays up for a Season which he shall ne'er see,
The Year One thousand eight hundred and three :
His Wit, and his Wealth, his Learning, and Sence,
Shall be turned to nothing a Hundred years hence.

Your Chancery-Lawyer, who subtilty thrives,
In spinning our Suits to the length of three Lives ;
Such Suits which the Clients do wear out in Slavery,
Whilst Pleader makes Conscience a cloak for his
      knav'ry :
May boast of Subtilty in th' Present Tense,
But *Non est Inventus* a Hundred years hence.

Then why should we turmoile in Cares and in Fears,
Turn all our Tranquility to Sighs and Tears ;
Let's eat, drink and play, 'till the Worms do corrupt us,
'Tis certain *post mortem nulla Voluptas :*
Let's deal with our Damsels, that we may from thence,
Have Broods to succeed us a Hundred years hence.

DORINDA *Lamenting the loss of her* AMYNTAS.

Dieu to the Pleasures and Follies of Love,
    For a Passion more noble my fancy does move ;
My Shepherd is dead, and I live to proclaim,
In sorrowful Notes my *Amyntas* his Name :
The Wood-Nymphs reply when they hear me com-
    plain,
Thou never shalt see thy *Amyntas* again ;
      For Death has befriended him,
      Fate has defended him,
None, none alive is so happy a Swain.

You Shepherds & Nymphs, that have danc'd to his
    lays,
Come help me to Sing forth *Amyntas* his Praise ;
No Swain for the Garland, durst with him dispute,
So sweet were his Notes, while he sang to his Lute :
Then come to his Grave, and your kindness pursue,
To Weave him a Garland, with Cypress and Yew ;
      For Life hath forsaken him,
      Death hath o'ertaken him,
No Swain again will be ever so true.

Then leave me alone to my wretched estate,
I lost him too soon, and I lov'd him too late ;
You Ecchoes, and Fountains, my witnesses prove,
How deeply I Sigh for the loss of my Love :
And now of our *Pan*, whom we chiefly adore,
This favour I never will cease to Implore ;
      That now I may go above,
      And there enjoy my Love,
Then, then I never will part with him more.

A

A Song.

ET's Love and lets Laugh,
   Let's Dance and let's Sing ;
While shrill Ecchoes ring ;
Our Wishes agree,
And from Care we are free,
   Then who is so Happy, so happy as we ?

We'll press the soft Grass,
Each Swain with his Lass,
And follow the Chase ;
When weary we be,
We'll sleep under a Tree,
   Then who is so Happy, &c.

By Flatt'ry or Fraud,
No Shepherds betray'd, i
Or Cheats the fond Ma d ;
No false subtle Knee,
To deceive us we see,
   Then who is so Happy, &c.

We envy no Pow'r,
They cannot be poor,
That wish for no more ;
Some Richer may be,
And of higher degree,
   And none are so Happy, so happy as we.

A

A SONG.

L ET the daring Advent'rers be toss'd on the Main,
  And for Riches no Danger decline ;
Tho' with hazard the Spoils of both *Indies* they gain,
  They can bring us no Treasure like Wine ;
Tho' with Hazard the Spoils of both *Indies* they gain,
  They can bring us no Treasure like Wine.

Enough

Enough of such Wealth would a *Beggar* enrich,
   And supply great wants in a King ;
'Twould smooth off the Griefs in a comfortless Wretch,
   And inspire weeping Captives to sing.
     'Twould smooth, *&c.*

There's none that groans under a burthensome Life,
   If this Sovereign Balsom he gains,
This will make a Man bear all the Plagues of a Wife,
   And of Rags and Diseases in Chains.
     This will make, *&c.*

It swells all our Veins with a kind purple Flood,
   And puts Love and great Thoughts in the Mind :
There's no Peasant so rank, but it fills with good
     Blood,
   And to Gallantry makes him inclin'd.
     There's no Peasant, *&c.*

There's nothing our Hearts with such Joy can bewitch,
   For on Earth 'tis a Power that's Divine ;
Without it we're wretched, tho' never so rich ;
   Nor is any Man poor that has Wine.
     Without it we're, *&c.*

A

A SONG.

Pas-

PAstora's Beauties when unblown,
 E'er yet the tender Budd did cleave,
To my more early Love were known,
 Their fatal Power I did perceive :
How often in the dead of Night,
 When all the World lay hush'd in Sleep ;
Have I thought this my chief Delight,
 To sigh for you, for you to weep.

Upon my Heart, whose Leaves of white,
 No Letter yet did ever stain :
Fate (whom none can controul) did write,
 The Fair *Pastora* here must Reign :
Her Eyes, those darling Suns shall prove
 Thy Love to be of noblest Race ;
Which took its Flight so far above,
 All Humane things on her to gaze.

How can you then a Love despise,
 A Love that was infus'd by you ;
You gave Breath to its infant Sighs,
 And all its Griefs that did ensue :
The Pow'r you have to wound I feel,
 How long shall I of that complain ;
Now shew the Power you have to heal,
 And take away the tott'ring Pain.

A SONG.

Ail to the Myrtle Shade,
   All hail to the Nymphs of the Field:
Kings will not here invade,
   Tho' Vertue all Freedom yields,
Beauty here opens her Arms,
   To soften the languishing Mind;
And *Phillis* unlocks her Charms:
   Ah *Phillis!* ah! why so kind?

Phillis, the Soul of Love,
   The Joy of Neighbouring Swains:
Phillis that crowns the Groves,
   And *Phillis* that gilds the Plains:
Phillis that ne'er had the Skill,
   To paint, or to patch, or to be fine;
Yet *Phillis*, whose Eyes can kill,
   Whom Nature has made Divine.

Phillis, whose charming Tongue,
   Makes Labour and Pain a Delight;
Phillis that makes the Day young,
   And shortens the live-long Night:
Phillis, whose Lips like *May*,
   Still laugh at the Sweets they bring,
Where Love never knew Decay,
   But sets with eternal Spring.

The

The Claret *Bottle.*

A Pox of the fooling and plotting of late,
　What a Pother and Stir has it kept in the State?
Let the Rabble run mad with Suspicions and Fears;
Let 'em scuffle and jarr till they go by the Ears:
Their Grievances never shall trouble my Pate,
So I can enjoy my dear Bottle at Quiet.

What Coxcombs were those, who would barter their
　　Ease,
And their Necks for a Toy, a thin Wafer and Mass?

At

At Old *Tyburn* they never had needed to swing,
Had they been but true Subjects to drink and their
    King :
A Friend and a Bottle is all my Design,
H'as no room for Treason that's top full of Wine.

I mind not the Menders and Makers of Laws,
Let 'em sit or prorogue as his Majesty pleases ;
Let 'em damn us to Woolen, I'll never repine
At my Lodging when Dead, so alive I have Wine :
Yet oft in my Drink I can hardly forbear,
To curse 'em for making my Claret so dear.

I mind not grave Asses, who idly debate,
About Right and Succession, the Trifles of State ;
We've a good King already, and he deserves laughter,
That will trouble his Head with who shall come after.
Come, here's to his Health, and I wish he may be
As free from all Care, and all Trouble as we.

What care I how Leagues with the *Hollander* go,
Or Intrigues betwixt *Sidney* and Mounsieur *d'Avaux;*
What concerns it my Drinking if *Cassal* be sold,
If the Conqueror takes it by storming or Gold.
Good *Bourdeaux* alone is the place that I mind,
And when the Fleet's coming I pray for a Wind.

The Bully of *France*, that aspires to Renown,
By dull cutting of Throats, and vent'ring his own ;
Let him fight and be damn'd, and make Matches &
    treat,
To afford News-mongers, and Coffee-House that,
He's but a brave Wretch, whilst I am more free,
More safe, and a thousand times happier than he.

Come he or the Pope, or the Devil to boot ;
Or come Fagot and Stake, I care not a Groat ;
Never think that in *Smithfield* I Porters will beat,
No, I swear Mr. *Fox*, pray excuse me for that :
I'll drink in Defiance of Gibbet and Halter,
This is the Profession that never will alter.

A

A SONG.

RAnging the Plain one Summers night,
  To pass a vacant hour,
I fortunately chanc'd to light,
  On lovely *Phillis* Bow'r,
The Nymph adorn'd with thousand Charms,
  In expectation sate,
To meet those Joys in *Strephon's* Arms,
  Which Tongue cannot relate.

Up-

Upon her Hand she lean'd her Head,
  Her breast did gently rise ;
That e'ry Lover might have read,
  Her Wishes in her Eyes :
At e'ry Breath that mov'd the Trees,
  She suddenly would start ;
A cold on all her Body seiz'd,
  A trembling on her Heart.

But he that knew how well she Lov'd,
  Beyond his hour had stay'd ;
And both with Fear and Anger mov'd,
  The melancholly Maid :
Ye Gods, she said, how oft he swore,
  He would be here by One ;
But now alas ! 'tis Six and more,
  And yet he is not come.

On *MARRIAGE.*

HE that is resolv'd to Wed,
   And be by the Nose by Woman led,
Let him consider't well e'er he be sped ;
For that lew'd Instrument, a Wife,
If that she be enclin'd to strife,
Will find a Man shrill Musick all his life,
   Will find a Man, &c.

If he approach her when she's vext,
Nearer than the Parson does his Text,
He's sure to have enough of what comes next ;
And by our Grammar Rules we see,
Two different Genders can't agree,
Nor without Solescims connected be,
   Nor without, &c.

Yet this by none can be deny'd,
That Wedlock, or 'tis much belyed,
Is a good School, in which Man's Vertue's tried :
And this convenience Woman brings,
That when her angry mood begins,
The Husband never wants a sight of's Sins,
   The Husband never, &c.

If he by chance offend the least,
His Pennance shall be well encreast,
She'll make him keep a Vigil without a Feast ;
And when's Confession he is framing,
She will not fail to make's Examen,
He has nothing else to do but say *Amen.*
   He has nothing, &c.

A

A Song.

A Curse on all Cares,
   And popular Fears,
Come let's to the *Bell*,
For their Wine there drinks well ;
There take of our Glass,
Nay it shall not one pass :
Cho. *For we will be dull, and heavy no more,*
   Since Wine does increase, and there's Claret good
     store.

Come fill up your Wine,
Look, fill it like mine,
Here Boys, I begin,
A good Health to the King ;
Jack, see it go round,
Whilst with Mirth we abound :
Cho. *For we will be dull, and heavy no more,*
   Since Wine does increase, and there's Claret good
     store.

Nay

Nay, don't us deceive,
Why this will you leave ?
The Glass is not big,
What-a-pox, you're no Whig ;
Come drink up the rest,
Or be merry at least :
Cho. *For we will be dull, and heavy no more,*
    Since Wine does increase, and there's Claret good
      store.

A SONG.

Elieve me *Jenny*, for I tell you true,
These Sighs, these Sobs, these tears, are all for you;
Can you mistrustful of my Passion prove,
When ev'ry Action thus proclaims my Love ?
 It's not enough, you cruel Fair,
  To slight my Love, neglect my Pain ?
 At least, that ridged Sentence spare ;
  Nor say that I first caus'd you to Disdain.

No, no, these silly Stories won't suffice,
Fate speaks me better in your lovely Eyes ;
Let not Dissimulation, baser Art,
Stifle the busie Passion of your Heart:
 Yet, let the Candor of your Mind,
  Now with your Beauty equal prove ;
 Which I believe ne'er yet design'd,
  The Death of me, and Murder of my Love.

A SONG.

A Pox of dull mortals of the grave and precise,
   Who past the Delight,
   We enjoy each Night,
Give Counsel, instruct us, to be counted more wise :
   When Nature excites,
   And Beauty invites,
Let us follow, let us follow, our own appetites.

         The

The brisk vigour of youth, and fierce heat of our Blood,
    The force of Desires,
    Which kind Love inspires,
Are too powerful Motives, and can't be withstood:
    If Love be a Crime,
    We're yet in our Prime;
Let's never grow wise, and repent e'er our time.

Then we'll boldly go on, whilst we're lusty and strong,
    Whilst fit for the Task,
    Of a Vizard Mask,
And still be as happy as still we are young;
    Whilst the impotent Sot,
    Rails, curses his Lot,
And being past his Pleasures, would have 'em forgot.

A SONG.

YE happy Swains, whose Nymphs are kind,
　　Teach me the Art of Love :
That I the like success may find,
　My Shepherdess to move :
Long have I strove to win her Heart,
　But yet alas ! in vain ;
For she still acts one cruel part,
　Of Rigour and Disdain.

Whilst in my Breast a Flame most pure,
　Consumes my Life away ;
Ten thousand Tortures I endure,
　Languishing night and day :
Yet she regardless of my Grief,
　Looks on her dying Slave ;
And unconcern'd, yields no Relief,
　To heal the Wound she gave.

What is my Crime, oh rigid Fate ?
　I'm punish'd so severe ;
Tell me, that I may expiate ;
　With a repenting Tear :
But if you have resolv'd, that I,
　No mercy shall obtain ;
Let her persist in Tyranny,
　And cure by Death my Pain.

A

A SONG.

My

MY Life and my Death, are both in your pow'r,
    I never was wretched 'till this cruel hour;
Sometimes it is true, you tell me you love,
But alas! that's too kind for me ever to prove:
Could you guess with what pain my poor Heart is
    opprest,
I am sure my *Alexis* would soon make me blest.

Distractedly jealous I do hourly rove,
Thus sighing and musing 'tis all for my Love;
No place can I find that does yield me Relief,
My Soul is for ever entangl'd with Grief:
But when my kind Stars let me see him, (oh then!)
I forgive the cruel Author of all my past Pain.

A Song.

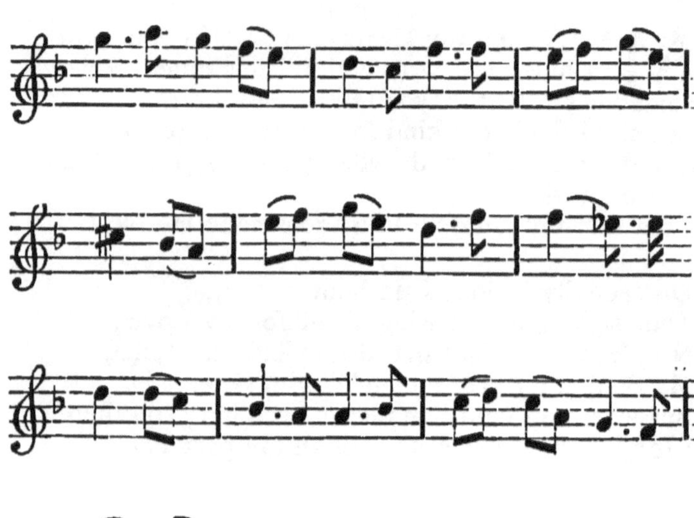

A S *May* in all her youthful Dress,
    My Love so gay did once appear;
A Spring of Charms dwelt on her Face,
    And Roses did inhabit there:
Thus while th' Enjoyment was but young,
    Each night new Pleasures did create;
Harmonious words dropp'd from her Tongue,
    And *Cupid* on her Fore-head sate.

But as the Sun to West declines,
    The Eastern Sky does colder grow;
And all its blushing Looks resigns,
    To the pale-fac'd Moon that rules below:
While Love was eager, brisk, and warm,
    My *Cloe* then was kind and gay;
But when by time I lost the Charm,
    Her smiles like Autumn dropp'd away.

A SONG.

WEEP all ye Nymphs, your Floods unbind,
  For *Strephon's* now no more;
Your Tresses spread before the Wind,
  And leave the hated Shore :
See, see upon the craggy Rocks,
  Each Goddess stripp'd appears ;
They beat their Breasts, and rend their Locks,
  And swell the Sea with Tears.

The God of Love that fatal hour,
  When this poor Youth was born ;
Had sworn by *Styx* to show his Power,
  He'd kill a Man e'er Morn :
For *Strephon's* Breast he aim'd his Dart,
  And watch'd him as he came ;
He cry'd, and shot him thro' the Heart,
  Thy Blood shall quench my Flame.

On *Stella's* Lap he laid his Head,
  And looking in her Eyes ;
He cry'd, Remember when I am Dead,
  That I deserv'd the Prize :
Then down his Tears like Rivers ran,
  He sigh'd, you Love, 'tis true ;
You love perhaps a better Man,
  But ah ! he Loves not you.

A SONG.

OH

OH Mother, *Roger* with his Kisses
   Almost stops my Breath, I vow;
Why does he gripe my Hand to pieces,
   And yet he says he loves me too?
    Tell me, Mother, pray now do !
    Pray now do, pray now do,
    Tell me, Mother, pray now do,
    Pray now, pray now, pray now do,
    What Roger *means when he does so ?*
    For never stir I long to know.

Nay more, the naughty Man beside it,
   Something in my Mouth he put ;
I call'd him Beast, and try'd to Bite it,
   But for my Life I cannot do't ;
    Tell me Mother, pray now do, &c.

He sets me in his Lap whole Hours,
   Where I feel I know not what ;
Something I never felt in yours,
   Pray tell me Mother what is that ?
    Tell me Mother what is that ?
    For never stir I long to know.

A

A SONG.

YOur Gamester, provok'd by his Loss may forswear,
  And rayl against Play, yet can never forbear ;
Deluded with Hopes, what is lost may be won,
In Passion plays on, 'till at last he's undone.

So

So I, who have often declaim'd the fond Pain,
Of those fatal Wounds, which Love gets by disdain ;
Seduc'd by the charms of your Looks, am drawn in,
To expose my poor Heart to those Dangers agen.

Clarissa, I live on the hopes of my Love,
Which flatters me so, that you kinder will prove ;
In some lucky Minute I hope to enjoy thee,
And rout all your forces in Arms to destroy me.

My Fortune I hope is reserv'd for this cast,
To make me a saver for all my Life past ;
Be lucky this once, Dice ! 'tis all I implore,
I'll gladly tye up then, and tempt you no more.

A SONG.

How

HOW lovely's a Woman before she's Enjoy'd,
When the spirits are strong, & the Fancy not
    cloy'd !
We admire every Part, tho' never so plain,
Which when throughly possest, we quickly disdain.

So Drinking we love too, just at the same rate,
For when we are at it we Foolishly prate ;
What Acts we have done, and set up for a Wit,
But next Morning's Pains, our Pleasure do quit.

But Music's a Pleasure, that tires not so soon,
'Tis Pleasant in Morning, 'tis welcome at Noon ;
'Tis Charming at Night, to sing Catches in Parts,
It diverts our dull Hours, and rejoices our Hearts.

But Music alone, without Women and Wine,
Will govern but dully, tho' never so fine ;
Therefore by consent, we'll enjoy them all three,
Wine and Music for you, and the Woman for me.

A SONG.

FAirest Work of happy Nature,
  Sweet without dissembling Art;
Kind in ev'ry tender Feature,
  Cruel only in a Heart:
View the Beauties of the Morning,
  Where no sullen Clouds appear;
Graces there are less adorning,
  Than below, when *Cælia's* there.

Ev'ry tuneful Breast confesses,
  Sounds by you improve their Power;
Ev'ry Tongue in soft Addresses,
  Humbly tells us his Amour:

Such

Such a Tribute, lovely Blessing,
　Faithful *Strephon* ne'er denies;
Such a Treasure in possessing,
　All the Bills of Love supplies.

Yet I see by ev'ry Tryal,
　Feeble Hopes my flames pursue;
Ever finding a Denyal,
　Where my softest Love was true:
But my Heart knows no retreating,
　No decay can ease my Pain;
Love allows of no defeating,
　Tho' the Prize is sought in vain.

For if e're my *Cælia's* Treasure,
　Must her Virgin sweets resign;
Love shall flow with equal Measure,
　And I'll boldly call her mine:
'Till her Panting Wedding Lover,
　Grown uneasy by my Claim;
Leaves me freely to discover
　Golden Coasts without a Name.

A SONG.

SAbina in the dead of Night,
  In restless Slumbers wishing lay,
Cynthia was Bawd, and her clear Light,
  To loose Desires did lead the way :
I step'd to her Bed-side with bended Knee,
  And sure *Sabina* saw,
And sure *Sabina* saw,
  And sure *Sabina* saw,
I'm sure she saw, but would not see.

I drew the Curtains of the Lawn,
  Which did her whiter Body keep ;
But still the nearer I was drawn,
  Methought the faster she did sleep ;
I call'd *Sabina* softly in her Ear,
And sure *Sabina* heard, but would not hear.

Thus, as some Midnight Thief, (when all
  Are wrapp'd into a Lethargy),
Silently creeps from Wall to Wall,
  To search for hidden Treasury :
So mov'd my busie Hand from Head to Heel,
  And sure *Sabina* felt, and would not feel.

Thus I ev'n by a Wish enjoy,
  And she without a Blush receives ;
As by dissembling most are coy,
  She by Dissembling freely gives :
For you may safely say, nay swear it too,
  Sabina she did hear,
Sabina she did see,
  Sabina she did feel,
She did hear, see, feel, sigh, kiss and do.

A SONG.

WHY is your faithful Slave disdain'd?
By gentle Arts my Heart you gain'd
Oh, keep it by the same!
For ever shall my Passion last,
If you will make me once possest,
Of what I dare not name.

Tho' charming are your Wit and Face,
'Tis not alone to hear and gaze,
That will suffice my Flame;
Love's Infancy on Hopes may live,
But you to mine full grown must give,
Of what I dare not name.

P 2

When

When I behold your Lips, your Eyes,
Those snowy Breasts that fall and rise,
  Fanning my raging Flame ;
That Shape so made to be imbrac't,
What would I give I might but taste,
  Of what I dare not name !

In Courts I never wish to rise,
Both Wealth and Honour I despise,
  And that vain Breath call'd Fame ;
By Love, I hope no Crowns to gain,
'Tis something more I would obtain,
  'Tis that I dare not name.

A SONG.

A Gentle Breeze from the *Lavinian* Sea,
   Was gliding o'er the Coast of *Sicily ;*
When lull'd with soft Repose, a prostrate Maid,
Upon her bended Arm had rais'd her Head :
Her Soul was all tranquile and smooth with Rest,
Like the harmonious Slumbers of the Blest.
Wrapp'd up in Silence, innocent she lay,
And press'd the Flow'rs with Touch as soft as they.

My thoughts in gentless Sounds she did impart,
Heighten'd by all the Graces of that Art ;
And as I sung, I grasped her yielding Thighs,
'Till broken Accents faulter'd into Sighs :
I kiss'd and wish'd, and forag'd all her store,
Yet wallowing in the Pleasure, I was poor ;
No kind Relief my Agonies could ease,
I groan'd, and curs'd Religious Cruelties.

The

The trembling Nymph all o'er Confusion lay,
Her melting Looks in sweet Disorder play ;
Her Colour varys, and her Breath's oppress'd,
And all her Faculties are dispossess'd,.
At last impetuously her Pulses move,
She gives a mighty Loose to stifled Love ;
Then murmurs in a soft Complaint, and cries,
Alas ! and thus in soft Convulsions dies.

A SONG.

WHen Money has done whate'er it can,
    And round about run to pleasure a Man,
    Whose Life's but a Span ;
With worldly Joys, and the glittering Toys,
Which do make such a Noise ;
As confound all Advice that's given by the Wise,
And in a trice, reduce the Wretch to Miseries,
    And there to leave him.

Then the World which before,
For his store did adore him,
    Strait seems afraid of one decay'd,
And him upbraid of the Wealth,
Which each by's Trade did before deceive him ;
But when the Mortal sees his own undoing,
Finds his Acquaintance and Friends are all a going.

Then he sighs and moans,
And then he pines and groans ;
At last he Craves, his Friends deny,
At which he raves, and swears he'll die ;
    And thus he cries,
    He ne'er was wise,
Until in Misery he dies ;
And thus the wretched Spendthrift lies,
    Fare him well for evermore, *Amen.*

A

A SONG.

PRetty *Armida* will be kind,
   When at her Feet you prostrate lie;
No cruel Looks was e'er design'd,
   To dwell within her charming Eye:
Gaze on her Face, and every Part,
   That is exposed to your View;
You'll presently conclude her Heart
   To be so soft, 'twill yield to you.

But first 'tis fit you try your Skill,
   You may not think that without Pain,
And some Attendance on her Will,
   So rich a Prize you shall obtain:
Wooers like Angling-men, must wait,
   Womens Time, and give them play,
'Till she has swallow'd well the Bait,
   Before she will become their Prey.

What tho' *Armida's* Looks be kind,
   And you read Yielding in her Eyes;
Yet you alas! may quickly find,
   Those Charms do nought but tantalize:
Her Heart may not so easy be
   As you imagine, but may prove
As hard as Adamant to thee,
   And Proof against the Darts of Love.

Your Skill, and all the Art you have,
   Make Trial of, Sir, if you please;
Tell her, you are her Captive Slave,
   And beg of her Relief and Ease:
But she'll not hear you, for she spies,
   That underneath your gilded Bait,
A crafty Hook inclosed lies,
   So from your Angle she'll retreat.

A

A SONG.

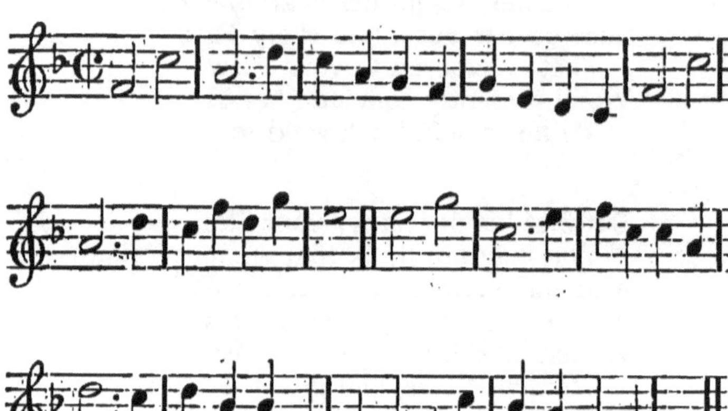

COme Sweet Lass,
    This bonny Weather,
Lets together:
    Come Sweet Lass,
Let's trip it on the Grass :
    Ev'ry where,
Poor *Jockey* seeks his Dear,
And unless you appear,
He sees no Beauty here.

    On our Green,
The Loons are Sporting,
Piping Courting ;
    On our Green,
The Blithest Lads are seen :
    There all day,
Our Lasses Dance and play,
And ev'ry one is gay,
But I, when you're away.

A

A SONG.

I Saw the Lass whom dear I lov'd,
   Long sighing and complaining,
While me she shunn'd and disapprov'd,
   Another entertaining :
Her Hand, her Lip, to him were free,
   No Favour she refus'd him ;
Judge how unkind she was to me,
   While she so kindly us'd him !

His Hand her milk-white Bubby press'd ;
   A Bliss worth Kings desiring ;
Ten thousand times he kiss'd her Breast,
   The snowy Mounts admiring ;
While pleas'd to be the Charming Fair,
   That to such Passion mov'd him ;
She clapp'd his Cheeks, and curl'd his Hair,
   To shew she well approv'd him.

The killing Sight my Soul inflam'd,
   And swell'd my Heart with Passion ;
Which like my Love could not be tam'd,
   Nor had Consideration :
I beat my Breast, and tore my Hair,
   On my hard Fate complaining ;
That plung'd me into deep Despair,
   Because of her Disdaining.

Ah, cruel *Moggy !* then I cry'd,
   Will not my Sorrows move you ?
Or if my Love must be deny'd,
   Yet give me leave to love you :
And then frown on, and still be coy,
   Your constant Swain despising ;
For 'tis but just you should destroy,
   What is not worth your Prizing.

A

A SONG.

A Soldier and a Sailor, a Tinker and a Taylor,
    Had once a doubtful Strife, Sir,
  To make a Maid a Wife, Sir,
Whose Name was Buxome *Joan*,
Whose Name was Buxome *Joan* :
For now the time was ended,
  When she no more intended
  To lick her Lips at Man, Sir,
And gnaw the Sheets in vain, Sir,
And lie a Nights alone,
And lie a Nights alone.

The Soldier swore like Thunder,
He lov'd her more than Plunder ;
  And shew'd her many a Scar, Sir,
  Which he had brought from far, Sir,
With fighting for her sake :
The Taylor thought to please her,
With offering her his Measure ;
  The Tinker too with Mettle,
  Said he wou'd mend her Kettle,
And stop up ev'ry Leak.

But while these three were prating,
The Sailor slily waiting ;
  Thought if it came about, Sir,
  That they shou'd all fall out, Sir,
He then might play his part ;
And just e'en as he meant, Sir,
To Loggerheads they went, Sir,
  And then he let fly at her,
  A Shot 'twixt Wind and Water,
Which won this fair Maids Heart.

A SONG.

MAN, (Man, Man) is for the Woman made,
 And the Woman made for Man ;
As the Spur is for the Jade,
As the Scabbard for the Blade,
As for digging is the Spade,
As for Liquor is the Can,
So Man, (Man, Man) is for the Woman made,
And the Woman made for Man.

As the Scepter's to be sway'd,
As for Night's the Serenade,
As for Pudding is the Pan,
And to cool us·is the Fan,
So Man, (Man, Man) is for the Woman made,
And the Woman made for Man.

Be she Widow, Wife or Maid,
Be she wanton, be she stay'd,
Be she well, or ill array'd,
Whore, Bawd, or Harridan,
Yet Man, (Man, Man) is for the Woman made,
And the Woman made for Man.

A

A SONG.

TAke not a Woman's Anger ill,
But let this be your comfort still,
This be your comfort still,
That if one won't another will:
Tho' she that's foolish does Deny,
She, she that is Wiser will comply,
And if 'tis but a Woman what care I,
What care I, what care I,
If 'tis but a Woman what care I.

Then who'd be Damn'd, to swear untrue,
And Sigh, and Weep, and Whine, and Wooe,
As all our simple Coxcombs do;
All Women love it, and tho' this,
Does sullenly forbid the Bliss,
Try but the next you cannot miss.

A SONG.

S *Awney* is a Bonny, Bonny Lad,
  But *Sawney* Kenns it well;
And *Sawney* might a Boon have had,
  But *Sawney* loves to tell:
He Weens that I mun love him soon,
  Gin Lovers now are rare;
But I'de as lif have none,
  As one whom twanty, twanty share.

When anent your love you come,
  Ah ! *Sawney* were you true;
What tho' I seem to Frown and Gloom,
  I ne'er could gang from you;
Yet still my Tongue do what I can,
  With muckle woe denies;
Wa's me when once we like a Man,
  It boots not to be wise.

A

A SONG.

Young

YOung I am and unskill'd,
　　How to make a Lover yield ;
How to keep or how to gain,
When to Love and when to Feign :
Take me take me some of you,
While I yet am young and true ;
E're I can my Soul disguise,
Heave my Breast, (heave my Breast,) and rowl my
　　Eyes.

Stay not till I learn the way,
How to lye and to betray ;
He that loves me first is blest,
For I may deceive the rest :
Cou'd I find a Blooming Youth,
Full of Love and full of Truth ;
Brisk and of a *Jantee* Meen,
I shou'd long, (I shou'd long) to be Fifteen.

A Song.

(Pish *must be only utter'd, not sung.*

Jocky.	Fairest *Jenny!* thou mun love me,
Jenny.	Troth, my bonny Lad, I do:
Jocky.	Gin thou say'st, thou dost approve me,
	Dearest thou mun kiss me too:
Jenny.	Take a kiss or twa, or twa gude *Jocky*,
	But I dare give nean I trow:
	Fye! nay! * *Pish* be not unlucky!
	VVed me first, and aw will do.

Jocky.	For aw Fife and Lands about it,
	Ize not yield thus to be bound;
Jenny.	Nor I Lig by thee without it,
	For twa Hundred Thousand Pound:
Jocky.	Thou wilt die if I forsake thee,
Jenny.	Better die, than be undone;
Jocky.	Gin 'tis so, come on, Ize tauk thee,
	'Tis too cauld to lig alone.

A

A SONG.

BOnny Lad, prithee lay thy Pipe down,
   Tho' blith are thy Notes, they have no pow'r,
Whilst my Joy, my dear *Peggy* is gone,
   And wedded quite from me, will love no more :
My Geud Friends that do ken my Grief,
   With Song and Story a Cure would find ;
But alas ! they bring no Relief,
For *Peggy* still runs in my Mind.

When I visit the Park or Play,
   They aw without *Peggy* a Desart seem ;
She's before my Eyes aw the Day,
   And aw the long Night too she haunts my Dream :
Sometimes fancying a Heav'n of Charms,
   I wake, and robb'd of my dear Delight,
Find she ligs in another's Arms,
   Ah ! then 'tis she kills me outright.

A SONG.

WHY does *Willy* shun his dear?
  Why is he never here,
    My tender Heart to Chear?
Why, why does *Willy* shun his Dear,
And leave his own poor *Jenny* Weeping?
Shall I never see him more,
    But live in Mickle Care,
    In Sorrow and Despair,
    Shall I never, never see him more,
But in my Dream when I am Sleeping?

Once he ne'er could gang away,
    But here the Lad wou'd stay;
    Still Bonny, Blythe and gay,
Once he ne'er cou'd gang away,
But all the Day he wou'd be Sueing:
But when he had got a Boon,
    Oh! then the Naughty Loon,
    In mickle haste was gone;
    But when he, when he had got a Boon,
There was an end of *Willey's* Wooing.

A

A SONG.

THE Bonny grey Ey'd Morn began to peep,
　When *Jockey* rowz'd with Love came blithly on;
And I who wishing lay depriv'd of sleep,
　Abhorr'd the lazy Hours that slow did run :
But muckle were my joys when in my view,
　I from my Window spy'd my only dear ;
I took the Wings of Love and to him flew,
　For I had fancy'd all my Heav'n was there.

Upon my Bosom *Jockey* laid his Head,
　And sighing told me pretty Tales of Love ;
My yielding Heart at ev'ry word he said,
　Did flutter up and down and strangely move :
He sigh'd, he Kissed my Hand, he vow'd and swore,
　That I had o'er his Heart a Conquest gain'd ;
Then Blushing begg'd that I wou'd grant him more,
　Which he, alass ! too soon, too soon obtain'd.

A

A SONG.

This to be Sung only at end of the first and last Verse.

THE Sun was just Setting, the Reaping was done,
    And over the Common I tript it alone;
Then whom should I meet, but young *Dick* of our Town,
Who swore e'er I went I shou'd have a Green-gown:
      He prest me, I stumbl'd,
      He push'd me, I Tumbl'd,
      He Kiss'd me, I Grumbl'd,
      But still he Kiss'd on,
Then rose and went from me as soon as he'd done.

    These 4 lines are only sung at the end of the 1. *and*
        last Verse.

If he be not hamper'd for serving me so,
    May I be worse Rumpl'd.
    Worse Tumbl'd, and Jumbl'd,
Where ever, where ever I go.

Before an old Justice I Summon'd the Spark,
And how do you think I was serv'd by his Clark;
He pull'd out his Inkhorn, and ask'd me his Fee,
You now shall relate the whole Business, quoth he.
    He prest me, &c.

The Justice then came, tho' grave was his look,
Seem'd to Wish I would Kiss him instead of the Book,
He whisper'd his Clark then, and leaving the place,
I was had to his Chamber to open my Case.
    He prest me, &c.

I

I went to our Parson to make my Complaint,
He look'd like a *Bacchus*, but Preach'd like a Saint ;
  He said we shou'd soberly Nature refresh,
Then Nine times he Urg'd me to Humble the Flesh.
      He prest me, I stumbl'd,
      He Push'd me, I Tumbl'd,
      He Kiss'd me, I grumbl'd,
      But still he Kiss'd on,
Then rose and went from me as soon as he'd done.
If he be not hamper'd for serving me so,
      May I be worse Rumpl'd,
      Worse Tumbl'd, and Jumbl'd,
      Where ever, where ever I go.

A Song, *on* Bartholomew *Fair.*

BOnny Lads and Damsels,
   Your welcome to our Booth ;
We're now come here on purpose,
   Your fancies for to sooth :
No heavy *Dutch* Performers,
   Amongst us you shall find ;
We'll make you Lads good humour'd,
   And Lasses very kind :
Your Damsons, and Filberds,
   You're welcome here to Crack ;
But a Glass of merry Sack, Boys,
   Is a Cordial for the Back.

You may Range about the Fair,
   New Tricks and Sights to see ;
And when your Legs are weary,
   Pray come again to me :
There's Thread-bear *Holophernes,*
   Whom *Judith* long hath Slain ;
With *Guy* of *Warwick*, St. *George*,
   And *Rosamona's* fair Dame :
You'll find some pretty Puppets too,
   With many a Nickey Nack ;
But a Glass of Jolly Sack, Boys,
   Is a Cordial for the Back.

The Houses being low too,
   Some Players hither come ;
But if my Stars deceive me not,
   They soon will know their doom :
There's other pretty Strowlers,
   That crowd upon us here ;
That may have Booths to let too,
   Before their time I fear.

All

All these may Prate, and Talk much,
  Show Tricks, and Bounce, and Crack ;
But here's a Glass of Sack, Boys,
  That's a Cordial for the Back.

Come sit down then brisk Lads all,
  A Bumper to the King ;
Old *England* let's remember,
  (May Peace, and Plenty spring.)
Let War no more perplex you,
  Your Taxes soon will end ;
The Souldiers all Disbanded,
  And each Man love his Friend :
Be Merry then Carouse Boys,
  See Drawer what tis' they lack ;
And fetch a Bottle neat Boy,
  That's Cordial for the Back.

A SONG *on* Bacchus.

C H O.

SInce there's so small difference 'twixt drowning
          and drinking,
We'll tipple and Pray too, like Mariners Sinking ;
Whilst they drink Salt-water, we'll Pledge 'em in Wine,
And pay our Devotion at *Bacchus's* Shrine :
    Oh ! Bacchus, *great* Bacchus, *for ever defend us,*
    And plentiful store of good Burgundy *send us.*

From censuring the State, and what passes above,
From a Surfeit of Cabbage, from Law-suits and Love ;
From medling with Swords and such dangerous things,
And handling of Guns in defiance of Kings.
    Oh ! Bacchus, *&c.*

From Riding a Jade that will start at a Feather,
Or ending a Journey with loss of much Leather;
From the folly of dying for grief or despair,
With our Heads in the Water, or Heels in the Air :
    Oh ! Bacchus, *&c.*

A

From a Usurer's gripe, and from every Man,
That boldly pretends to do more than he can ;
From the Scolding of Women, and bite of mad Dogs,
And wandering over wild *Irish* Boggs.
   Oh ! Bacchus, *&c.*

From Hunger and Thirst, Empty Bottles and Glasses,
From those whose Religion consists in Grimaces ;
From e'er being cheated by Female decoys,
From humouring old Men, and reasoning with Boys :
   Oh ! Bacchus, *&c.*

From those little troublesome Insects and Flyes,
That think themselves Pretty, or Witty, or Wise ;
From carrying a Quartan for Mortification,
As long as a *Ratisbon* Consultation.
   Oh ! Bacchus, *great* Bacchus, *for ever defend us,*
   And plentiful Store of good Burgundy *send us.*

A SONG.

HOW long must Woman wish in vain,
  A constant Love to find ;
No Art can Fickle Man retain,
  Or fix a Roving mind :
Thus fondly we our selves deceive,
  And empty hopes pursue ;
Tho' false to others we believe,
  They will to us prove true.

But oh ! the Torments to discern,
  A perjured Lover gone ;
And yet by sad experience learn
  That we must still Love on :
How strangely are we fool'd by Fate,
  VVho tread the Maze of Love ;
VVhen most desirous to Retreat,
  VVe know not how to move.

A

A SONG.

Oh

OH Fie ! what mean I Foolish Maid,
  In this Remote and Silent shade,
  To meet with you alone ;
My Heart does with the place combine,
And both are more your Friends than mine,
And both are more your Friends than mine :
  Oh ! oh ! oh ! I shall, I shall be undone,
  Oh ! oh ! oh ! oh ! I shall be undone.

A Savage Beast I wou'd not fear,
Or shou'd I meet with Villains here ;
  I to some Cave wou'd run :
But such inchanting Art you show,
I cannot strive, I cannot go ;
  Oh ! I shall be undone.

Ah ! give your sweet Temptations o'er,
I'll touch those dangerous Lips no more,
  What must we yet Fool on ?
Ah ! now I yield, ah ! now I fall,
Ah ! now I have no Breath at all,
  And now I'm quite undone.

A SONG.

Tho'

THo' *Jockey* Su'd me long, he met disdain,
  His tender Sighs and Tears were spent in vain ;
    Give o'er said I give o'er,
    Your silly fond Amour,
I'll ne'er, ne'er, ne'er, ne'er, ne'er comply ;
    At last he forc'd a Kiss,
    Which I took not amiss,
    And since I've known the bliss,
    I'll ne'er deny.

Then ever when you Court a Lass that's Coy,
Who hears your Love, yet seems to shun its Joy ;
    If you press her to do so,
    Ne'er mind her no, no, no,
      But trust her Eyes :
    For Coyness gives denyal,
    When she wishes for the Tryal,
    Tho' she swears you shan't come nigh all,
      I'm sure she lies.

The Leather Bottle.

NOW God above that made all things,
 Heaven and Earth and all therein ;
The Ships upon the Seas to Swim,
To keep Foes out they come not in :
Now every one doth what he can,
All for the use and praise of Man ;
 I wish in Heaven that Soul may dwell,
 That first devis'd the Leathern Bottle,

Now what do you say to the Canns of Wood ?
Faith, they are nought, they cannot be good ;
When a Man for Beer he doth therein send,
To have them fill'd as he doth intend :
The bearer stumbleth by the way,
And on the Ground his Liquor doth lay ;
Then straight the Man begins to Ban,
And Swears it 'twas long of the wooden Cann :
But had it been in a Leathern Bottle,
Although he stumbled all had been well ;
So safe therein it would remain,
Until the Man got up again :
 And I wish in Heaven, &c.

Now

Now for the Pots with handles three,
Faith they shall have no praise of me;
When a Man and his Wife do fall at strife,
As many I fear have done in their Life:
They lay their Hands upon the Pot both,
And break the same though they were loth;
Which they shall answer another day,
For casting their Liquor so vainly away:
But had it been in a Bottle fill'd,
The one might have tugg'd, the other have held;
They both might have tugg'd till their Hearts did ake,
And yet no harm the Bottle would take:
  And I wish in Heaven that Soul may dwell,
  That first devis'd the Leathern Bottle.

Now what of the Flagons of Silver fine?
Faith they shall have no praise of mine;
When a Noble-man he doth them send,
To have them fill'd as he doth intend:
The Man with his Flagon runs quite away,
And never is seen again after that day;
Oh, then his Lord begins to Ban,
And Swears he hath lost both Flagon and Man:
But it ne'er was known that Page, or Groom,
But with a *Leathern Bottle* again would come;
  And I wish in Heaven, &c.

Now what do you say to these Glasses fine?
Faith they shall have no praise of mine;
When Friends are at a Table set,
And by them several sorts of Meat:
The one loves Flesh, the other Fish,
Among them all remove a Dish;
Touch but the Glass upon the brim,
The Glass is broke, no Wine left in:
Then be your Table-Cloth ne'er so fine,
There lies your Beer, your Ale, your Wine;
And doubtless for so small abuse,
A young Man may his Service lose:
  And I wish in Heaven that Soul may dwell,
  That first devis'd the Leathern Bottle.

            Now

Now when this Bottle is grown old,
And that it will no longer hold ;
Out of the side you may cut a Clout,
To mend your Shoe when worn out :
Or hang the other side on a Pin,
'Twill serve to put many odd trifles in ;
As Nails, Awls, and Candles ends,
For young beginners need such things.
   I wish in Heaven his Soul may dwell,
   That first Invented the Leathern Bottle.

The Black JACK :

To the foregoing Tune.

'TIS a pitiful thing that now adays, Sirs,
  Our Poets turn *Leathern* Bottle praisers ;
But if a Leathern Theam they did lack,
They might better have chosen the bonny *Black-Jack :*
For when they are both now well worn and decay'd,
For the *Jack*, than the *Bottle*, much more may be said ;
   And I wish his Soul much good may partake,
   That first devis'd the bonny Black Jack.

And now I will begin to declare,
What the Conveniencies of the *Jack* are ;
First, when a gang of good Fellows do meet,
As oft at a Fair, or a Wake, you shall see't :
They resolve to have some merry Carouses,
And yet to get home in good time to their Houses ;
Then the *Bottle* it runs as slow as my Rhime,
With *Jack*, they might have all been Drunk in good
   time :
   And I wish his Soul in Peace may dwell,
   That first devis'd that speedy Vessel.

                                 And

And therefore leave your twittle twattle,
Praise the *Jack*, praise no more the *Leathern Bottle;*
For the Man at the *Bottle*, may drink till he burst,
And yet not handsomely quench his thirst :
The Master hereat maketh great moan,
And doubts his *Bottle* has a spice of the Stone ;
But if it had been a generous *Jack*,
He might have had currently what he did lack :
 And I wish his Soul in Paradise,
  That first found out that happy devise.

Be your Liquor small, or thick as Mud,
The cheating *Bottle* that cries good, good ;
Then the Master again begins to storm,
Because it said more than it could perform :
But if it had been in an honest *Black Jack*,
It would have prov'd better to sight, smell, and smack ;
 And I wish his Soul in Heaven may rest,
  That added a Jack, *to* Bacchus *his Feast.*

No Flagon, Tankard, Bottle, or Jugg,
Is half so fit, or so well can hold tugg ;
For when a Man and his Wife play at thwacks
There's nothing so good as a pair of *Black Jacks :*
Thus to it they go, they Swear, and they Curse,
It makes them both better, the *Jack's* ne'er the worse ;
For they might have bang'd both, till their hearts did ake,
And yet no hurt the *Jacks* could take ;
 And I wish his Heirs may have a Pension,
  That first produc'd that lucky Invention.

SOCRATES and *ARISTOTLE,*
Suck'd no Wit from a *Leather Bottle;*
For surely I think a Man as soon may,
Find a Needle in a Bottle of Hay :
But if the *Black Jack*, a Man often toss over,
'Twill make him as Drunk as any Philosopher ;
When he that makes *Jacks* from a Peck, to a Quart,
Conjures not, though he lives by the black Art :
 And I wish his Soul, &c.

Be-

Besides my good Friend let me tell you, that Fellow,
That fram'd the Bottle, his Brains were but shallow;
The Case is so clear I nothing need mention,
The Jack is a nearer and deeper Invention;
When the Bottle is cleaned, the Dregs fly about,
As if the Guts and the Brains flew out;
But if in a Cannon-bore Jack it had been,
From the top to the bottom all might have been clean,
 And I wish his Soul no Comfort may lack,
 That first devis'd the bouncing black Jack.

Your Leather Bottle is us'd by no Man,
That is a Hairs Breadth above a Plow-man;
Then let us gang to the *Hercules* Pillars,
And there visit those gallant Jack swillers;
In these small, strong, sour, mild, stale,
They drink Orange, Lemon, and Lambeth Ale:
The Chief of Heralds there allows,
The Jack to be of an ancienter House.
 And may his Successors never want Sack,
 That first devis'd the long Leather Jack.

Then for the Bottle you cannot well fill it,
Without a Tunnel, but that you must spill it;
'Tis as hard to get in, as it is to get out,
'Tis not so with a Jack, for it runs like a Spout:
Then burn your Bottle, what good is in it,
One cannot well fill it, nor drink, nor clean it,
But if it had been in a jolly black Jack,
'Twould come a great pace, and hold you good Tack.
 And I wish his Soul, &c.

He that's drunk in a Jack looks as fierce as a Spark,
That were just ready cockt to shoot at a Mark;
When the other thing up to the Mouth it goes,
Makes a Man look with a great Bottle Nose;
All wise Men conclude, that a Jack New or Old,
Tho' beginning to leak, is however worth Gold;
For when the poor Man on the way does trudge it,
His worn-out Jack serves him well for a Budget;
 And I wish his Heirs may never lack Sack,
 That first contrived the Leather Black Jack.

When

When *Bottle* and *Jack* stand together, fie on't,
The *Bottle* looks just like a Dwarf to a Giant;
Then have we not reason the *Jack* for to chuse,
For they can make Boots, when the *Bottle* mends Shoes:
For add but to every *Jack* a Foot,
And every *Jack*, becomes a Boot:
Then give me my *Jack*, there's a reason why,
They have kept us wet, and they'll keep us dry:
I now shall cease, but as I'm an honest Man,
The *Jack* deserves to be called Sir *John;*
 And may they ne'er want for Belly, nor Back,
 That keep up the Trade of the bonny Black Jack.

A SONG.

Jenny

J*Enny*, my blithest Maid,
　Prithee listen to my true Love now ;
I am a canny Lad,
　Gang along with me to yonder Brow :
Aw the Boughs shall shade us round,
　While the Nightingale and Linnet teach us,
How the Lad the Lass may woo,
　Come, and I'll shew my *Jenny* how to do.

I ken full many a thing,
　I can dance, and can whistle too ;
I many a Song can sing,
　Pitch-Bar, and run and wrestle too :
Bonny *Mog* of our Town,
Gave me Bead-laces and Kerchers many,
　Only *Jenny* 'twas could win,
　Jockey from aw the Lasses of the Green.

Then lig thee down my Bearn,
　Ize not spoil the gawdy shining Geer ;
I'll make a Bed of Fern,
　And I'll gently press my *Jenny* there :
Let me lift thy Petticoat,
And thy Kercher too that hides thy Bosom ;
　Shew thy naked Beauty's store,
　Jenny alone's the Lass that I adore.

A SONG.

TELL me ye Gods,
  Why do you prove so cruel,
So severe, to make me burn in Flames of Love,
  Then throw me in Despair?
Tell me what Pleasure do you find,
  To force tormenting Fate;
To make my *Sylvia* first seem kind,
  Then vow perpetual hate?

Once gentle *Sylvia* did inspire,
  With her bewitching Eyes;
Oft with a Kiss she'd fan that Fire,
  Which from her Charms arise:

With

With her diviner Looks she'd bless,
  And with her Smiles revive;
When she was kind, who could express
  The Extasie of Life?

But now I read my fatal Doom,
  All Hopes now disappear;
Smiles are converted to a Frown,
  And Vows neglected are:
No more kind Looks she will impart,
  No longer will endure:
The tender Passion of my Heart,
  Which none but she can cure.

Ah! cruel, false, perfidious Maid!
  Are these Rewards of Love?
When you have thus my Heart betray'd,
  Will you then faithless prove?
'Tis pity such an Angels Face
  Shou'd so much perjur'd be;
And blast each captivating Grace,
  By being false to me.

Return, return, e'er 'tis too late,
  The God of Love appease;
Lest you too soon do meet your Fate,
  And fall a Sacrifice:
Despise not then a proferr'd Heart,
  But mighty Love obey;
For Age will ruin all your Art,
  And Beauty will decay.

A

A SONG.

S IT thee down by me, mine own Joy,
   Thouz quite kill me, should'st thou prove coy :
Shouldst thou prove Coy, and not love me,
Oh ! where should I find out sike a yan as thee.

Ize been at Wake, and Ize been at Fare,
Yet ne'er found yan with thee to compare :
Oft have I sought, but ne'er could find,
Sike Beauty as thine, couldst thou prove kind.

Thouz have a gay Gown and go foyn,
With silver Shoon thy Feet shall shoyn :
With foyn'st Flowers thy Crag Ize crown,
Thy pink Petticoat sall be laced down.

Weeze yearly gang to the Brook side,
And Fishes catch as they do glide :
Each Fish thyn Prisoner then shall be,
Thouz catch at them, and Ize catch at thee.

What

What mun we do when Scrip is fro ?
Weez gang to the Houze at the Hill broo,
And there weez fry and eat the Fish ;
But 'tis thy Flesh makes the best Dish.

Ize kiss thy cherry Lips, and praise
Aw the sweet Features of thy Face ;
Thy Forehead so smooth, and lofty both rise,
Thy soft ruddy Cheeks, and pratty black Eyes.

Ize lig by thee aw the cold Night,
Thouz want nothing for thy Delight :
Thouz have any thing if thouz have me,
And sure Ize have something that sall please thee.

A SONG.

BOnny Lass gin thou wert mine,
   And twenty Thousand Pounds about thee;
I'd scorn the Gow'd for thee my Queen,
To lay thee down on any Green:
And shew thee how thy Daddy gat thee,
I'd scorn thy Gow'd for thee my Queen,
To lay thee down on any Green,
And shew thee how thy Daddy gat thee.

Bonny Lad gin thou wert mine,
And twenty Thousand Lords about thee;
I'd leave them aw to kiss thine Eyn,
And gang with thee to any Green;
To shew me how my Daddy gat me,
   I'd leave them, *&c.*

A

A SONG.

TELL me *Jenny*, tell me roundly,
   When you will your Heart surrender;
Faith and Troth I love thee soundly,
   'Twas I that was the first Pretender.
Ne'er say nay, nor delay,
   Here's my Heart, and here's my Hand too;
All that's mine shall be thine,
   Body and Goods at thy Command too.

Ah! how many Maids, quoth *Jenny*,
   Have you promis'd to be true to;
Fye! I think the Devil's in you,
   To kiss a body so as you do!
What d'ye? let me go,
   I can't abide such foolish doing;
Get you gone you naughty Man,
   Fye, is this your way of Wooing.

A SONG.

THE bright *Laurinda*, whose hard fate,
  It was to Love a Swain,
Ill-natur'd, faithless, and ingrate,
  Grew weary of her Pain :
Long, long, alas ! she vainly strove,
To free her Captive Heart from Love ;
  'Till urg'd too much by his Disdain,
  She broke at last the strong-link'd Chain,
  And vow'd she ne'er would love again.

The lovely Nymph now free as Air,
  Gay as the blooming Spring ;
To no soft Tale would lend an ear,
  But careless sit and Sing :
Or if a moving Story wrought,
Her frozen Breast to a kind thought ;
  She check'd her Heart, and cry'd, ah ! hold,
  Amyntor thus his Story told,
  Once burn'd as much, but now he's Cold.

Long thus she kept her Liberty,
  And by her all-conquering Eyes,
A thousand Youths did daily die,
  Her Beauties Sacrifice :
'Till Love at last young *Cleon* brought,
The Object of each Virgin's thought,
  Whose strange resistless Charms did move,
  They made her burn and rage with Love,
  And made her blest as those above.

A SONG.

Ah

AH *Jenny* gin your Eyes do kill,
   You'll let me tell my pain ;
Gud Faith, I lov'd against my will,
   Yet wad not break my Chain :
Ize once was call'd a bonny Lad,
   'Till that fair Face of yours,
Betray'd the Freedom once I had,
   And all my blither hours.

And now wey's me, like Winter looks,
   My faded show'ring Eyn ;
And on the Banks of shaded Brooks,
   I pass my wearied time :
Ize call the Streams that glideth on,
   To witness, if they see,
On all the brink they glide along,
   So true a Swain as I.

A SONG.

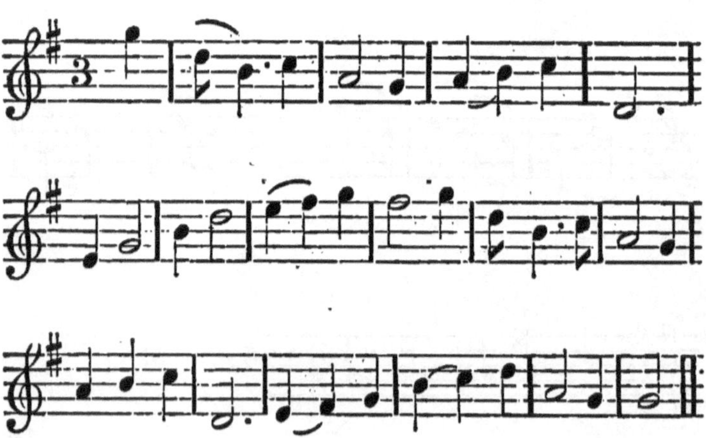

I Often for my *Jenny* strove,
   Ey'd her, try'd her, yet can't prove,
So lucky to find her Pity move,
Ize have no Reward for Love:
If you wou'd but think on me,
And now forsake your Cruelty,
Ize for ever shou'd be, cou'd be, wou'd be,
Joyn'd with none but only thee.

When first I saw thy lovely Charms,
I kiss'd thee, wish'd thee in my Arms;
I often vow'd, and did protest,
'Tis *Joan* alone that I love best:
Ize have gotten Twanty Pounds,
My Father's House, and all his Grounds,
And for ever shou'd be, cou'd be, wou'd be,
Joyn'd with none but only thee.

A

A SONG.

THere was a Jovial Beggar,
  He had a wooden Leg ;
Lame from his Cradle,
  And forced for to beg :
And a Begging we will go,
  We'll go, we'll go,
And a Begging we will go.

A Bag for his Oatmeal,
  Another for his Salt ;
And a pair of Crutches,
  To shew that he can halt.
And a Begging, &c.

A Bag for his Wheat,
  Another for his Rye ;
A little Bottle by his side,
  To drink when he's a dry.
And a Begging, &c.

To

To *Pimblico* we'll go,
  Where we shall merry be ;
With ev'ry Man a Can in's Hand,
  And a Wench upon his Knee.
And a Begging, &c.

And when we are dispos'd
  To tumble on the Grass,
We've a long patch'd Coat,
  To hide a pretty Lass.
And a Begging, &c.

Seven Years I begg'd
  For my old Master *Wild*,
He taught me to beg
  When I was but a Child.
 And a Begging, &c.

I begg'd for my Master,
  And got him store of Pelf ;
But *Jove* now be praised,
  I now beg for my self.
 And a Begging, &c.

In a hollow Tree
  I live and pay no Rent ;
Providence provides for me,
  And I am well content.
And a Begging, &c.

Of all Occupations,
  A Beggar lives the best ;
For when he is a weary,
  He'll lie him down and rest.
And a begging, &c.

I fear no Plots against me,
  I live in open Cell ;
Then he wou'd be a King,
  When the Beggars live so well :
And a Begging we will go,
  We'll go, we'll go,
And a Begging we will go.

                                     A

A SONG.

A^T *London* che've bin,
  At *London* che've bin,
And che've seen the King and the Queen *a;*
   Che've seen Lords and Earls,
   And roaring fine Girls,
Turn up their Tails at fifteen *a;*

   Che've seen the Lord-Mayor,
   And Bartoldom-Fair,
And there che met with the *Dragon,*
   That St. *George* that bold Knight,
   Fought and kill'd outright,
Whilst a Man could toss off a Flagon.

   From thence as I went
   To see th' Monument
I met with a Girl in Cheapside *a;*
   That for half a Crown,
   Pluck'd up her Silk Gown,
And shew'd me how far she could stride *a;*

A

A SONG.

TEll me no more, no more, I am deceiv'd,
    That *Chloe's* false, that *Chloe's* false and common:
By Heav'n I all along believ'd,
    She was, she was, a very, very Woman.
As such I lik'd, as such carest,
    She still, she still was constant when possest;
She cou'd, she cou'd, she cou'd, she cou'd
    Do more for no Man.

But oh! but oh her Thoughts on others ran,
    And that you think, and that you think a hard thing;
Perhaps she fancy'd you the Man,
    Why what care I, what care I one Farthing.
You say she's false, I'm sure she's kind,
    I'll take, I'll take her Body, you her Mind;
Who, who has the better Bargain?

A SONG.

THen beauteous Nymph look from above,
  And see me here below :
See how that mighty Tyrant Love, drags me to your
    Window,
  Drags me to your Window :
Let not your Heart then hardned be,
  Since you my Love have got ;
For I'm a Knight of high Degree,
  And dye upon the Spot.

To Morrow then let us be wed,
  At Hours Canonical ;
That I may say when I have sped,
  My Heart is free from Thrall :
Oh think then what the Joy will be,
  When I am in thy Arms ;
That thou may'st have the Liberty
  To rifle all my Charms.

The

The Old and New Courtier.

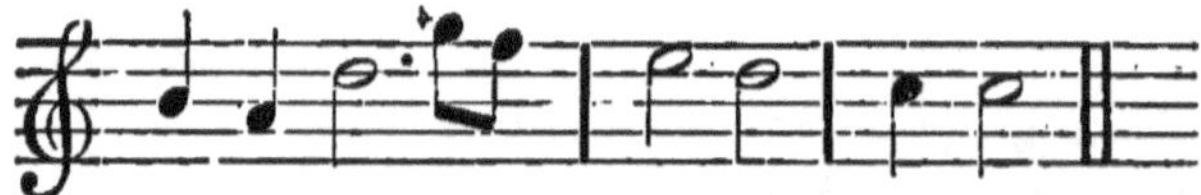

With an Old Song made by an Old Ancient Pate,
Of an Old worshipful Gentleman who had a
great Estate :
Who kept an Old House at a bountiful rate,
And an Old Porter to relieve the Poor at his Gate,
Like an old Courtier of the Queens.

With an Old Lady whose Anger good Words asswages,
Who every Quarter pays her Old Servants their Wages,
Who never knew what belongs to Coachmen, Footmen
and Pages :
But kept twenty or thirty Old Fellows with blue Cloaths
and Badges ;
Like an old Courtier, &c.

With a Study fill'd full of Learned Books,
With an Old Reverend Parson, you may judge him by
his looks
With an Old Buttery hatch worn quite off the old Hooks,
And an Old Kitchin, which maintains half a dozen
Old Cooks ;
Like an Old Courtier, &c.

With

With an old Hall hung round about with Guns, Pikes,
     and Bows,
With old Swords and Bucklers, which hath born many
     shrew'd Blews,
And an old Frysadoe Coat to cover his Worship's trunk
     Hose,
And a Cup of old Sherry to comfort his Copper Nose ;
     Like an old Courtier, &c.

With an old Fashion when *Christmas* is come,
To call in his Neighbours with Bag-pipe and Drum,
And good Cheer enough to furnish every old Room,
And old Liquor able to make a Cat speak, and a wise
     Man dumb ;
     Like an Old Courtier, &c.

With an old Huntsman, a Falconer, and a Kennel of
     Hounds,
Which never hunted, nor hawk'd but in his own
     Grounds :
Who like an old Wise-man kept himself within his own
     Bounds,
And when he died gave every Child a thousand old
     Pounds.
     Like an old Soldier, &c.

But to his Eldest Son, his House and Land he assign'd,
Charging him in his Will to keep the same bountiful
     Mind,
To be good to his Servants, and to his Neighbours
     kind,
But in the ensuing Ditty, you shall hear how he was
     enclin'd ;
     Like a young Courtier of the Kings.

Like a young Gallant newly come to his Land,
That keeps a brace of Creatures at's own Command,
And takes up a thousand Pound upon's own bond,
And lieth drunk in a new Tavern, till he can neither
     go nor stand ;
     Like a young Courtier, &c.

With

With a neat Lady that is fresh and fair
Who never knew what belong'd to good House-keeping,
    or care,
But buys several Fans to play with the wanton Air,
And seventeen or eighteen Dressings of other Womens
    Hair.
    Like a young Courtier, &c.

With a new Hall built where the old one stood,
Wherein is burned neither Coal nor Wood,
And a new Shuffle-board-table where never Meat stood,
Hung round with Pictures, which doth the poor
    little good;
    Like a young Courtier, &c.

With a new Study stuff'd full of Pamphlets and Plays,
With a new Chaplain, that swears faster than he prays,
With a new Buttery Hatch that opens once in four or
    five Days,
With a new *French-Cook* to makes Kickshaws and Toys
    Like a young Courtier, &c.

With a new Fashion when *Christmas* is come,
With a Journey up to London we must be gone,
And leave no body at home but our New Porter *John*
Who relieves the Poor with a thump on the Back with
    a Stone,
    Like a young Courtier, &c.

With a Gentleman-Usher whose carriage is compleat,
With a Foot-man, a Coachman, a Page to carry Meat,
With a waiting Gentlewoman, whose dressing is very
    neat,
Who when the Master has din'd gives the Servants
    little Meat ;
    Like a young Courtier, &c.

With a new Honour bought with his Father's Old Gold,
That many of his Father's Old Manours hath sold
And this is the Occasion that most Men do hold,
That good House-keeping is now a days grown so cold ;
    Like a young Courtier of the Kings.

BACCHUS's *Health*:

*To be Sung by all the Company together,
with Directions to be Observed.*

First Man stands up with a Glass in's Hand and Sings.

HEre's a Health to Jolly *Bacchus*,
   Here's a Health to Jolly *Bacchus*,
Here's a Health to Jolly *Bacchus*, *I—ho, I—ho, I—ho;*
For he doth merry make us,
For he doth merry make us,
For he doth merry make us, *I—ho, I—ho, I ho,*

At

*At this Star they all bow to each other,
and sit down.
†At this Dagger all the Company beckons
to the Drawer.*

*Come sit ye down together,
Come sit ye down together,
Come sit ye down together, *I—ho, I—ho, I—ho;*
And † bring more Liquor hither,
And bring more Liquor hither,
And bring more Liquor hither, *I—ho, I—ho, I—ho.*

*At this Star the first Man drinks his
Glass, while all the other sing and
point at him.
†At this Dagger they all sit down clap-
ping their next Man on the Shoulder.*

It goes into the * *Cranium,*
It goes into the *Cranium,*
It goes into the *Cranium, I—ho, I—ho, I—ho.*
And † thou'rt a boon Companion,
And thou'rt a boon Companion,
And thou'rt a boon Companion, *I—ho, I—ho, I—ho;*

*Then the 2d Man takes his Glass, all the Company
Singing* Here's a Health, *&c. so round.*

A SONG to the foregoing Tune.

THere was a bonny Blade,
    Had marry'd a Country Maid,
And safely conducted her home, home, home ;
    She was neat in ev'ry part,
    And she pleas'd him to the Heart,
But ah ! alas ! she was dumb, dumb, dumb.

    She was bright as the Day,
    And brisk as the May,
And as round, and as plump as a Plumb, plumb, plumb,
    But still the silly Swain,
    Could do nothing but complain,
Because that his Wife she was dumb, dumb, dumb.

    She could Brew and she could Bake,
    She could Sew and she could make,
She could sweep the House with a Broom, Broom,
        Broom,
    She could wash and she could wring,
    She could do any kind of thing,
But ah ! alas ! she was dumb, dumb, dumb.

    To the Dr. then he went,
    For to give himself Content,
And to cure his Wife of the mum, mum, mum,
    O ! 'tis the easiest part
    That belongs unto my Art,
For to make a Woman speak that is dumb, dumb, dumb.

    To the Dr. he did her bring,
    And he cut her chattering String,
And at Liberty he set her Tongue, her Tongue, her
        Tongue,
    Her Tongue began to walk,
    And she began to talk,
As tho' she had never been dumb, dumb, dumb.

    Her Faculty she tries,
    And she fill'd the House with Noise,

And

And she rattl'd in his Ears like a drum, drum, drum,
  She bred a deal of Strife,
  Made him weary of his Life,
He'd give any thing again she was dumb, dumb, dumb.

    To the Dr. then he goes,
    And thus he vents his Woes,
Oh ! Dr. You've me undone, undone, undone ;
    For my Wife she's turn'd a Scold,
    And her Tongue can never hold,
I'd give any kind of thing she was dumb, dumb, dumb.

    When I did undertake,
    To make thy Wife to speak,
It was a thing easily done, done, done ;
    But 'tis past the Art of Man,
    Let him do whate'er he can,
For to make a Scolding Wife hold her Tongue, Tongue,
  Tongue.

The West-Countryman's Song *on a Wedding.*

ODS hartly wounds, Ize not to plowing, not I, Sir,
　　Because I hear there's such brave doing hard
　　by, Sir ;
Thomas the Minstrel he's gan twinkling before, Sir,
And they talk there will be two or three more, Sir :
Who the Rat can mind either *Bayard* or *Ball*, Sir,
Or anything at all, Sir, for thinking of drinking i'th'
　　Hall, Sir ;
E'gad not I ! Let Master fret it and storm it, I am re-
　　solv'd :
I'm sure there can be no harm in't :
Who would lose the zight of the Lasses and Pages,
And pretty little *Sue* so true, when she ever engages ;
E'gad not I, I'd rather lose all my Wages.

There's my Lord has got the curiousest Daughter,
Look but on her, she'll make the Chops on ye water ;
This is the day the Ladies are all about her,
Some veed her, some to dress and clout her :
Uds-bud she's grown the veatest, the neatest, the
　　sweetest,
The pretty littl'st Rogue, and all Men do say the dis-
　　creetest.

There's ne'er a Girl that wears a Head in the Nation,
But must give place zince Mrs. *Betty's* Creation ;
She's zo good, zo witty, zo pretty to please ye,
Zo charitably kind, zo courteous, and loving, and easie :
That I'll be bound to make a Maid of my Mother,
If *London* Town can e'er zend down zuch another.

Next

Next my Lady in all her Gallant Apparel,
Ize not forget the thumping thund'ring Barrel ;
There's zuch Drink the strongest head cannot bear it,
'Twill make a vool of Zack, or White wine, or Claret :
And zuch plenty, that twenty or thirty good vellows,
May tipple off their Cups, until they lie down on their
      Pillows ;
Then hit off thy Vrock, and don't stand scratching thy
      head zo,
For thither I'll go, Cods——because I have said so.

A SONG.

J Ockey was as brisk and blith a Lad,
   As ever did pretend to love a Maiden true ;
But I fear that I shall die a Maid,
   And never taste the Joys of Love as others do :
     When the Wars alarms,
     Call'd him forth to Arms,
     And the Trumpets sound,
     Made the shores rebound.

All that ever I cou'd say to keep my Lover,
   Was too little to confine him here ;
And till he returns I never shall give over,
   Mourning for the absence of my dear :
     To Arms, to arms, he cry'd,
     To Love I straight reply'd,
     But in vain I strove,
     To perswade my Love.

Love can ne'er contend when Glory is a Rival,
   Or I wou'd have kept my Swain from harms ;
But he thought that he in Glory should survive all,
   When by Honour he was call'd to Arms :
     To Arms, to Arms he cry'd,
     To Love I straight reply'd,
     But in vain I strove,
     To persuade my Love.

All that ever I cou'd say to keep my Lover,
   Was too little to confine him here ;
And till he returns I never shall give over,
   Mourning for the absence of my dear :

A SONG.

YOU mad caps of *England* who merry wou'd make
  And for your brave Valour would pains under-
take :
Come over for *Flanders*, and there you shall see,
How merry we'll make it, how frolick we'll be :
      Sing Tanta, ra, ra, ra, ra, ra Boys,
      Tanta ra, ra, ra, ra, ra Boys,
      Tanta ra, ra, ra, ra, ra Boys drink, Boys drink.

If

If you have been a Citizen broke by mischance,
And wou'd by your Courage, your Credit advance ;
Here's stuff to be won by ventring your Life,
So you leave at home a good friend by your Wife :
      Sing Tanta ra, ra, *&c.* Wear Horns, wear Horns,
      Sing Tanta ra, ra, *&c.* Wear Horns.

But if upon Wenches you have spent all your means,
And still your minds runs upon Whores and Queans ;
Here's Wenches enow that with you will go,
 From Leaguer to Leaguer, in spite of your Foe :
      Sing Tanta ra, ra, *&c.* Whores all, Whores all,
      Sing Tanta ra, ra, *&c.* Whores all.

As soon as you come to your Enemies Land,
 Where fat Goose and Capon, you have at command ;
Sing take them, or eat them, or let them alone,
Sing go out and fetch them, or else you get none :
      Sing Tanta ra, ra, *&c.* Make shift, make shift,
      Sing Tanta ra, ra, *&c.* Make shift.

Your Serjeants and Officers are very kind,
If that you can Flatter and Speak to their mind ;
They will free you from Duty and all other trouble,
 Your money being gone your Duty comes double ;
      Sing Tanta ra, ra, *&c.* Hard case, hard case,
      Sing Tanta ra, ra, *&c.* Hard case.

And when you break an Arm, or a Leg,
You shall have your Pass, thro' the Country to Beg ;
Your Officer promises you some other pay,
But the Souldier never gets it, no, not till Dooms-day:
      Sing Tanta ra, *&c.* Long time, long time,
      Sing Tanta ra, ra, *&c.* Long time.

At last when you come to your Enemies Walls,
Where many a brave Gallant and Gentleman falls ;
And when you have done the best that you can,
Your Captain rewards you, there dies a brave Man ;
      Sing Tanta ra, ra *&c.* That's all, that's all,
      Sing Tanta ra, ra, *&c.* That's all.

A

A SONG.

Her

HER Eyes are like the Morning bright,
  Her Eyes are like the Morning bright,
Her Cheeks like Roses fair ;
Her Breasts like water'd Lillies white,
Her Breasts like water'd Lillies white,
  Like Silk her flowing Hair:
Her Breasts like water'd Lillies white,
Her Breasts like water'd Lillies white,
  Like Silk her flowing Hair.

Her Breath's as sweet as Odours blown,
  By *Zephyrus* o'er the Vales ;
Her Skin's as fine and soft as Down,
  Her Voice like Nightingale's.

Where e'er she Breaths, where e'er she sings,
  How happy are the Groves ;
How blest ! how much more blest than Kings,
  The Shepherd's that she loves.

With gentle steps lets beat the ground,
  In Gladsome Couples joyn'd ;
For Joy that your *Dorinda's* found,
  And ev'ry Lover kind.

A SONG.

G Reat *Alexander's* Horse,
  Bucephalus by Name ;
That long has been enrolled
  Within the Books of Fame :
But Sir *Credulous Easy's* Mare,
  So far did him excel,
She ne'er run for the Plate
  But she bore away the Bell :
  Ç *With a Nighy, Wheeghy, Yeopoop a,*
Full Caper and Career ;
All England *cannot shew you,*
Sike another Mare,

And

And to *Brentford* she did come,
  And an Ale-house she did find ;
She could not pass it by,
  But she knew her Master's mind :
And as she called for a Pot,
  She wou'd be, wou'd be sure of twain ;
Which made her such a Sott,
  She ne'er could run again.
    Ç *With a Nighy*, &c.

Since last I saw her Face,
  I heard report is spread,
With drinking in that Place,
  This bonny Mare is dead :
And the last Words she did say,
  As she came down the Hill ;
Was ah ! that Bowl had broke her Heart,
  And so she made her Will :
    Ç *With a Nighy*, &c.

Her Fore-Hoof she bequeath'd
  To some Religious Fool ;
Who after her untimely Death,
  Begs Pardon for her Soul :
An   her hinder Hoof with which,
  She play'd full many a Trick ;
She gave to those curs'd Wives,
  That against their Husbands kick :
    Ç *With a Nighy*, &c.

At the Burial of this Mare,
  Her Master wept full sore ;
Because it was reported,
  He ne'er shou'd see her more :
But that which Comforted him,
  For his departed Friend ;
Was after all his great Loss,
  She made so good an end :
    With a Nighy, &c.

A SONG.

If

IF Love's a sweet Passion, why does it Torment?
   If a bitter, oh tell me! whence comes my content;
Since I suffer with Pleasure, why should I complain,
Or grieve at my Fate, when I know 'tis in vain?
Yet so pleasing the Pain is, so soft is the Dart,
That at once it both wounds me, and tickles my Heart.

I press her hand gently, look languishing down,
And by Passionate silence, I make my Love known;
But Oh! how I'm blest when so kind she does prove,
By some willing mistake to discover her Love:
When in striving to hide, she returns all her Flame,
And our Eyes tell each other, what neither dare Name.

A SONG.

COME if you dare, our Trumpets sound,
Come if you dare, the Foes rebound;
We come, we come, we come, we come,
Says the double, (double, double) Beat of the thunder-
ing Drum:
Now they charge on amain,
Now they Rally again,
The Gods from above the Mad labour behold,
And pity Mankind that will perish for Gold.

The Fainting *Saxons* quit their Ground,
Their Trumpets Languish in the sound;
They fly, they fly, they fly, they fly,
Victoria, Victoria the bold *Britons* cry:
Now the Victory's won,
To the Plunder we run,
We return to our Lasses like Fortunate Traders,
Triumphant with Spoils of the Vanquish'd Invaders.

A SONG.

HOW blest are Shepherds, how happy their Lasses,
  While Drums and Trumpets are sounding Alarms!
Over our lowly sheds all the Storms passes,
  And when we Die, 'tis in each others Arms:
All the Day on our Herds and Flocks employing,
All the Night on our Flutes, and in enjoying.
  All the Day, &c.

Bright Nymphs of *Britain*, with Graces attended,
  Let not your days without Pleasure expire;
Honour's but empty, and when Youth is ended,
  All Men will praise you, but none will desire:
Let not Youth fly away without Contenting,
Age will come time enough, for your Repenting.
  Let not Youth, &c.

A SONG.

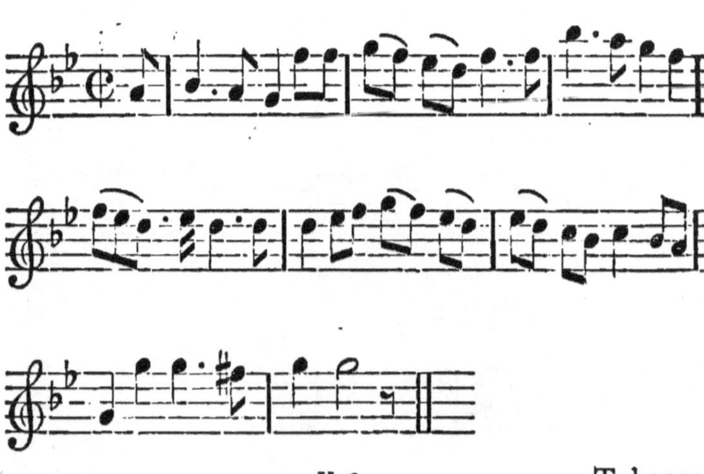

Tobacco

TObacco is but an *Indian* Weed,
 Grows green in the Morn, cut down at Eve ;
  It shows our decay,
  We are but Clay,
Think of this and take Tobacco.

The Pipe that is so Lilly-white,
Where so many take delight ;
  Is broke with a touch,
  Man's Life is such,
Think of this, &c.

The Pipe that is so foul within,
Shews how Man's Soul is stain'd with Sin ;
  It does require,
  To be purg'd with fire,
Think of this, &c.

The Ashes that are left behind,
Does serve to put us all in mind ;
  That into Dust,
  Return we must,
Think of this, &c.

The Smoak that does so high ascend,
Shews you Man's Life must have an end ;
  The Vapour's gone,
  Man's Life is done,
Think of this and take Tobacco.

A SONG.

SIR *Eglamore*, that valiant Knight,
  Fa la, lanky down dilly;
He took up his Sword, and he went to fight,
  Fa la, lanky down dilly:
And as he rode o'er Hill and Dale,
All Armed with a Coat of Male,
  Fa la la, la la la, lanky down dilly.

There leap'd a Dragon out of her Den,
That had slain God knows how many Men ;
But when she saw Sir *Eglamore*,
Oh that you had but heard her roar !

Then

Then the Trees began to shake,
Horse did Tremble, Man did quake ;
The Birds betook them all to peeping,
Oh ! 'twould have made one fall a weeping.

But all in vain it was to fear,
For now they fall to't, fight Dog, fight Bear ;
And to't they go, and soundly fight,
A live-long day, from Morn till Night.

This Dragon had on a plaguy Hide,
That cou'd the sharpest steel abide ;
No sword cou'd enter her with cuts,
Which vex'd the Knight unto the Guts.

But as in Choler he did burn,
He watch'd the Dragon a great good turn ;
For as a Yawning she did fall,
He thrust his Sword up Hilt and all.

Then like a Coward she did fly,
Unto her Den, which was hard by ;
And there she lay all Night and roar'd,
The Knight was sorry for his Sword :
But riding away, he cries, I forsake it,
He that will fetch it, let him take it.

A SONG.

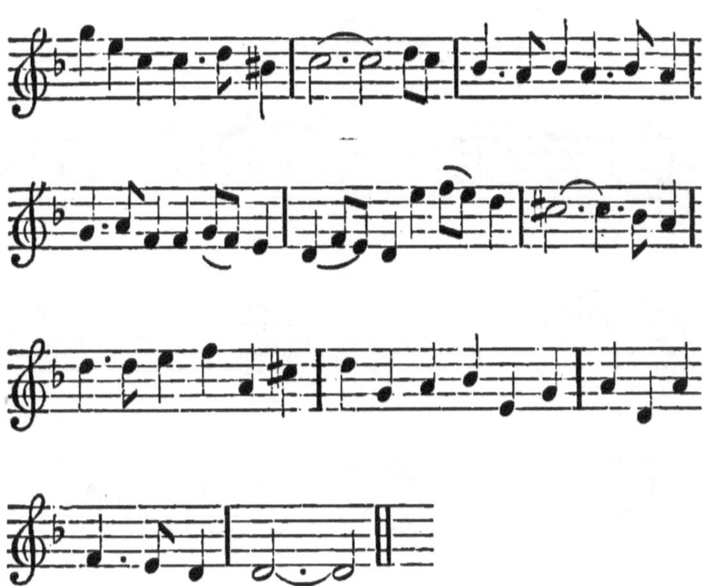

THE Danger is over, the Battle is past,
   The Nymph had her fears, but she ventur'd at last;
She try'd the Encounter, and when his was done;
She smil'd at her Folly, and own she had won:
By her Eyes we discover, the Bride has been pleas'd,
Her Blushes become her, her Passion is eas'd;
She dissembles her joy, and affects to look down,
If she sighs, 'tis for sorrow 'tis ended so soon.

Appear all you Virgins, both Aged and Young,
All you, who have carry'd that burden too long;
Who have lost precious time, and you who are loosing,
Betray'd by your fears between doubting and chusing:
Draw nearer, and learn what will settle your mind,
You'll find your selves happy, when once you are kind;
Do but wisely resolve the sweet venture to run,
You'd feel the loss little, and much to be won.

A

A SONG.

WUlly and *Georgy* now beath are gean,
  To see their lovely Flocks a feeding;
Jenny and *Moggy* too follow'd them,
  For fear they should be now a breeding:
Out of *London* Town they aw did trip it,
  Down to play at new bopeep at *Tunbridge* Well;
But how they play'd, or what they said,
  The De'el his sell can only tell.

Moggy

Moggy had Bearns, Four, Five or Six,
　Put *Jenny* was a young beginner;
Sure to her Trading now she will fix,
　The Kirk has made her a young Sinner:
To *London* Town they're gean,
　Each with a muckle Weam:
And *Georgy* now to *Scotland* he mun run,
　Fare him weel, ene take him De'el,
Poor *Jenny* now is quite undone.

A SONG.

SING, sing whilst we trip it, trip, trip it,
    Trip, trip it, upon the Green;
But no ill Vapours rise or fall,
But no ill Vapours rise or fall,
No nothing, no nothing offend,
No nothing offend our Fairy Queen:
No nothing, no nothing,
No nothing offend our Fairy Queen;
No nothing, no nothing, no nothing,
No nothing offend our Fairy Queen.

A SONG.

YOU Lasses and Lads take leave of your Dads,
    And away to the Maypole hye,
There is every he has gotten a she,
    And a Fidler standing by ;
There is *Jockey* has gotten his *Jenny*,
    And *Johnny* has gotten his *Jone*,
And there they do jugget, and jugget,
    And jugget up and down.

You're out said *Dick*, you lye said *Nick*,
    The Fidler play'd it false ;
And so said *Natt*, and so said *Kate*,
    And so said nimble *Ealse :*
With that the Fidler he
    Did play the Tune again ;
And then they did foot it, and foot it,
    And foot it unto the Men.

Three times in an Hour they went to a Bower,
    To play for Ale and Cakes,
And kisses to whom they were due,
    The Lasses held the Stakes :
The Lasses they began
    To quarrel with the Men,
And bid them take their Kisses back,
    And give them their own again.

A SONG.

WHat ungrateful Devil moves you !
    Come, come my Friend the Truth declare ;
You love *Sylvia, Sylvia* loves you ;
    Why, why then will you wed the Fair ?
Marriage joyning does discover,
    But Lovefreeing joyns for Life :
Wou'd you, wou'd you, wou'd you,
    Love the Nymph for ever ?
Never, never, never, never, never, never,
    Let her be your Wife.

A

A SONG.

Sett by Mr. Barincloth.

ALL Hands up aloft,
   Swab the Coach fore and aft,
For the Punch Clubbers straight will be sitting;
   For fear the Ship rowl
   Sling off a full Bowl,
For our Honour let all things be fitting:
   In an Ocean of Punch
   We to Night will all sail,
   I'th' Bowl we're in Sea Room
   Enough we ne'er fear;

Here's

Here's to thee Mess-mate,
Thanks honest *Tom*,
'Tis a Health to the King,
Whilst the Larboard Man drinks,
Let the Star-board Man sing,
   With full double Cups,
   We'll Liquor our Chaps,
   And then we'll turn out,
   With a Who up, Who, Who,
   But let's drink e'er we go,
   But let's drink e'er we go.

The Winds veering aft,
  Then loose ev'ry Sail,
She'll bear all her Topsails a trip:
  Heave the Logg from the Poop,
  It blows a fresh Gale,
And a just Account on the Board keep:
  She runs the eight Knots,
And eight Cups to my thinking,
  That's a Cup for each Knot,
Must be fill'd for our drinking;
  Here's to thee Skipper,
  Thanks honest *John*,
  'Tis a Health to the King,
  Whilst the one is a drinking,
  The other shall fill,
   With full double Cups
   We'll liquor our Chaps,
   And then we'll turn out,
   With a Who up, Who, Who,
   But let's drink e'er we go,
   But let's drink e'er we go.

The Quartier must Cun,
  Whilst the foremast-man steers;
Here's a Health to each Port where'er bound,
  Who delays 'tis a Bumper,
  Shall be drubb'd at the Geers;
The Depth of each Cup therefore sound:

To our noble Commander,
To his Honour and Wealth,
May he drown and be damn'd,
That refuses the Health :
Here's to thee honest *Harry,*
Thanks honest *Will,*
Old true Penny still,
Whilst the one is a drinking,
The other shall fill.

 With full double Cups
 We'll liquor our Chaps,
 And then we'll turn out,
 With a Who up, Who, Who,
 But let's drink e'er we go,
 But let's drink e'er we go.

VVhat News on the Deck ho?
It blows a meer Storm ;
She lies a try under her Mizen,
VVhy what tho' she does,
VVill it do any Harm ?
If a Bumper more does us all Reason :
The Bowl must be fill'd Boys,
In spight of the VVeather,
Yea, yea huzza, let's howl altogether ;
Here's to thee *Peter,*
Thanks honest *Joe,*
About let it go ;
In the Bowl still a Calm is,
VVhere'er the VVinds blow.

 With full double Cups
 We'll liquor our Chaps,
 And then we'll turn out,
 With a Who up, Who, Who,
 But let's drink e'er we go,
 But let's drink e'er we go.

A Scotch *SONG.   Set by Mr.* Akeroyde.

AS I went o'er yon misty Moor,
   'Twas on an Evening late, Sir,
There I met with a welfar'd Lass
   VVas spanning of her Gate, Sir;
I took her by the lilly white Hand,
   And by the Twat I caught her,
I swear and vow, and tell you true,
   She piss'd in my Hand with Laughter.

The silly poor VVench she lay so still,
   You'd swear she had been dead, Sir;
The deel a word but aw she said, but ay,
   And bow'd her Head, Sir;
Kind Sir, quoth she, you'll kill me here,
   But I'll forgive the Slaughter,
You make such Motions with your A——se,
   You'll split my Sides with Laughter.

A SONG.

Sett by Mr. Samuel Akeroyde.

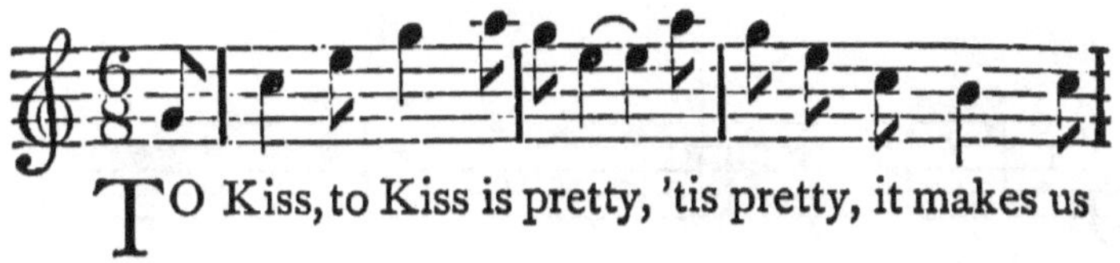

'Tis

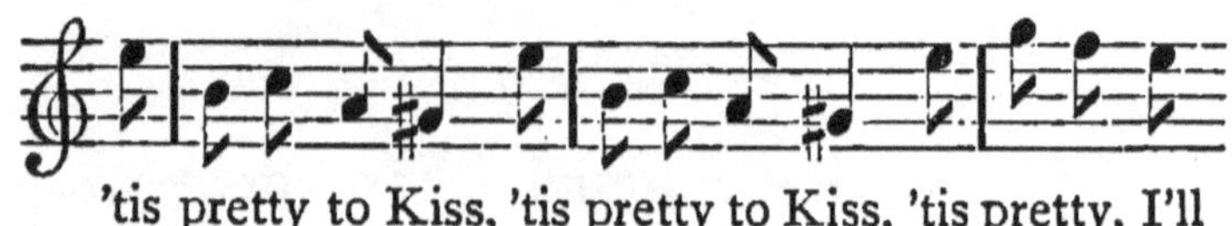
'tis pretty to Kiss, 'tis pretty to Kiss, 'tis pretty, I'll

tell you why,'tis pretty to Kiss, 'tis pretty to Kiss to

Love, but not to dye ; no,no,no,no, no, no, no,

no, no, Kissing till you're out of breath, 'tis

foolish to Kiss, 'tis foo - lish, 'tis foolish to

Kiss to death.

The

The Midwives *Christening* SONG.

Et's consecrate a mighty Bowl,
  On this our solemn Meeting,
To recreate those Female Hearts,
That sometime since were weeping :
The Lady's Pangs are now no more,
All Grief is banish'd from her ;
The lusty Boy has made his way,
And nothing now can wrong her.

Cho. *By all the Gossips.*

O Mighty Power of active Love,
  How bravely hast thou wrought !
From Something done, there's Something come,
  While many toyl for nought.

Then dish about the Mother's Health,
The Lads shall soon come after ;
Nor shall the Father be forgot,
In hopes the next —— a Daughter :
Go on brave Pair, obey Command,
And multiply together ;
    May Strength increase,
    And VVealth ne'er cease,
Nor may you part for ever.

Cho. *By all the Gossips.*

O mighty Power of active Love,
  How bravely hast thou wrought !
From Something done, there's Something come,
  While many toyl for nought.

A

A SONG.

O Raree Show, O brave Show,
    O pretty Show, who see my fine a Show?
O Raree Show, O Brave Show,
Who see my pretty Show?
Quand la Cigala Canta fa pasboun travailar,
Fadboun estr' a l'ombretta a l'ombretta,
Fad boun estr' l'ombretta Calignar.

Here's

Here's de *English* and *French* to each oder most civil,
Shake Hands and be friends, and hug like the Devil :
O Raree Show, O brave Show, O pretty gallant a Show.

Here be de *Savoyards* a trudging thro' *France*,
To sweep ade Shimney, to sing and to dance.
  O Raree Show, &c.

Here be de great *Turk*, and de great King of no Land,
A Galloping bravely from *Hung'ry* to *Poland*.
  O Raree Show, &c.

Here's de brave *English Beau* for de Pacquet Boat tarries,
To go make his Campaign vid his Taylor at *Paris*.
  O Raree Show, &c.

Here be de honest Captain a cursing the Peace,
Here's another disbanding his Coach and his Miss.
  O Raree Show, &c.

Here be de *English* Ships bring Plenty and Riches,
And here be de *French* Caper a mending his Breeches.
  O Raree Show, &c.

Here be de Jacks set out Lights and dissemble,
And here be de Mob make 'em squitter and tremble.
  O Raree Show, &c.

Here be de Sea Captain a reeling on Shore,
Here's one spend all his Pay and Boarding a Whore.
  O Raree Show, &c.

Here be de brave Trainbands a drinking Carouses,
And here be de Soldiers a storming their Spouses.
  O Raree Show, brave Show, who see my fine Show.

A

A SONG in the Morose Reformer.

YOU Ladies who are young and gay,
  Since Time too swiftly flyes away,
Bestow your hours of leisure, bestow your hours of leisure
  On Courts, on Gardens, Springs, and Groves,
  On Conversation lawful Loves,   [Pleasure.
And ev'ry harmless Pleasure, ev'ry, ev'ry harmless

Be you the finest Shows at Plays,
Alluring Youth to love and gaze ;
  But try no mad Conclusions :
But ev'ry where and often shown,
But Vision-like, be touch'd by none,
  Be only fair Delusions.

For Pleasure ramble round the Town,
But give your Friends no cause to frown ;
  From Honour never sally :
How they're contemn'd who were admir'd,
In Courts had all their Hearts desire,
  For ev'ry Kiss a Tally.

The

The Second Part of St. George *for* England,
by the late John Grub, M.A. *of* Christ's-
Church Oxon; *to the same Tune*, Pag. 117.

THE Story of King *Arthur* it is very memorable,
  The Number of his valiant Knights, and roundness
  of his Table ;
His Knights around his Table in a Circle sate, d'ye see,
And altogether made up one large Hoop of Chivalry ;
He had a Sword both broad and sharp, yclip'd *Calliburn*,
Would cut a Flint more easy, than Penknife cuts a Corn ;
A Case-Knife does a Capon carve, so it would carve a
    Rock,
And split a Man at single slash, from noddle down to nock,
He was the Cream of *Brecknock*, and the Flower of all
    the *Welch*,
But *George* he did the Dragon fell, and gave him a
    plaguy Squelsh ;

> *St.* George *he was for fair* England,
> *St.* Dennis *was for* France,
> *Sing* Honi soit qui mal y pense.

Tamerlain with *Tartarian* Bow the *Turkish* Squadrons
    slew,
And fetcht the *Pagan* Crescent down, with half Moon
    made of Yew ;
His trusty Bow proud *Turks* did gall, with show'rs of
    Arrows thick,
And Bow-strings without throtling sent, Grand *Visier*
    to Old *Nick ;*
Much Turbants and much *Pagan* Pates, he made to
    tumble in Dust,
And heads of *Saracens* he fixt on Spears as on a Sign Post ;
He coop'd in Cage grim *Bajazet*, prop of *Mahomet's*
    Religion,
As if he'd been the whispering Bird that prompted
    him the Pidgeon ;

In

In *Turkey* leather Scabbard, he did sheath his Blade
    so trenchant,
But *George* he swing'd the Dragon's Tail, and cut off
    every Inch on't ;

      St. George *he was,* &c.

Achilles of old *Chiron* learnt the great Horse for to ride,
Was taught by th' *Centaurs* rational Parts the Hinnible
    to bestride ;
Bright silver Feet and shining Face had the stout He-
    roe's Mother,
As Rapiers silver'd at one end, and wound us at the
    other ;
Her Feet were bright, his Feet were swift as Hawk
    pursuing Sparrow,
Hers had the Metal, his the Speed of *Brabant's* Silver
    Arrow :
Thetis to double Pedagogue commits her dearest Boy,
Who bred him from a slender Twig to be the Scourge
    of *Troy;*
But e'er he lash'd the *Trojans* was, in *Stygian* Waters
    steept,
As Birch is soaked first in Piss when Boys are to be
    whipt ;
His Skin exceeding hard, he rose from Lake so black
    and muddy,
As *Lobsters* rising from the Sea with Shells about their
    Body ;
And as from *Lobsters* broken Claw, pick out the Flesh
    you might,
So might you from one unshell'd Heel dig pieces of
    the Knight ;
His Myrmidons robb'd *Priams* Barns, and Hen-Roosts
    say the Song,
Carry'd away both Corn and Eggs, like Ants from
    which they sprung ;
Himself tore *Hector's* Pantaloons, and sent him down
    bare breech'd,

                    To

To *Pedant Radamanthus* in Posture to be switch'd,
But *George* made the Dragon look as if he'd been
    bewitch'd ;
       St. George *he was,* &c.
The *Amazon Thalestris* was beautiful and bold,
She sear'd her Breasts with Iron hot, and bang'd her
    Foes with Cold ;
Her hands were like the tool wherewith *Jove* keeps
    proud Mortals under.
It shone just like his Lightning, and batter'd like his
    Thunder ;
Her Eye darts Lightning, that would blast the proudest
    he that swagger'd,
And melt that Rapier of his Soul, in its corporeal Scab-
    bard ;
With Beauty the great *Lapland* charm'd, poor Men she
    did bewitch all,
Still a blind whining Lover had, as *Pallas* had her
    Screech-Owl ;
Her Beauty and her Drum to Foe did cause Amaze-
    ment double,
As timorous Larks amazed are, with Light and with a
    low Bell ;
She kept the Chastness of a *Nun,* in Armour as in a
    Cloyster,
But *George* undid the Dragon, just as you'd undo an
    Oyster ;
       St. George *he was,* &c.
Full fatal to the *Romans* was the *Carthaginian Hannibal,*
Him I mean who did them give a devilish Thump at
    Cannæ,
Moors thick as Goats on *Penwinmaur* flood on the
    Alpes's Front,
Their one-ey'd Guide, like blinking Mole, bor'd thro'
    the hindring Mount ;
Who baffled by the massy Rock, took Vinegar for Re-
    lief,
Like Plow-men when they hew their way thro' stubborn
    Rump of Beef ;

As

As dancing Louts from humid Toes, cast atome of ill
    Savour,
To blinking *Hial* when on vile Croud, he Merriment
    does endeavour ;   [quiver,
And on harmonious Timber saws a wretched Tune so
Just so the *Romans* stunk at sight of *African* Conniver;
The tawny surface of his Phiz did serve instead of
    Vizard,
But *George* he made the Dragon have and a grumbling
    in his Gizard ;   *St.* George *he was*, &c.

Pendragon, like his Father *Jove,* was fed with Milk of
    Goat,   [Coat ;
And like him made a noble Shield of she Goats shagged
On top of burnish'd Helmet he did wear a Crest of
    Leeks,
And Onions-heads with dreadful Nods, drew Tears
    down hostile Cheeks ;
Itch and Welch Blood did make him hot, and very
    prone to ire,
Was ting'd with Brimstone like a Match, and would as
    soon take Fire ;   [Occasion,
And Brimstone he took inwardly, when Scurf gave him
His postern puff of wind was a sulphureous Exhalation ;
The *Britain* never tergivers'd, but was for Adverse
    drubbing,   [Scrubbing ;
Nor ever turn'd his Back to ought, but to a Post for
His Sword would serve for Battel, or for Dinner if you
    please,   [Cheese ;
When it had slain a *Cheshire* Man, 'twould tost a *Cheshire*
He wounded, and in their own Blood did Anabaptize
    Pagans,   [Dragons ;
But *George* he made the Dragon an Example to all
    St. George *he was,* &c.

Gorgon a twisted Adder wore for Knot upon her Shoulder,
She kemb'd her hissing Periwig, and curling Snakes did
    powder ;
These Snakes they made stiff Changelings of all Men
    that they hiss'd on,   [stone ;
They turned Barbers into Hones, and Masons into Free-
                      Sworded

Sworded Magnetick *Amazon*, her Shield to Load-stone
    changes,
The amorous Sword by mystic Belt, clung fast unto
    her Hanches ;   [from Town,
This Shield long Village did protect, and kept the Army
And chang'd the Bullies into Rocks, that came to invade
    long *Compton ;*   [unravels,
The postdiluvian Stone unmans, and *Pyrrha's* Work
And stares *Deucalions* hardy Boys, into their primitive
    Pebbles ;
Red Noses she to Rubies turns, and Noddles into Bricks,
But *George* made the Dragon laxative, and gave him a
    bloody Flix ;.
        St. George *he was*, &c.

Brave *Warwick's* Guy at Dinner-time, challeng'd a Giant
    Savage,
And straight came out the unwieldy Lout, brim full of
    Wrath and Cabbage ;   [middle,
He had a Phiz of Latitude, and was full thick i'th'
The Cheeks of puffed Trumpeter, and Paunch of Squire
    Beadle ;
But the Knight fell'd him like an Oak, and did upon
    his Back tread,
The Valiant *Guy* his Weason cut, and *Atropus* his
    Packthread ;   [Witty,
Besides, he fought with a Dun Cow, as say the Poets
A dreadful Dun, and horned too, like *Dun* of *Oxford*
    City ;
The fervent Dog-days made her mad, by causing heat
    of Weather,   [Father ;
Syrius and *Procyon* baited her, as a Bull-dog did her
Grasiers nor Butchers this fell Beast, e'er of her
    Frolick hinder'd,
John Dorset she'd knock down as flat, as *John*
    knocks down his Kindred ;
Her Heels would lay ye all along, and kick into a
    Swoon,
Cow-heels at *Frewins* keep up your Corps, but here
    t'would beat you down ;
                        She

She vanquish'd many a sturdy Knight, and proud was
    of the Honour,
Was pufft by mauling Butchers so, as if themselves
    had blown her;
At once she kick'd and push'd at *Guy*, but all that
    would not fright him,
Who wav'd his Whinyard o'er her Loyn, as if he'd
    gone to Knight him;
He let her Blood her Frenzy to cure, and eke he did
    her Gall rip,
His trenchant Blade, like Cooks long Spit, ran thro'
    the Monsters bald Rib;   [Triumphal,
He rear'd up the vast crook'd Rib, instead of Arch
But *George* hit th' Dragon such a Pelt, which made
    him on his Bum fall;
      St. George *he was,* &c.

Great *Hercules* the Offspring of *Jove*, and fair *Alcmene*,
One part of him celestial was, the other part Terrene:
To scale the Walls of's Cradle, two fiery Snakes com-
    bin'd,   [twin'd;
And just like unto Swadling-Cloaths about the Infant
But he put out these Dragons Fires, and did their
    hissing stop,
As red-hot Iron with hissing noise, is quench'd in
    Blacksmith's Shop;
He cleans'd a Stable, and rubb'd down the Horses of
    new Comers,
And out of Horse-dung he rais'd Fame, as *Tom Wrench*
    does Cucumbers;   [Groom,
He made a River help him thro', *Alpheus* was under
The Stream grumbling at Office mean, ran murm'ring
    thro' the Room?   [Work,
This liquid Ostler to prevent being tired with a long
His Father *Neptune's* trident took, instead of three
    tooth'd Dung-fork;
This *Hercules* as Soldier, and as Spinster could take pains,
His Club it would sometimes spin Flax, and sometimes
    knock out Brains;

                                         He

He was forc'd to spin his Miss a Shift, by *Juno's*
    Wrath and her Spite,
Fair *Omphale* whipt him to his Wheel, as Cooks whip
    barking turnspit ;
From Man or Churn, he well knew how to get him
    lasting Fame,   [came ;
He'd baste a Giant till the Blood, and Milk to Butter
Often he fought with huge Battoon, and oftentimes he
    Boxed,
Tap'd a fresh Monster once a Month, as *Harvey* doth
    fresh Hogshead ;   [*Cornwall,*
To stiff *Antæus* he gave a Hug, such as Folks give in
But *George* he did the Dragon kill, as dead as any
    door Nail ;
        St. George *he was,* &c.

The Valour of *Domitian* it must not be forgotten,
Who from the Jaws of worm-blowing Flies, freed sup-
    pliant Veal and Mutton ;
A Squadron of Flies Errant, against the Foe-appears,
With Regiment of buzzing Wights, and swarms of
    Volunteers ;   [Hum,
The Warlike Wasp incourag'd them, with's animating
And the loud brazen Hornet he was their Kettle-drum ;
The *Spaniard don Cantharido,* did him most sorely
    pester,
And rais'd on Skin of ventrous Knight full many a
    plaguy Blister ;
A Bee whipt thro' his Button-hole, as thro' Key-hole
    a Witch,
And stabb'd him with a little Tuck, drawn from his
    Scabbard Breech ;   [brawny,
But the undaunted Knight lifts up an Arm so big and
And slasht her so, that here lay Head, and there lay
    Bag of Honey ;
Then 'mongst the Rout he flew, as swift as Weapons
    made by *Cyclops,*
And bravely quell'd seditious Buz, by dint of massy
    fly Flaps ;

Surviving Flies did Curses Breath, and Maggots too
.   at *Cæsar,*
But *George* he shav'd the Dragon's Beard, and *Askulon*
    was his Razor;
        St. George *he was,* &c.

The *Gemini* sprung of an Egg, were put into a
    Cradle,
Their Brains with Knocks and bottl'd Ale, were
    oftentimes full addle;
And scarcely hatch'd these Sons of him, that hurls the
    Bolt trisulcate,
With helmet shell on tender head, did bustle with red
.   Ey'd Polecat;
Castor a Horseman, *Pollux* tho' a boxer was I wist,
The one was fam'd for Iron heel, the other for leaden
    fist;
Pollux to shew he was a God, when he was in a passion,
Would first make Noses fall down flat, by way of
    adoration;
This Fist as sure as *French* Disease, demolisht Noses
    ridges,   [of bridges;
He like a certain Lord, was fam'd for breaking down
Castor the flame of fiery steed, with well spur'd Boots
    took down,   [Town;
As men with leathern Buckets, do quench Fire in a
His Famous Horse that liv'd on Oats, is sung on
    Oaten quill,
Ah *Bards* immortal provender the Nag surviveth still;
This brood of Egs on none but rogues, employ'd their
    brisk Artillery,   [on Pillory;
They flew as naturally at a rogue, as Egs at Knaves
Much sweat they spent in furious flight, much blood
    they effund,
Their whites they vented thro' their pores, their yolks
    thro' gaping wound;
Then both from blood and dust were cleans'd to make
    a heavenly sign,
The lads just like their Armour were scow'r'd and
    hang'd up to shine;
                                   Thus

Thus were the heav'nly double Dicks, the sons of
    Jove and *Tinder*,
But *George* he cut the Dragon up, as't had bin Duck
    or Winder;
        St. *George he was*, &c.

By Boar Spear *Meleager* acquir'd a lasting name,
And out of haunch of basted Swine he hew'd eternal
    fame;
The beast the Heroes Trouzers ript, and rudely
    shew'd his bare Breech,
Prickt but the Wem and out there came, Heroick
    Guts and Garbadge;
Legs were secur'd with Iron boots, no more than
    peas by peas-cods,
Brass helmets which inclosed Skulls, would crackle
    in's mouth like Chesnuts;
His tawny Hairs erected were, by rage that was
    resistless,
And wrath instead of Coblers wax, did stiffen his
    rising bristles;
His Tusks lay'd dogs to sleep, that Whip nor Bugle
    Horn could wake 'em,
It made them vent both their last blood, and their
    last *Albumgrecum;*
But the Knight gor'd him with his spear, to make of
    him a tame one,
And Arrows thick instead of Cloves, he struck in
    Monsters gammon;
For Monumental Pillar, that his Victory might be
    known,
He rais'd up in Cylindrick form a Collar of the brawn;
He sent his shade to shades below, in *Stygian* mud to
    wallow,
And eke the stout St. *George* eftsoon he made the
    Dragon follow;
        St. *George he was*, &c.

A Scotch *SONG.*

' TWas in the Month of *May* Joe, when *Jockey*
    first I spy'd ;
He luk'd as fair as day too, Gude gin I'd bin his Bride :
With Cole black Eyne and Milk white hand,
   Ise ne'er yet saw the Like ;
I wish I had gin aw my Land,
   Ise ne'er had ·seen the Tike.

He fix'd his Eyne upon me, with aw the signs of Love ;
Ise thought they wou'd gang thro' me, so fiercely they
    did move :
He tuke me in his eager Arms,
   Ise made but faint denials ;
Ise then alas found aw his Charms,
   Woe worth such fatal trials.

The Bonny Lad at last *Joe,* was forc'd toll gang away :
But I'se had eane stuck fast tho', full Nine Months
    from that day :
And now poor *Jenny's* Maiden-head,
   Shame on't they find its lost ;
The little brat has aw betray'd
   Was ever Lass thus cross'd.

POEMS

POEMS
On Several Occasions.

The FRYER *and the* MAID.

AS I lay Musing all alone,
    A merry Tale I thought upon ;
Now listen a while and I will you tell,
Of a Fryer that lov'd a Bonny Lass well.

He came to her when she was going to Bed,
Desiring to have her Maiden-head ;
But she denyed his desire,
And said that she did fear Hell-fire.

Tush, tush, quoth the Fryer, thou need'st not doubt,
If thou wert in Hell, I could sing thee out ;
Why then, quoth the Maid thou shalt have thy
    request,
The Fryer was as glad as a Fox in his Nest.

But one thing more I must request,
More than to sing me out of Hell-fire ;
That is for doing of the thing,
An Angel of Money you must me bring.

Tush, tush, quoth the Fryer, we two shall agree,
No Money shall part thee and me ;
Before thy company I will lack,
I'll pawn the grey Gown off my Back.

The

The Maid bethought her on a Wile,
How she might this Fryer beguile;
When he was gone, the truth to tell,
She hung a Cloth before a Well.

The Fryer came as his bargain was,
With Money unto his bonny Lass;
Good morrow, Fair Maid, good morrow quoth she,
Here is the Money I promis'd thee.

She thank'd him, and she took the Money,
Now let's go to't my own dear Honey;
Nay, stay a while, some respite make,
If my Master should come he would us take.

Alas! quoth the Maid, my Master doth come;
Alas! quoth the Fryer where shall I run;
Behind yon Cloth run thou, quoth she,
For there my Master cannot see.

Behind the Cloth the Fryer went,
And was in the Well incontinent:
Alas! quoth he, I'm in the Well,
No matter quoth she if thou wert in Hell.

Thou saidst thou could sing me out of Hell,
I prithee sing thy self out of the Well;
Sing out quoth she with all thy might,
Or else thou'rt like to sing there all Night.

The Fryer sang out with a pitiful sound,
Oh! help me out or I shall be Drown'd;
She heard him make such pitiful moan,
She hope him out and bid him go home.

Quoth the Fryer I never was serv'd so before,
Away quoth the Wench, come here no more;
The Fryer he walk'd along the street,
As if he had been a new wash'd Sheep:
    Sing hey down a derry, and let's be merry,
    And from such Sin ever keep.

The

The Virtue of SACK :
By Dr. HEN. EDWARDS.

FEtch me *Ben. Johnson's* Skull, and fill't with Sack,
    Rich as the same he drank, when the whole pack ;
Of jolly Sisters pledg'd, and did agree,
It was no Sin to be as Drunk as he :
If there be any weakness in the Wine,
There's virtue in the Cup, to make't divine ;
This muddy drench of Ale does taste too much
Of Earth, the Mault retains a scurvy touch
Of the dull Hand that Sows it, and I fear
There's Heresie in Hops, give *Calvin* Beer :
And his precise Disciples, such as think
There's Powder Treason in all *Spanish* drink ;
Call Sack an Idol, nor will Kiss the Cup,
For fear their *Conventicle* be blown up
With Superstition, give to the Brew-house Alms,
Whose best Mirth is Six Shillings Beer, and Psalms ?
Let me rejoice in sprightly Sack, that can
Create a Brain, even in an empty Pan,
Canary ! it's thou that dost inspire
And actuate the Soul with Heavenly fire ;
That thou Sublim'st the Genius making Wit
Scorn Earth, and such as love or live by it ;
Thou makest us Lord, of Regions large and fair,
Whilst our conceits build Castles in the Air :
Since Fire, Earth, Air, thus thy inferiors be,
Henceforth I'll know no Element but thee :
Thou precious *Elixir* of all Grapes !
Welcome by thee our Muse begins her scapes,
Such is the worth of Sack, I am (methinks)
In the *Exchequer* now, hark how it chinks :
And do esteem my venerable self
As brave a Fellow, as if all the pelf
Were sure mine own ; and I have thought a way
Already how to spend it ; I would Pay
No Debts, but fairly empty every Trunk,
And change the Gold for Sack to keep me Drunk :

                  And

And so by consequence till rich *Spains* Wine,
Being in my Crown, the *Indies* too were mine :
And when my Brains are once a foot (heaven bless us!)
I think my self a better Man then *Cræsus ;*
And now I do conceit my self a Judge,
And Coughing Laugh to see my Clients trudge
After my Lordship's Coach unto the Hall,
For Justice, and am full of Law withal.
And do become the Bench as well as He,
That Fled long since for want of Honesty :
But I'll be Judge no longer tho' in Jest,
For fear I should be talk'd with like the rest,
When I am Sober ; who can chuse but think,
Me Wise, that am so wary in my Drink !
Oh admirable Sack ! here's dainty sport,
I am come back from *Westminster* to Court :
And am grown young again ; my Ptisick now,
Hath left me, and my Judges graver brow
Is smooth'd, and I turn'd Amorous as *May,*
When she invites young Lovers forth to play,
Upon her flow'ry Bosom I could win,
A Vestal now, or tempt a Queen to Sin,
Oh for a score of Queens ! you'd laugh to see,
How they would strive which first should Ravish me.
Three Goddesses were nothing : Sack has tipt
My Tongue with Charms like those which *Paris* sipt,
From *Venus* when she taught him how to Kiss
Fair *Hellen,* and invite a fairer bliss :
Mine is *Canary-Rhetorick,* that alone,
Would turn *Diana* to a burning Stone :
Some with amazement, burning with Loves fire,
Hard, to the touch, but short in her desire.
Inestimable Sack ! thou mak'st us rich,
Wise, Amorous any thing ; I have an itch
To t'other Cup, and that perchance will make,
Me Valiant too, and Quarrel for thy sake ;
If I be once inflam'd against thy Nose,
That could Preach down thy worth in Small-beer Prose,
I should do Miracles as bad or worse,
As he that gave the King an Hundred Horse.

T'other

T'other odd Cup, and I shall be prepar'd,
To snatch at Stars ; and pluck down a reward,
With mine own Hands from *Jove* upon their Backs,
That are, or *Charles's* his Enemies, or Sack's,
Let it be full if I do chance to spill,
O'er my Standish by the way, I will,
Dipping in this diviner Ink my Pen,
Write my self Sober and fall to't agen.

On a Combat of Cocks, *the* Norfolk, *and the* Wisbich : *By Dr.* R. W.

GO you tame Gallants you that have the Name,
And would accounted be Cocks of the Game,
That have brave Spurs to shew for't and can Crow,
And count all Dunghill breed that cannot shew
Such painted Plums as yours ; that think no Vice,
With Cock-like lust to Tread your Cockatrice :
Tho' Peacocks, Wood-cocks, Weather-cocks you be,
If you're not fighting Cocks y'are not for me :
I of two Feather'd Combatants will write,
He that to th' Life means to express the Fight,
Must make his Ink o'th' Blood which they did spill,
And from their dying Wings borrow his Quill.

NO sooner were the doubtful People set,
  The Matches made, and all that would had Bet,
But straight the skilful Judges of the Play,
Bring forth their sharp heel'd Warriors, and they
Were both in Linen bags, as if 'twere meet,
Before they Dy'd to have their Winding sheet.
With that into th' Pit they are put, and when they were
Both on their Feet, the *Norfolk* Chanticleer,
Looks stoutly at his ne'er before seen Foe,
And like a Challenger begins to Crow,
And shakes his Wings, as if he would display,
His warlike Colours which were Black and Gray :
Mean time the wary *Wisbich* walks and breaths
His active Body, and in Fury wreaths

His

His comely Crest, and often looking down,
He whets his angry Beak upon the Ground :
With that they meet, not like the Coward breed
Of *Æsop ;* these can better Fight than Feed :
They scorn the Dunghill, 'tis their only Prize,
To dig for Pearl within each others Eyes.
They Fight so long that it was hard to know,
To th' skilful whether they did Fight or know,
Had not the Blood which died the fatal Floor,
Born witness of it ; yet they Fight the more,
As if each Wound were but a Spur to prick
Their Fury forward ; Lightning's not more quick
Nor Red then were their Eyes ; 'twas hard to know
Whether it was Blood or Anger made them so :
And sure they had been out, had not they stood,
More safe by being fenc'd in by Blood.
Yet still they Fought but now (alas !) at length
Altho' their Courage be full try'd their strength
And Blood began to ebb. You that have seen
A Watry Combate on the Sea, between
Two Roaring Angry boyling Billows, how
They march and meet and dash their curled brows,
Swelling like Graves as if they did intend
T' intomb each other, e'er the Quarrel end :
But when the Wind is down, and Blust'ring weather,
They are made Friends and sweetly run together,
May think these Champions such; their Blood runs low,
And they that leapt before, now scarce can go ;
Their Wings which lately at one Blow they clapt,
(As if they did Applaud themselves) now flapt ;
And having lost the advantage of the Heel,
Drunk with each others Blood they only Reel.
From either Eyes such drops of Blood did fall,
As if they Wept them for their Funeral.
And yet they fain would Fight, they came so near,
As if they meant into each others Ear
To whisper Death ; and when they cannot rise,
They lie and look Blows in each others Eyes.
But now the Tragick part after the Fight,
When *Norfolk* Cock had got the best of it.

And

And *Wisbich* lay a Dying so that none,
Tho' Sober, but might venter Seven to One,
Contracting (like a dying Taper) all
His force, as meaning with that Blow to fall;
He struggles up, and having taking Wind,
Ventures a Blow and strikes the other Blind.
And now poor *Norfolk* having lost his Eyes,
Fights only guided by Antipathies :
With him (*alas*) the Proverb holds not true,
The Blows his Eyes ne'er saw his Heart must rue.
At length by chance he stumbled on his Foe,
Not having any power to strike a Blow,
He falls upon him with his Wounded Head,
And makes his Conquerors Wings his Feather-bed :
Where lying Sick his Friends were very charie
Of him, and fetcht in hast an Apothecary ;
But all in vain his Body did so Blister,
That 'twas incapable of any Glister ;
Wherefore at length opening his fainting Bill,
He call'd a Scriv'ner, and thus made his Will.

*I*Nprimis, *Let it never be forgot,*
　My Body freely I bequeath to th' Pot,
Decently to be Boil'd, and for its Tomb,
Let it be Buried in some hungry Womb :
Item. *Executors I will have none,*
But he that on my side laid Seven to One;
And like a Gentleman that he might live,
To Him and to his Heirs my Comb I give,
Together with my Brains, that all may know,
That oftentimes his Brains did use to Crow :
Item. *It is my Will to the weaker ones,*
Whose Wives complain of them, I give my Stones;
To him that's dull I do my Spurs impart;
And to the Coward I bequeath my Heart :
To Ladies that are light it is my Will,
My Feathers should be given; and for my Bill
I'd give't a Taylor, but it is so short,
That I'm afraid he'll rather Curse me for't :

And

And for the Apothecaries Fee who meant.
To give me a Glister, let my Rump be sent.
Lastly, because I feel my Life decay,
I yield and give to Wisbich *Cock the Day.*

On a FART

In the Parliament House: By Sir JOHN SUCKLING.

DOWN came Grave Ancient Sir *John Crook*,
   And read his Message in a Book,
Very well quoth *Will. Norris* is it so,
But Mr. *Pym's* 'Tayl cry'd no.
Fie, quoth Alderman *Atkins*, I like not this Passage,
To have a *Fart* intervoluntary in the midst of a message;
Then up starts one fuller of Devotion
Than Eloquence, and said a very ill motion ;
Not so neither, quoth Sir *Henry Jenking*,
The Motion was good, but for the Stinking ;
Quoth Sir *Henry Poole* 'twas an audacious trick,
To *Fart* in the Face of the Body Politick ;
Sir *Jerome* in Folio swore by the Mass,
This *Fart* was enough to have blown a Glass :
Quoth then Sir *Jerome* the lesser such an abuse,
Was never offer'd in *Poland* nor *Pruce.*
Quoth Sir *Richard Houghton*, a Justice i'th' *Quorum,*
Would tak't in Snuff to have a *Fart* let before him ;
If it would bear an Action, quoth Sir *Thomas Holecraft,*
I would make of this *Fart* a Bolt or a Shaft ;
Then quoth Sir *John More,* to his great Commendation,
I will speak to this House in my wonted fashion,
Now surely says he, for as much as how be it,
This *Fart* to the Serjeant we must commit.
No, quoth the Serjeant, low bending his Knees,
Farts oft will break Prisons, but never Pay Fees :
Besides this Motion with small reason stands,
To charge me with what I cant keep in my Hands :
Quoth

Quoth Sir *Walter Cope*, 'twas so readily let,
I would it were sweet enough for my Cabinet.
Why then Sir *Walter* (quoth Sir *William Fleetwood*)
Speak no more of it but Bury it with Sweetwood,
Grave Senate, quoth *Duncomb*, upon my Salvation
This *Fart* stands in need of some great Reformation.
Quoth Mr. *Cartwright*, upon my Conscience,
It would be reform'd with a little Frankincence.
Quoth Sir *Roger Acton*, it would much mend the matter,
If this *Fart* were Shaven and wash'd with Rose-water,
Per verbum Principis, how dare I tell it,
A *Fart* by here-say and not see it nor Smell it.
I am glad quoth Sir *Sam. Lewknor*, we have found a thing,
That no Tale-bearer can carry it to the King.
Such a *Fart* as this was never seen,
Quoth the Learned Council of the Queen.
Yet, quoth Sir *Hugh Beeston*, the like hath been
Let in a Dance before the Queen.
Then said Mr. *Leak*, I have a president in store,
His Father *Farted* last Sessions before.
A Bill must be drawn, then quoth Sir *John Bennet*,
Or a selected Committee quickly to Pen it.
Why quoth Dr. *Crompton*, no Man can draw,
This *Fart* within the Compass of the Civil Law :
Quoth Mr. *Jones*, by the Law't may be done,
Being a *Fart* intayl'd from Father to Son,
In troth, quoth Mr. *Brook*, this Speech was no lye,
This *Fart* was one of your *Post Nati :*
Quoth *William Paddy*, he dares assure 'em,
Tho' 'twere *Contra Modestiam*, 'tis not *præter Naturam :*
Besides by the Aphorisms of my Art,
Had he not been deliver'd h'ad been sick of a *Fart*.
Then quoth the *Recorder*, the mouth of the City,
To have smother'd that *Fart* had been great pitty.
It is most certain, quoth Sir *Humphry Bentwizzle*,
That a round *Fart* is better than a stinking Fizzle.
Have Patience Gentlemen, quoth Sir *Francis Bacon*,
There's none of us all but may be mistaken :
Why right quoth the Great Attorney I confess,
The Eccho of ones A— is remediless.

The

The GENEVA *Ballad :*

By the Author of HUDIBRAS.

OF all the *Factions* in the Town,
   Mov'd by *French Springs* on *Flemish Wheels*,
None treads Religion upside down,
Or tears *Pretences* out at Heels,
   Like *Splay Mouth* with his brace of Caps,
   Whose Conscience might be scan'd perhaps,
   By the Dimensions of his Chaps.

He whom the Sisters so adore,
Counting his Actions all Divine,
   Who when the Spirit hints can roar,
And if occasion serves can whine ;
   Nay he can Bellow, bray, or bark,
   Was ever *sike a Beuk learn'd Clerk*,
   That speaks all *Lingua's* of the Ark.

To draw in Proselytes like Bees,
With *pleasing Twang*, he tones his Prose :
   He gives his Handkercheif a squeez,
And draws *John Calvin* thro' his Nose :
   Motive on Motive he obtrudes,
   With *Slip-stocking Similitudes*,
   Eight Uses more, and so concludes.

When *Monarchy* began to bleed,
And *Treason* had a fine new Name ;
   When *Thames* was *balderdash'd* with *Tweed*,
And Pulpits did like Beacons flame :
   When *Jeroboam's* Calves were rear'd,
   And *Laud* was neither lov'd nor fear'd,
   This *Gospel Comet* first appear'd.

Soon his unhallow'd Fingers strip'd,
His Sov'reign Leige of Power and Land :
   And having smote his Master, slip'd
His Sword into his Fellows hand.

But

But he that wears his Eyes may Note
Oftimes the Butcher binds a Goat,
And leaves his Boy to Cut her Throat.

Poor *England* felt his Fury then,
Out-weigh'd Queen *Mary's* many grains ;
  His very Preaching slew more men,
Than *Bonner's* Faggots, Stakes and Chains.
    With *Dog-star Zeal* and Lungs like *Boreas,*
    He fought and taught, and what's notorious,
    Destroy'd his Lord to make him *Glorious.*

Yet drew for *King* and *Parliament ;*
As if the Wind could stand *North South,*
  Broke *Moses's* Law with blest intent,
Murther'd and then he wip'd his mouth,
    Oblivion alters not his case,
    Nor Clemency nor Acts of Grace,
    Can blanch an *Æthiopian's* Face.

Ripe for Rebellion he begins,
To rally upon the Saints in Swarms,
  He bawls aloud, *Sirs leave your Sins,*
But whispers, *Boys stand to your Arms,*
    Thus he's grown insolently rude,
    Thinking his Gods cant be subdu'd,
    Money, I mean, and *Multitude.*

Magistrates he regards no more,
Than St. *George* or the Kings of *Colen ;*
  Vowing he'll not conform before
The Old-Wives wind their dead in Wollen,
    He calls the Bishop, *Grey-bear'd Goff,*
    And makes his Power as meer a Scoff,
    As *Dagon* when his Hands were off.

Hark ! how he opens with full Cry !
Hallow my Hearts, beware of ROME,
  Cowards that are afraid to die.
Thus make domestick Broils at home.

How

How quietly Great *CHARLES* might Reign,
Would all these Hot-spurs cross the Main,
And Preach down Popery in *Spain*.

The starry Rule of Heaven is fixt,
There's no dissention in the Sky:
  And can there be a Mean betwixt
Confusion and Conformity?
      A Place divided never thrives:
      'Tis bad where Hornets dwell in Hives,
      But worse where Children play with Knives.

I would as soon turn back to Mass,
Or change my phrase to *thee* and *thou;*
  Let the Pope ride me like an Ass,
And his Priests milk me like a Cow:
      As buckle to *Smectymnuan* Laws,
      The bad effects o'th' Good Old Cause,
      That have Dove's Plumes, but Vulture's Claws.

For 'twas the *Haly Kirk* that Nurs'd
The *Brownists* and the *Ranters* Crew;
  Foul Errors motly Vesture first
Was Coated in a Northern Blue,
      And what's th' Enthusiastick breed,
      Or Men of *Knipperdolin's* Creed,
      But Cov'nanters run up to Seed?

Yet they all cry, they love the King,
And make boast of their Innocence:
  There cannot be so vile a thing,
But may be colour'd with Pretence,
      Yet when all's said, one thing I'll Swear,
      No Subject like the Old Cavalier,
      No Traitor like *Jack* ——

A

A PROLOGUE.

By Sir JOHN FALSTAFF.

SEE, *Britains*, see, one half before your Eyes,
  Of the old *Falstaff*, lab'ring to arise ;
Curse on the strait lac'd Traps, and *French* Machines,
None but a Genius can ascend these Scenes.

Once more my *English* Air I breath again,
And smooth my double Ruff, and double Chin ;
Now let me see what Beauties gild the Sphere,
Body o'me, the Ladies still are Fair :
The Boxes shine, and Galleries are full,
Such were our *Bona Roba's* at the *Bull;*
But supream *Jove !* what washy Rogues are here,
Are these the Sons of Beef and *English* Beer ?
Old *Pharaoh* never dream'd of Kine so lean,
This comes of meagre Soop and sour *Champeign;*
Degenerate Race, let your old Sire advise,   }
If you desire to fill the Fair one's Eyes,
Drink unctuous Sack, and emulate my Size.
Your half-flown Strains aspire to humble Bliss,
And proudly aim no lower than a Kiss ;
'Till quite worn out with acting Beau's and Wits,
You're all sent crawling to the Gravel-pits :
Pretending Claps, there languishing you lie,
And like the Maids, of the Green-sickness die :
The Case was other when we rul'd the Roast,
We robb'd and ravish'd, but you sigh and toast.

But here I see a side Box better lin'd,   }
Where old plump *Jack* in Miniature I find,
Tho' they're but Turn-spits of the Mastiff kind.
Half-bred they seem, mark'd with the Mungril Curse,
Oons, which amongst you dare attempt a Purse ?
If you'd appear my Sons, defend my Cause,
And let my Wit and Humour meet Applause :

Shew you disdain those nauseous Scenes to tast, ⎞
Where *French* Buffoons like honest *Switzer* drest, ⎬
Turns all good Fellowship to Farce and Jest.   ⎠
Banish such Apes, and save the sinking Stage,
Let Mimicks and squeaking Eunuchs feel your Rage ;
On such let your descending Scourge be try'd,
Preserve plump *Jack*, and banish all beside.

Richmond WELLS.

By Mr. HERBERT.

B*LANDUSIA !* Nymph of this fair Spring,
    Appear, while we your Vertues sing ;
While swelling Notes do raise your Name,
And flowing Numbers spread your Fame.

See ! round your Wells we thronging stand,
Now gentle wave your Sacred Wand,
And touch the yielding Mountain's Brow,
And let your healing Waters flow.

They cure the thinking Matrons Spleen,
The longing Virgin's sickly Green ;
Cool the good Fellow's glowing Veins,
And purge a raving Poet's Brains.

You mingle with 'em purest Air,
    Which streams from Hills that touch the Sky ;
That spacious Valley yield the Fair,
    Which feeds the vast luxurious Eye.

The greatest Dainties here we see !
    Delicious Villa's sweetest Groves ;
Each thing in full Maturity,
    Which courts the Eye, or Fancy moves.

With

With what Varieties the bright,
The noble *Thames* regales the Sight!
Cover'd with Barks which Plenty brings,
The sweets of *Zephyr's* laden Wings.

His gliding by *Elysian* Fields,
In frequent Twines strange Pleasure yields;
And those so near fair watry Plains,
Where ride such royal Fleets of Swains.

Two chiefs I've seen with pleasing Pain,
A long and bloody Fight maintain;
Ruffled and under Sail like *Jove*,
Stemming the stronger Tide of Love.

The Inspir'd POET:

Or, the Power of LOVE. *Sent in a Letter, from a mean Person to a* COUNTESS.

READ, fairest of the Graces, read my Lines,
Thou, that so justly with that Title shines;
Let Love's soft Fire by degrees diffuse,
And warm your snowy Breast as you peruse:
Me the *Pierian* Sisters do approve,
Not one of all the Nine disdains my Love;
A Thousand beauteous Nymphs have sought my Bed,
A Thousand Girls challeng'd the Vows I made:
All *Galatea* were despis'd by me,
As soon as I had hopes of bedding thee;
And if thou wilt thy sacred Poet Wed,
The *Muses* shall adorn the Bridal-Bed:
Orpheus shall strike his high resounding Wire,
And great *Apollo* touch his softer Lyre;
Clio shall be thy Hand-maid, and for State,
The *Graces* in thy Bed-chamber shall wait:
But least you should my Love contemn or jeer,
Something I have to whisper in your Ear;

On Mount *Parnassus* I've a little Farm,
'Twill match thy Portion, so there is no harm :
Here Ivy Lawrels grow, which crown my Theams,
And Wit's still flowing in my purling Streams ;
From hence, the Glories of the World you see,
Parnassus Tops are *Paradise* to me :
My way to Heaven's short, *Pegasus* flies,
And, free as Air, soon mounts me to the Skies ;
Minerva has a noble Seat near mine,
So has *Apollo*, so the sacred Nine :
Then all the Poets my Companions are,
They, and sweet Musick, still my Spirits cheer :
Homer and *Virgil* in their turns rehearse,
The two great Masters in Heroick Verse :
The Satyrist diverts, when scourging Knaves,
And sometimes he corrects my pilf'ring Slaves ;
Dear *Horace* makes me smile my Spleen at height,
His tickling *Muse* oft makes me laugh out-right :
Musæus, *Hero* and *Leander* sings,
And *Hesiod's* Verse relate most wondrous things ;
Maro, *Theocritus* Pastoral refines,
Pythagoras's Morals draws in golden Lines :
Blind aged *Homer* bloody Battles writes,
Whilst youthful *Ovid Billet-deux* indites ;
And *Mercury* from *Phœbus* came just now,
And brought these Lawrel Branches for thy Brow :
From *Nisa's* top, he's now a calling thee,
And summons all the Tribe of Poesie ;
A Banquet for you Poets does prepare,
And rich old *Nectar* crowns the Bill of Fare :
You've Water from the clear *Pegasean* Fount,
And thou shalt sleep on quiet *Cyrrha's* Mount ;
Here Verse runs streaming from the sacred Spring,
And when thou wak'st, thou wilt like *Ennius* sing :
Orpheus, *Arion* will be here and Play,
And all the Nymphs and Satyrs the Hay ;
This *Mercury* did grant at my desire,
And I will add thee to the *Muses* Choir :
With Goddesses, thy Sociates, shalt thou play,
They shall be Bride-maids on the Wedding-day ;

Clio

Clio and all her Sisters I'll invite,
Minerva too, shall throw the Hose at Night.
  Divine *Apollo* late did visit me,
My Cottage seem'd to please his Deity ;
My Lawrel Crown was sent me by that God,
And *Mercury* for Sceptre left his Rod :
My House is on the Fam'd *Parnassus* Hill,
Where my two Steeds, of *Nectar* drink their fill;
A King I am, in *Phocis* reign, and sit
On Great *Tibullus* Throne, that Prince of Wit:
Cyrrha's the Kingdom, that's design'd for thee,
And when we Bed, thou shalt be Queen of me ;
And when the Ivy Wreath's fix'd on thy Brow,
The Nymphs shall frown and envy as they bow:
In the same Chariot thou shalt with me ride,
And *Pegasus* himself shall draw my Bride.
He'll carry thee my Spouse, up to the Skies,
Thou shalt be *Pallas* as the Chariot flies.
As *Phœbus* through the World does dart his Rays,
And from the Throne his Lucid Realms surveys ;
So through the Orbs, my Verse refulgent shines,
All shall be full of my most dazling Lines :
My Fame shall last, Ages to come shall know it,
The self-same Day shall end the *Sun* and *Poet :*
Romantick Flames shall burn the Starry Plain,
And Earth and Seas be *Chaos* once again :
My Verse shall on the Gen'ral Pile expire,
Mine and the World's, one Flame shall set on Fire,
Angels shall mourn the Fate of this World's Frame,
And snatch my Works from the devouring Flame.
The drossy part of Earth, of Verse consumes,
The best Remains ascend in hallowed Fumes :
From Thunder, Lightning, are my Verses safe,
The pointed Flame wont touch a Lawrel Leaf ;
The Teeth of Time, or Envy, or her Tongue,
Have not the Power to do my Verses wrong :
Then don't thy Lawrell'd Lover now refuse,
Thou, dearer to me, than the dearest *Muse.*

  Ex Parnasso.   *J. P.*

To

To chuse a Friend, but never Marry.
By the Earl of ROCHESTER.

TO to all young Men that love to Wooe,
   To Kiss and Dance, and Tumble too ;
Draw near and Counsel take of me,
Your faithful Pilot I will be :
Kiss who you please, *Joan*, *Kate*, or *Mary*,
But still this Counsel with you carry,
                  Never Marry.

Court not a Country Lady, she
Knows not how to value thee ;
She hath no am'rous Passion, but
What *Tray*, or *Quando* has for *Slut :*
To Lick, to Whine, to Frisk, or Cover,
She'll suffer thee, or any other,
                Thus to Love her.

Her Daughter she's now come to Town,
In a rich Linsey Woolsey Gown ;
About her Neck a valued Prize,
A Necklace made of Whitings Eyes :
With List for Garters 'bove her Knee,
And Breath that smells of Firmity,
                's not for thee.

Of Widows Witchcrafts have a care,
For if they catch you in their Snare ;
You must as daily Labourers do,
Be still a shoving with your Plow :
If any rest you do require,
They then deceive you of your Hire,
                And retire.

The Maiden Ladies of the Town,
 Are scarcely worth your throwing down ;
For when you have possession got,
Of *Venus* Mark, or Hony-pot :
              There's

There's such a stir with marry me,
That one would half forswear to see
>   Any she.

If that thy Fancy do desire,
A glorious out-side, rich Attire ;
Come to the Court, and there you'll find,
Enough of such to Please your Mind :
But if you get too near their Lap,
You're sure to meet with the Mishap,
>   Call'd a Clap.

With greasy painted Faces drest,
With butter'd Hair, and fucus'd Breast ;
Tongues with Dissimulation tipt,
Lips which a Million have them sipp'd :
There's nothing got by such as these,
But Achs in Shoulders, Pains in Knees
>   For your Fees.

In fine, if thou delight'st to be,
Concern'd in VVomans Company :
Make it the Studies of thy Life,
To find a Rich, young, handsome VVife :
That can with much discretion be
Dear to her Husband, kind to thee,
>   Secretly.

In such a Mistress, there's the Bliss,
Ten Thousand Joys wrapt in a Kiss ;
And in th' Embraces of her VVast,
A Million more of Pleasures taste :
VVho e'er would Marry that could be
Blest with such Opportunity,
>   Never me.

The Well-Featur'd LADY.

THERE are I know, Fools that do not care
    Much for the Body, so the Face be fair ;
Some other Asses in a Female Creature,
Respect no Beauty, but a handsome Feature :
Each Man his Humour hath, and faith 'tis mine,
To love a Woman that I now define :
First, I would have her wrinkl'd Wainscot Face,
With Mouth from Ear to Ear, much like a Plaice ;
Her Nose I'd have a Foot long, not above,
With Pimples red and blue, for such I love :
And at the End a comely Pearl of Snot,
Consid'ring whether it should fall or not ;
Provided next her Teeth be rotted out,
I care not if her pretty pearly Snout
Meet with her Chin, and both of them together,
Hem in her Lips, as dry as is tann'd Leather :
She should have one Wall-eye, for that's a Sign
In other Beasts the best, why not in mine ?
Let her Eye-brows be a Pent-house to her Face,
With Hair two Inches long, for th' better Grace :
Her Neck I'd have to be pure Jet at least,
With yellow Spots enamell'd, and her Breast
Shrivell'd like two old Bottles made of Leather,
Yet they should loving be and stick together.
As for her Belly, 'tis no matter so
There be a Belly, and a Thing below ;
Yet would I have it to be something high,
But always let there be a Tympany :
Into her Legs let her good Humours fall,
And all her Calf into a gouty Small :
Her Feet both short and thick, and neatly splay'd,
Here's the Character of a handsome Maid ;
As for her back Parts, I desire no more,
If they but answer those that are before :
I have what I desire ; and having so,
Judge Reader, am I happy, yea, or no ?

On

On a *WOLF Sentenc'd.*

THE Country People once a Wolf did take,
   That of their Sheep and Lambs did havock
  make ;
Some Voted that he should be Crucify'd,
Others would have him in the Fire be fry'd :
Some to be hew'd in Pieces with a Sword,
And to be thrown to Dogs to be devour'd :
Among the rest, one who unlucky Fate,
Had doom'd to th' Troubles of a married State ;
(The common Lot of Men) oh ! Friends (says he)
Lay by your Forks, and Ropes that knotty be,
The Sword, the Fire, the Guns, the Cross, the Whips,
Are but slight Tortures, I have one out-strips
All those, if you would punish him to th' Life,
Fit for his Crimes, then *let him Wed a Wife.*

Round O.

BETTER our Heads than Hearts should ake,
   Love's Childish Empire we despise :
Good Wine of him a Slave can make,
   And force a Lover to be Wise :
Wine sweetens all the Cares of Peace,
   And takes the Terror off from War ;
To Love's Affliction it gives ease,
   And to our Joys does best prepare.
Better our Heads, &c.

By

By CLEVELAND.

IF you will be still,
  Then tell you I will
Of a fusty old *Gill*,
That dwells under a Hill :
She is a right Sage,
Well worn with Age,
And a Visage will swage
A stout Man's Courage.

She has a beetle Brow,
Deep Furrows enow,
She's Ey'd like a Sow,
Flat Nos'd like a Cow :
She has a Devilish Grin,
Long Hairs on her Chin,
She's nearly a-kin
To the foul footed Fiend.

Teeth yellow as Box,
Half out with the Pox,
Her Breath sweet as Socks,
Or the Scent of a Fox :
Lips swarthy and Dun,
With a Mouth like a Gun,
And her Twattle does run,
As swift as the Sun.

Hair lousie with Nits,
She stinks i'th' Arm-pits,
She'll still hauks and spits,
And hems up great Bits :
 She has long unpar'd Nails,
 Hands cover'd with Scales,
She's still full of Ails,
And to stink never fails.

Her

Her Back has a Hill,
You may plant a Wind-mill,
And the Farts of this *Gill*,
Would the Sails well trill:
I've taken my fill,
Of the fusty old *Gill*,
Which she took so ill,
That I laid down my Quill.

On the Battle of BLENHEIM.

Display the Standard, let the News be shown,
   With *Salvo's* raise the Genius of the Town:
Old *Thames*, he Corresponds, and best can tell
What Pow'rs caus'd Imperial *Danube* swell,
And turn a Purple Stream, a Sea of Blood;
No Fields thus overflown since *Canna's* Flood?
   A Victory, says *Danubius*, so Compleat,
   Sure the Hero sprung from *Thamesis* the Great.

Sing sing *Britannia's* Arms, her Shield and Spear,
The Glories of this weighty Conquest bear;
Sing to the Harp, tun'd in *Thessalion* Grove,
That Harp which us'd to cheer the Bird of *Jove*.
Erect the Trophy-Pillar, raise it high,
The Spoils wou'd mount it to the very Sky.
   Europ's Palladium strikes the Giant down,
   VVho wars with Heaven, must be overthrown.

Bring, bring the Chariot, and Triumphal Crown,
And March the Captive-Army thro' the Town;
The Banners, Ensigns, let those Trophies fall
Before the Standard of the Capital:
Then Plant 'em on the Banks of *Thames*, and there
Let 'em all grow like *Romulus's* Spear.
   The Stream in *Tempe's* Valley never had,
   In *Daphne's* Reign a Nobler Laurel Shade.

The

The Power of Gold.

ON Verse depending, *Orpheus* urg'd his Flight
   Down to *Tartarian* Shades, and dreary Night
There with unequal Harmony, he try'd,
To sooth grim *Pluto* and regain his Bride :
Won by his Strains, the God till then unmov'd,
Pity'd the Bard, and his request approv'd ;
Acknowledg'd Poetry's prevailing Charms,
And gave the Fair into her Husband's Arms.
Transported *Orpheus* hasted to convey,
His willing Consort to the Realms of Day :
But whilst too soon he cast his longing Eyes,
Thoughtless upon his new recover'd Prize,
The hapless Dame was ravish'd from his Sight, ⎫
Depriv'd again of *Orpheus* and the Light, ⎬
And reconvey'd to Hell and Melancholick Night. ⎭
Again his Harp the lonesom Poet strung,
Again employ'd the Music of his Tongue ;
But all in vain : Those lays which mov'd before,
Have lost their Influence, and prevail no more.

   Mistaken *Orpheus !* Didst thou vainly hold
Thy Skill superiour to the pow'r of Gold ?
Hadst thou for Gold but quitted luckless Verse,
Tempted his Eyes and not engag'd his Ears ;
The God had soon revers'd his late decree,
And once more bless'd thee with *Euridice.*

   When amorous *Jove* made *Danaë* his Care,
And left his Heav'n to gain that earthly Fair ;
He call'd not weaker Numbers to his Aid,
But with the yellow Metal try'd the Maid :
She wou'd have heard unmov'd Poetick Charms,
Sunk pleas'd into the glittering Lover's Arms.

   Numbers which once but seldom fail'd to move,
And fire the coldest Beauty into Love ;
Strange turn of Fate ! are now an empty Name,
And cannot kindle nor preserve a Flame :
Whilst Gold Monopolizes Female Hearts,
And Love with this curs'd Metal tips his Darts.

   'Tis Gold that makes us Happy, makes us Wise,
This the defect of Wit and Form supplies :

Let

Let Gold your Merits plead with her you love,
Tho' once as *Pallas* Coy, she'll kind as *Venus* prove.
  'Twas this that stopt fair *Atalanta's* Pace:
'Twas this that gave *Hyppomenis* the Race:
Had all thy Sparks, *Penelope*, with this,
Urg'd thee to crown their Hopes with lasting Bliss;
Thou betwixt widdow'd Sheets no Night hadst led,
And they by turns had shar'd the wand'rers Bed:
They try'd not Gold, or if its Force they try'd,
The Story's false; *Penelope* comply'd.
  If now a Bard in midnight Numbers moves,
For entrance to the Nymph he dearly loves.
Perhaps some mony'd Coxcomb Wits despair,
Within enjoys the mercenary Fair;
And both combine to mock the needy Poets Care.
  Were *Ovid's* self the power of Verse to prove,
With all his soft Philosophy of Love,
Finding no *Julia* with its Charms comply,
He'd quit his *Art of Love*, to hug the *Remedy*.
  Cease then Harmonious few, with Female Cares,
To prostitute the Majesty of Verse:
Let Wine instead of Love your Fancy raise,
And *Venus* yield to *Bacchus* in your Lays:
Or, if your Breast sufficient Fury warms,
In Epic strains record great *Churchill's* Arms.
But if of Woman you vouchsafe to Write,
Invoke none other Deity but spite,
In injur'd Poetry's defence engage,
And make its bold Insulters feel thy Rage,
To flatt'ry's Varnish be no more inclin'd;
No more to Female Imperfections blind:
Nay, where a Woman in your work might shine,
With cutting Satyr sharpen every Line:
Her Errors in severest Terms express,
And paint her Vices in their proper Dress:
Let Pride and Falshood, Avarice and Scorn
That she must hate the Piece she can't but own.
Thus with the Sex a vig'rous War maintain,
Till Wealthy Ideots meet their sure Disdain,
And long neglected Verse its antient Sway regain.

On

An EPIGRAM.

On the Prosperous Reign of Queen Eliza-
beth, *and our present Queen* Ann.

SURE Heavens unerring Voice, decreed of Old,
　The fairest Sex shou'd *Europe's* Ballance hold,
As great *Eliza's* Forces humbled *Spain*,
So *France* now stoops, to *ANN's* Superiour Reign :
Thus tho' proud *Jove* with Thunder fills the Sky,
Yet in *Astrea's* Hand, the fatal Scale does lie.

On the Duke of Marlborough's *Victory, at* Blenheim.

THE Conquering Genius of our Isle returns,
　Inspir'd by *ANN*, the God-like Heroe burns ;
Retrieves the Fate, our Ill-led Troops had lost,
And spreads reviving Virtue thro' the Host :
In distant Climes the wand'ring Foe alarms,
And with new Thunder, *Austria's* Eagle Arms ;
The *Danube's* Banks forgetting *Cæsar's* Fame,
Shall Eccho to the sound of *Marlborough's* Name :
The Shepherd's Pipes rejoice o'er *Gallick* Blood,
Which with eternal Purple stain the Flood.

An

An Imitation of the Sixth Ode *of* Horace,
beginning, Scriberis vario fortis. *Apply'd
to his Grace the Duke of* Marlborough :
Suppos'd to be made by Capt. R. S.

SHOU'D *Addison's* Immortal Verse,
   Thy Fame in Arms, great Prince rehearse ;
With *ANNA's* lightning you'd appear,
And glitter o'er again in VVar :
Repeat the proud *Bavarian's* fall !
And in the *Danube* plunge the *Gaul.*

'Tis not for me thy VVroth to show,
Or lead *Achilles* to the Foe ;
Describe stern *Diomed* in Fight,
And put the wounded Gods to Flight :
I dare not with unequal Rage,
On such a mighty Theam ingage ;
Nor Sully in a Verse like mine,
Illustrious *ANNA's* Praise, and Thine.

   Let the laborious *Epick* strain,
In lofty Numbers sing the Man ;
That bears to distant VVorlds his Arms,
And frights the *German* with alarms :
His Courage and his Conduct tell,
And on his various Virtues dwell ;
In trifling Cares my humble Muse,
A less Ambitious Tract pursues :
Instead of Troops in Battle mixt,
And *Gauls* with *British* Spears transfixt ;
She Paints the soft Distress and Mein,
Of Dames expiring with the Spleen.

   From the gay Noise affected Air,
And little Follies of the Fair ;
A slender stock of Fame I raise,
And draw from others Faults, my Praise.

An

An Old KNIGHT, *to a Young* LADY.
By Sir J. B.

MADAM, your Beauty, I confess,
   May our young Gallants wound or bless;
But cannot warm my frozen Heart,
Not capable of Joy or Smart:
Cause neither VVit, nor Looks, nor Kindness can
Make Young a superanuated Man.

   Those Sparks that every Minute fly
From your bright Eyes do falling die;
Not kindle Flames, as heretofore,
Because Old, I can love no more:
Beauty on whither'd Hearts no Trophy gains,
Nor Tinder over-us'd no Fire retains.

   If you'll endure to be admir'd
By an Old Dotard new inspir'd;
You may enjoy the Quintessence
Of my past Love without Expence:
For I can wait and prate, I thank my Fate,
I can do all, but no new Fire create.

F I N I S.